PRESUMPTION

JULIA BARRETT

M. EVANS AND COMPANY, INC.

NEW YORK

M. Evans and Company, Inc.
216 East 49th Street
New York, New York 10017

Library of Congress Cataloging-in-Publication Data

Barrett, Julia.
    Presumption : an entertainment / Julia Barrett. — 1st ed.
       p.   cm.
    Sequal to: Pride and prejudice / Jane Austen.
    ISBN 0-87131-736-2 (hard) : $19.95
    1. Young women—England—Fiction. I. Austen, Jane,
1775–1817. Pride and prejudice. II. Title.
PS3552.A73463P74 1993
813'.54   dc20   93-5778
                                                     CIP

Book design by Charles A. de Kay

Typeset by AeroType, Inc.

Manufactured in the United States of America

First Edition

9 8 7 6 5 4 3 2 1

It is a truth universally acknowledged, that a single man in possession of a good fortune, must be in want of a wife.

*

Pemberley was now Georgiana's home; and the attachment of the sisters was exactly what Darcy had hoped to see. They were able to love each other, even as well as they intended. Georgiana had the highest opinion in the world of Elizabeth; though at first she often listened with an astonishment bordering on alarm, at her lively, sportive, manner of talking to her brother. He, who had always inspired in herself a respect which almost overcame her affection, she now saw the object of open pleasantry. Her mind received knowledge which had never before fallen in her way. By Elizabeth's instructions she began to comprehend that a woman may take liberties with her husband, which a brother will not always allow in a sister more than ten years younger than himself.

—Jane Austen
Pride and Prejudice

PART I

CHAPTER 1

I F, AS THE prevailing wisdom has had it these many years, a young man in possession of a good fortune is always in want of a wife, then surely the reverse must prove true as well: any well-favored lady of means must incline, indeed yearn, to improve her situation by seeking a husband.

Yet our own heroine found herself in the singular position of contesting this complacent assurance. Miss Georgiana Darcy, of Pemberley in Derbyshire, although beautiful, accomplished, and, moreover, an heiress to a considerable fortune, remained nevertheless, at the age of seventeen years, markedly disinclined to secure her future happiness by bestowing that fortune upon any one. Georgiana had reason.

It was not that she had never sought to fall in love, far from it. Once, she had dreamt of nothing other. But her first amorous venture had served only to dishearten her. Orphaned by the time she had completed her ninth year, and growing up an uncommonly pretty and winning child, she had been much accommodated by her only brother and loving guardian, Fitzwilliam Darcy. A series of governesses had taught her, and while they had invariably found her tractable, even compliant, this circumstance was maintained largely by none of their ever presuming to make so inconvenient a suggestion as that she do one single thing genuinely against her own wishes.

Alas, indulgence served her ill. At the age of fifteen, her head quite turned by the attentions of a dashing young officer named Lieutenant George Wickham, the son of her father's steward, our impetuous heiress eloped with him. Had not the affair most fortunately been discovered by her devoted brother, there is no telling the consequence.

The two, happily, were recovered in good time. Georgiana was returned to her beloved Pemberley, and her brother was able to console himself with the knowledge both that his sister was unharmed and that not one in the neighborhood had any inkling of the disaster which had so nearly overtaken her.

Yet the incident served to check the high spirits of the young heiress. She had come to see the dangers hovering over too precipitate a flight into unrestrained passion. In truth, Georgiana found herself much subdued. She feared her own romantic heart.

Now that she approached the full bloom of young womanhood, her appearance amply fulfilled every childhood promise. She was tall, her figure was formed, and her every aspect graceful. These attractions, augmented by her expectations, made Miss Darcy much solicited. But while enjoying ardent attentions from an enviable number of unexceptionable suitors, she refused to fix a serious gaze upon any. On all of them she smiled, to most was amiable, but to none held out serious promise.

Still, on this, the evening of her coming out into society, her anticipations were high; indeed, she had much pleasure to look forward to. Besides the never-failing joys of the dance, there was the agreeable company of her sister-in-law, Elizabeth; the arrival in the neighborhood of the new relations Elizabeth had brought to the family; and, the certain admiration of young gentlemen from all over the county that was none the less welcome for her determination not to reciprocate it.

Tonight especially, she had a further aim: since the unfortunate incident with the young officer, her brother had grown stern, and she was eager to demonstrate to him just how much improved had been her cast of mind in the two years that had intervened. Although inexperienced, she had never been foolish and, sobered by the loss of her illusions, she had resolved to address her failings. In this endeavor she had found herself with an ally in the person of her brother's new bride.

The arrival of Elizabeth Bennet at Pemberley had seemed to Georgiana to bring with it an alteration in the very air of that great house. Rooms which had for so long been silent were now filled with laughter. Her brother was more often there, his presence most happily felt: under his beloved's tutelage, Darcy's demeanor was perceptibly altered. He smiled more easily and was even heard, on occasion, to laugh out loud. His sister observed this change in awe. She scarcely dared herself to address him in the insouciant manner to which Elizabeth was accustomed; but nevertheless drew comfort from the knowledge that he was after all capable of levity.

Georgiana, remembering her many long years of solitude, or, at best, the company of one or another governess, could not but rejoice at the change. And, as she watched and listened to ever more adventurous sallies upon her brother's person, she conceived for their perpetrator an admiration which only grew as their friendship progressed.

It was in the midst of such musings that she was surprised by the appearance of their subject herself, who just then came to the door in her dressing gown.

"Well, my dear Georgiana," cried Elizabeth Darcy, "are you prepared to be hailed as quite the most charming and loveliest creature the neighborhood has ever been privileged to behold?"

"Dear sister," said Georgiana in some surprise, "Surely, you cannot think Derbyshire is so deprived of beauty that I could ever be thought so?"

"Nonsense," was her reply, "a young woman on her coming out into society is always described thus—she *is* the loveliest creature ever seen. Depend upon it, I have been to many such occasions and I have never heard any young woman granted a lesser estimation, no matter how plain or graceless she may be."

"If that be the case," replied Georgiana, smiling, "I shall arrange to be just as beautiful as you say. It appears that this evening, the task is accomplished easily enough."

"*You*, Georgiana, need exert yourself but little at any time to be admired. Nature has granted you enough already; more would be profligate. What a fine ball this evening's shall be. I expect you shall dance every dance; your dressmaker, I see, has looped up your gown for the cotillion."

"I am quite prepared for any circumstance, dear Elizabeth. Sir Edward Stanton so enjoys the old dances, but his son, George, prefers the Boulanger, while Richard Brook dearly loves a reel. I shall answer to all."

"So young and yet so dutiful," cried Elizabeth. "Can the young men of Derbyshire have an idea of their good fortune tonight? But beware, Georgiana: too ready a compliancy, and a man is apt to assume dullness."

"Let him assume what he may," returned Georgiana. "Dear Elizabeth, I shall dance and allow myself to be admired by every eye if that can give the company pleasure. I should hate to disgrace my brother and you by being uncompanionable. But I am not in love; and do not, I pray, require me to fall hopelessly so, to pledge myself to one, and one alone, all in the course of an evening's entertainment."

"I could hardly demand *that*, sister," laughed Mrs. Darcy. "When I think upon it, advice on hasty judgments from myself would surely be of little consequence. Having done everything quite wrong on one such an occasion, I can only wonder at my own present good fortune."

And secure in her mind about her young friend's disposition, while yet speculating about what the evening would bring, she returned to her own quarters to dress.

CHAPTER 2

T HE MASTER OF Pemberley had himself only just returned from business affairs in London, bringing with
him a young architect. Pemberley, although possessed
of all the grace that age and loving maintenance could provide, was nevertheless in constant need of attention and
Darcy had long sought to find a rare artist who was capable
both of appreciating its qualities and of resisting the tempta-
tion to improve upon them. Such a one, he was assured, was
James Leigh-Cooper. Although not yet thirty, the young man
had distinguished himself in several important houses, and
Darcy, who had admired his accomplishments for some
years, was pleased to have at last secured his services.

Having settled his visitor comfortably into his own quarters, he returned confidently to domestic matters. He had
departed for the City secure in the knowledge that the
arrangements for Georgiana's ball were in excellent hands,
and that whatever obstacles might occur, his dear Lizzy
would be there to surmount them.

How well she had adapted to her new-found duties as mistress of Pemberley had given him the profoundest of pleasure.
Her intelligence, her quickness of wit, her playfulness, which
had first won his affection despite himself, were in evidence as
they had always been; but they were augmented by the dignity
inherent in her superior position. Always, he had loved her;
now he could also delight in her serenity.

Elizabeth, for her part, greeted her husband warmly and
with all the affection of a truly loving heart. In their brief time

together he had become for her everything she could have hoped. *Now* she wondered at her own first notions about him. *He*, forbidding or proud? Never! He was surely the gentlest, the most generous and the most agreeable of men. No one in possession of good sense could but recognize it.

"Well, Mrs. Darcy," said the prompter of these tender thoughts so soon as he arrived, "and are we all quite ready for the festivities of the evening?"

"Perfectly, thank you," replied she. "Mrs. Langham has taken to bed with the tooth-ache; the jellies are not yet set; and Arthur has brought word that the musicians are delayed at Eaton. So everything is proceeding as well as may be anticipated by anyone foolish enough to give a ball."

"And my sister? How does she do?"

"Tolerably well. She is ready and willing, I assure you, for whatever the evening can bring. Who knows," with a conscious look, "but what someone might be drawn to admire her fine eyes?"

Darcy could not but smile at this reminder of what it was that had at first brought Elizabeth to his notice.

"Are Georgiana's eyes fine?" was all he said, however. "I really had not observed."

"That," she replied playfully, "is because you are her brother and not her suitor. I consider myself lucky indeed to have but sisters. What may have been an affliction for my father, was certainly of benefit to the vanity of the rest of us. Had you been my brother, you surely would have been impervious to *any* charms I may have possessed."

"Perhaps you are right, Lizzy," he smiled, "but what I have most certainly taken note of are the material improvements in the demeanor of that young lady since she has had the advantage of your company. Evidence of my sister's high spirits, I had already seen, but as I look upon her now, I glimpse something other, a good sense, a lack of frivolity. With your good offices, she is, I do believe, becoming a credit to her sex."

The lovers continued this way together in their discussion of Georgiana, reiterating their pleasure at her new seriousness. Had she not begun to study more diligently, apply herself better at her needlework and at the piano? Darcy delighted to see not only his sister's development but his own

Elizabeth's influence upon it. He saw her hand in every application, in each improvement, and his happiness knew no restraint. But, a man in love, and so new to the joys of marital bliss, can hardly be expected to make the most uncontestable judgments. Fitzwilliam Darcy was no exception.

For Mrs. Darcy, the new life at Pemberley was not without its difficulties. With her marriage, Elizabeth Bennet, a handsome, intelligent, but virtually dowerless young gentlewoman, had found herself quite unexpectedly the mistress of a large estate and the possessor of enormous wealth. The sudden acquisition of title and position, happy as such a circumstance may be, will inevitably bring with it to any sensible young woman a variety of hazards. In short, Elizabeth had had to learn to live with unmitigated good fortune.

Her father was a gentleman possessed of a good-sized property in Hertfordshire; but Darcy's circle until then had been far higher born than she. *They* represented the pick of the English aristocracy; *her* only claim to title was Darcy's boundless admiration.

She was far too discerning not to have seen from the start that others at Pemberley were aware of her modest beginnings. She had immediately observed the raised eyebrows and secret smiles of the coachmen, the butler, the housemaids and the other servants, all accustomed to receiving their orders from those far grander than the daughter of a mere country gentleman.

The neighborhood, moreover, had been, she knew, too eagerly awaiting her coming. She was a perfect supplement for any gossip that might be lacking in the county and she knew that there were those anticipating an awkward act, or inapt gesture. She was illiberal enough to determine not to oblige them; but still, the knowledge could not but disturb.

Darcy's aunt, Lady Catherine de Bourgh, was openly abusive and Anne de Bourgh dutifully followed her mother's lead. Others of their set, their compassion aroused by the indignity of the family's being obliged to admit among them one who had been married merely for love, made their displeasure as keenly felt. Too often Elizabeth encountered coldness, if not genuine ill-will.

Her natural high spirits inclined her to seek some consolation by laughing at her position and the folly of some of her neighbors. But her attempts to lighten her burden did not always succeed. In the privacy of her splendid quarters, she often succumbed to tears. Her attachment to Hertfordshire and her friends and family there was strong; and while, in the past, the eccentricity of her father, and the uncertainty of temper and meanness of understanding of her mother, had caused her concern and even irritation, now she remembered only the dear familiarity of both. Even the recollection of her sisters' boisterous conduct seemed sweet to her. What had once appeared excessive frivolity, she could recognize as only the pardonable whims of gaiety and youth. At this flattering distance, Longbourn was attractive indeed.

Her miseries she kept well hidden. Darcy, she was determined, would see none of her tears. She would make her own way in his household and in his country, and if she wept, she would do so alone.

CHAPTER 3

AMONG DARCY'S CIRCLE was one whom he esteemed in particular, Sir Geoffrey Portland. A close friend of his father's, Sir Geoffrey had never failed the younger man during even the most trying times of his parents' loss. For Darcy, he had indeed replaced his father, if not in the son's affections, then certainly in the everyday practice of parenthood.

Darcy relied upon him for advice and counsel, nor had he ever approached him in vain. Left to care for a much younger sister before he himself had come of age, he truly believed that without Sir Geoffrey's support he would have found himself overwhelmed by the task. Situated as his friend was at a convenient distance, he could turn to him with each successive domestic mishap, and none was judged too small to be considered, although throughout the county Sir Geoffrey's consequence was substantial. Darcy admired him prodigiously, and moreover, he loved him.

Sir Geoffrey's property, Denby Park, was a grand estate no lesser than Pemberley itself. In his gardens, the most particular of gentlemen could wander at will, secure in the assurance that nowhere would he encounter a sight disquieting or unlovely. There were vast sweeps of parkland, great lawns running down to the water's edge, views across the river to the encircling woods and beyond them the embracing hills. Sir Geoffrey had years earlier sought out Capability Brown to add all the conveniences of the modern age to the house and gardens that had been been in his family since before the Restoration. The result was harmony both without and within, one of Sir Geoffrey's most cherished comforts. Indeed, for years it had been almost his only comfort.

Childless, and a widower himself, his preoccupations had been too often engaged not in the future but with his family's splendid past. He was a handsome man, of noble bearing and a haughty mien, which often gave the impression that he considered himself above the company of others. In truth, this impression was far from false since his standards were exalted, and there were few in his opinion who rose to them. But the orphaned young Darcys had aroused his sympathies and brought him to know emotions he had never before encountered. For his old friend's children, he had abandoned reserve. He loved them as his own.

He had but lately returned from Antigua in the West Indies, where he had gone on family business, and though he had there been informed of his godson's marriage, he had yet to make Elizabeth's acquaintance.

His anxieties about Darcy's bride were not negligible, and stemmed mostly from a letter he had received while abroad from Lady Catherine de Bourgh. His friendship with Her Ladyship had been long enough established for him to discount in large part her estimation of almost any circumstance. But in one matter above others, he had always found her to be trustworthy; that of social standing.

Her description of Elizabeth had alarmed him greatly. A young woman of inferior birth, with an unfortunate family, little dowry and an uncle, Lady Catherine had heard, in trade in Cheapside. Swiftly following upon the first communication had come to Sir Geoffrey another from the bridegroom himself extolling his love's amiability of temper, her superior understanding, her gaiety, in short, her perfection in every aspect. His bride, Darcy wrote, was surely the embodiment of all that man might dare to hope for in a woman.

The second letter did little to allay Sir Geoffrey's concerns. His desire for his young friend's happiness was great, yet greater was his fear that Darcy might compromise his station through an improper match. Having such inferior connections as those Lady Catherine reported, it seemed unlikely that Miss Elizabeth Bennet of Longbourn could be the exemplary young person Darcy described. Sir Geoffrey could only suppose him befuddled by passion. Usually, he knew him to be considerate of his own rank, and faithful to the duties which bound him as heir to Pemberley. But he was yet young and could be gulled.

His earnest contemplations, however, on this subject, were disturbed by the approach of a carriage to Denby Park. Its livery was as handsome and elegant as befit its owner, Lady Catherine de Bourgh. Her arrival was awaited, her visit having been fixed between them by post. It was, Her Ladyship had adjudged, to be assumed that the newly-arrived mistress of Pemberley—having taken on so presumptuous a task as Georgiana's coming-out ball—would not, assuredly, be equal, in addition to that, of entertaining such exacting guests as her party from Rosings. The good lady, with characteristic delicacy towards her inferiors, would stay rather at a house whose master might be supposed to be a match for her. Sir Geoffrey, therefore, might await her on the Friday shortly after three of the clock. That gentleman, knowing himself without recourse, had declared himself delighted.

As the horses approached, the servants were enlisted to aid her to her comforts. The footmen carried in box after box, while Lady Catherine, never patient with the discomforts attendant upon travel, and fatigued besides by the ardors of her journey from Kent, nevertheless felt it necessary to direct the process. She soon found herself in some displeasure over the haphazard methods she saw employed. They were the result, she could not but observe, of Sir Geoffrey's having softened his staff's labors in the restoration of Denby Park, an extravagance of which at the time she had heartily disapproved. As Sir Geoffrey was an old and valued friend, she must now further fulfill her duty to him by asserting that never in her life had she seen such indolent domestics.

She was able to congratulate herself at least on her foresight in having brought her own Sally to accompany herself and Anne in their visit. Sir Geoffrey might be content to live in bachelor's anarchy; but it behooved Lady Catherine to be properly served in all particulars if she was to make a fitting appearance at Pemberley.

"Anne, my dear," she cried to her daughter, so soon as she had sent Sally about her business, "you must retire immediately. You are looking ill, and that will never do for a ball, even for this evening's. If Pemberley is not what it once was, recall that *we* are still de Bourghs. Rest, my dear, and recover your complexion. I shall join you presently to superintend your repose."

Chapter 4

L ADY CATHERINE COULD not herself retire before consulting Sir Geoffrey. The matter of her nephew's late marriage weighed too heavily on her spirits to allow her any ease until she had exercised her generosity by sharing that burden with her old friend.

"Now Sir Geoffrey," she cried, the very minute he had rung for tea, "and what do you make of all *this*?"

"I cannot venture any opinion," replied Sir Geoffrey, "until you give me some clue about what 'this' may be. If you are referring to your daughter's complexion, most lately your subject of conversation, I can only say that it seemed markedly fine to me."

"Always, you pretend to misunderstand me, Sir," she said in vexation. "You surely cannot think I mean anything but this most deplorable entanglement of Darcy's."

"You shock me, Madam," cried he, "can my godson, so lately married, be entangled so soon? I confess that marriage à la mode baffles me."

"Pray be serious, Sir," was her response. Lady Catherine often mistook Sir Geoffrey's sardonic wit for mere playfulness and derived from it all the pleasure of one who understood a bare fraction of it. But, after her wearisome journey, and, on so bleak a topic, she found it impossible to humor him. "It is precisely *of* his marriage that I speak."

"Ah, yes," said he gravely. "It has been upon my mind, do not think it has not. But after all, Fitzwilliam Henry Darcy has many years ago come of age and might be supposed to know his own mind in these matters."

"Nonsense," cried Her Ladyship. "Miss Elizabeth Bennet is nothing but a cunning young woman. Her family is quite without breeding, and the connection can only bring misery. Upon my honor, at Longbourn they dine at five!"

Sir Geoffrey was silenced by the latter intelligence, and Lady Catherine, supposing herself to have effectively carried her point, retired in triumph.

It was not until some hours later when Her Ladyship had arisen refreshed, and Anne had once again recovered such complexion as was deemed sufficient for Pemberley, that the final member of their party made his arrival. Having followed their carriage on horseback, Captain Thomas Heywood, of His Majesty's Navy, a second cousin of the de Bourghs, had been delayed for some time by his horse's throwing a shoe at Lambton.

Lady Catherine welcomed him cordially and hastened to present him to his host. He was a young man whose good looks and elegance of person commanded immediate attention. He had but just returned from the Mediterranean, where he had been engaged in his country's defense.

"A commendable young fellow in every respect," she whispered after the introductions had been made, and Captain Heywood had retired to what she judged the safe distance of some five yards away, "and an heir to a considerable estate of his own. I look forward to having him more intimately among us." As she spoke, she cast a glance at Anne who, usually wan, colored at her mother's tone.

"What a fine room is this," observed the Captain as he strolled its length. "The portrait over the fireplace is indeed splendid. Is it by the hand of Sir Joshua Reynolds?"

Sir Geoffrey was pleased to reply only that it was a faithful likeness of his beloved wife in her younger years.

"Reynolds to be sure," asserted Lady Catherine. "Sir Geoffrey would allow no lesser artist in his drawing room. The frame, you will notice, is particularly fine: it was especially imported from Venice, and you will look far before you find its like in any but the very finest drawing rooms in England, not excluding *certain* that I have visited in St. James's."

Having thus established beyond question the quality of the frames around Sir Geoffrey's paintings, Her Ladyship fell into silent exultation upon the superiority of her own artistic discrimination.

Captain Heywood was then guided about the other rooms of Denby Park and, led by Sir Geoffrey through his garden so lately brought to perfection by Brown's skilled hand, declared himself much affected. The Palladian bridge in the distance, together with the serenity of the view, inspired in him the most romantic thoughts; they seemed to him wonders akin to those he had lately seen in Spain and Italy. And he found himself, to the delight of the assembled company, reciting the verses of the celebrated Lord Byron:

> *When man was worthy of thy clime,*
> *The hearts within thy valleys bred,*
> *The fiery souls that might have led*
> *Thy sons to deeds sublime . . .*

all the while fixing his gaze upon both ladies, enchanting Her Ladyship entirely, while her daughter blushed almost pink. Sir Geoffrey himself applauded and complimented his erudition.

They made a charming picture altogether, the good lady thought. Here, in their midst, was most certainly a superb young man, heroic in thought as well as in deed.

CHAPTER 5

N OT TEN MILES from Pemberley, yet another group had assembled for the coming ball, though they might perhaps be considered less harmonious a party.

At Pelham Hall, the newly acquired property of Charles and Jane Bingley, several guests had already made their appearance, among them Charles's sisters, Miss Caroline Bingley and Mrs. Louisa Hurst and her husband, and Jane's own relations, Kitty and Mary Bennet.

Their hostess busily sought the comfort of all: but the task of achieving it was too often an arduous one. To the needs of each, Jane was sensitive: but towards the congeniality of the whole, she could contribute only her own good will. That amiability, however warm, could not be sufficient to marry so discordant a group. Civility Mrs. Bingley maintained for the most part, but rarely more.

Kitty and Mary Bennet, lately come from Longbourn, must needs talk to their sister of all the comings and goings, the little mishaps that the town of Meryton had seen over the last months. They described at length the dressmaker's failures, the linendraper's latest sarcenets, the trimming and retrimming of their bonnets, and most of all, debated which of the garments they had brought with them they might wear for Georgiana's ball.

Miss Bingley, happily, could rise above their trifling dispute. *She* had simply to rely upon the judgments of the very best dressmaker in London; no such doubts as the Bennet girls' could concern *her*.

"Whatever you may say of it, Mary," protested Kitty, "I am resolved to wear the spotted muslin tonight. Ensign Atkinson of the _____shire, you may remember, admired it prodigiously when the regiment was still in Meryton. Ah, the dear Regiment! I swear that since they have gone, my life is scarcely worth living."

"I hardly noticed their absence," returned Mary. "But that is customary with me. For one taken up with the true life of the mind, conviviality provides little sustenance. I am too occupied in my study of society to be troubled with persons."

At this exchange between the sisters, Miss Bingley made no comment.

"No matter, my dears," interjected Jane, "tonight should provide merriment enough for us all. Even Mary may find herself taken unawares by enjoyment. Since Lizzy's coming to Pemberley, it has become positively gay. And besides, Georgiana is growing into a splendid young woman."

"*I*, at any rate, intend to enjoy myself," said Kitty with a meaningful glance. "What captivated Ensign Atkinson at home can surely have no less an effect in Derbyshire."

This, at last, moved Miss Bingley to speech:"Your determination to cut a figure here is understandable," said she, "now that the _____shire have deserted Meryton. But then your family is to be congratulated," she added pointedly, "for your near relation's recent marriage to one of its officers. It was commendable in one so young as Lydia Bennet thus successfully to seize her opportunity as soon as it presented itself."

Jane looked away, mortified at this allusion to her sister's elopement, but said nothing. She had determined in herself, immediately after her marriage to Charles Bingley, that whatever feelings might be in her heart towards Caroline Bingley and Louisa Hurst, she would extend towards them all the welcome at Pelham Hall that she might give to her own sisters.

Kitty only laughed meanwhile. "*I* need not be concerned for my prospects yet," she cried, "since *I* am but of an age with Georgiana, although I have been out in society for longer than she. I cannot as yet feel that anxiety that many another may feel. Can you imagine poor Jane still not married when she was twenty-three? Had it been me, my dear Miss Bingley, I should have been ready for the spinster's cap!"

Appalled by the vulgarity of Kitty Bennet's tone, and the more by the consciousness that she herself had lately passed her twenty-fourth birthday, Miss Bingley drew aside. She was still contemplating a reply, when her brother and Mr. Hurst arrived, newly come from surveying the estate. Pelham Hall, while not above fifty years old, was still possessed of all the elegance of many an older house. It was large and handsome, and furnished in a way that was neither gaudy nor mean, but perfectly fitted to the taste of its new inhabitants. Mr. Bingley was justly proud of it. As for the grounds, nothing would satisfy him but that his brother-in-law should be shown every wonder of the rose garden, the arbor, the orchards, and the sloping lawns that ran down to the river where the fallow deer were wont to refresh themselves.

Mr. Hurst suffered these beauties with a tolerable grace and had his reward when at last they reached the brewhouse, where he could discuss the year's crop with the brewmaster, and the stables, where he was able to assess the value of his brother-in-law's equestrian stock. Having judged the latter to be rather poorer than his own, he was in excellent spirits when they returned, and even went so far as directly to address his hostess.

"Mrs. Bingley," said he, "I must congratulate you upon your establishment. While under no circumstances to be compared with Pemberley, it is still one of which you need not be ashamed." And having thus exhausted his stock of gallantries, he lapsed into silence for the remainder of his visit.

Charles Bingley, looking about him and seeing none but those he loved, could scarcely contain his joy. "What a splendid occasion this is," cried he. "I have never known the air so pure; the apple trees, I have just observed, are beginning to blossom—I think, my dear Jane, that there will be a wonderful crop. Oh, how I love the country. And, best of all, here with us are both our families together! Could one hope for anything more delightful?"

Jane, while unable precisely to agree with his assessment of the situation, still welcomed, as always, his cheerful presence. Since their marriage, the loving pair had exceeded even their own expectations in their life together. His Jane's, Bingley thought, was surely the most agreeable nature and affectionate heart in all the world; while her husband's easy temper was to his wife a never-failing source of satisfaction. His remarks now lifted her spirits and even affected the mood of the whole company. And when he next observed upon the earliness of the hour and proposed that the group join him in a game of whist before they dressed, the response was unexpectedly a happy one.

More animated a card player than conversationalist, Miss Bingley became straightaway much improved in temper. "Come now, dear brother," she said, "for heaven's sake leave your chatter and let us pass a pleasant hour in play before it is time for us to leave for Pemberley."

Thus insuring the gratification of the whole group by *their* observing her so much improved in civility, and *her* supposing the idea to have been her own, she led them to the game room and arranged them at table to enjoy their play.

CHAPTER 6

T HE ABSENCE OF Mrs. Darcy's parents at the Pemberley festivities could not fail to be noticed. Indeed, Mr. and Mrs. Bennet had expected to attend, and had both greatly anticipated the visit—Mr. Bennet to see his Lizzy again and Mrs. Bennet to revel in her Lizzy's exalted status—but Mrs. Bennet, having been prostrated by her nerves, after an unfortunate incident in Meryton on the morning of their family's scheduled departure for Derbyshire, had been forced to remain behind.

At first, she would have Kitty and Mary stay with her. But, allowing for their urgent pleas, and their real desolation at the possibility of missing the ball altogether, she had decided to permit the young ladies to proceed, selflessly urging their father to accompany them as well.

"My dear Mr. Bennet," the good lady had cried, "how can I deprive my younger, my most eligible and dearest daughters such an evening? No, go they must, and you shall go with them. No matter what becomes of me here, alone and unattended. Bridget may bring me a dish of chicken broth in the afternoon, if Hill reminds her, or she may not, but since my appetite is quite gone, it is of little consequence. What matters is that their father shall accompany my sweet girls to the ball. Yes, you shall go and there's an end to it."

In the face of such unyielding self-sacrifice, Mr. Bennet had no recourse but to offer to stay behind with her. And, with his proposal magnanimously accepted, the elder Bennets remained at Longbourn while they sent their daughters on in the company of Mrs. Hill.

This arrangement, however, was remarked upon, and not only by those whose feelings towards Elizabeth were kindly. Mrs. Celia Montague, a particular friend of Lady Catherine's, was especially surprised by it.

"How very odd," she observed to Elizabeth immediately upon her arrival at Pemberley "that your own mother and father have not seen fit to take the journey for the ball. Surely, they cannot be insensitive to the grandeurs of such an occasion. Or," she concluded with a half-smile, "can it be that their own establishment provides finer diversion?"

Elizabeth could only reply that her mother had been indisposed. "What a very great pity," persisted Mrs. Montague, a thin woman, upright of figure and expressionless of face. "I so looked forward to making her acquaintance, having already heard so very much about her. I am wretched with disappointment that I shall not after all see her here."

In truth, Elizabeth's own regret was keen since she had eagerly awaited the solace of her family's company. Yet, hearing Mrs. Montague's tone, she must comfort herself with the knowledge that any pleasures their visit might afford would be offset on this particular occasion by attendant worries. The pain of their absence was great; but, now, she could not but be aware that their presence might have proved the greater agony.

Elizabeth's discomfort this evening was not inconsiderable. The witticisms of a Celia Montague, she could easily withstand, but there was more to contend with. She must remember—could not forget—that Sir Geoffrey Portland might arrive at any minute. *He* would require her concentrated attention.

She had looked forward with trepidation to meeting that gentleman. His letters to Darcy had included mentions of her that were cordial enough, if cold. And while Darcy had assured her on more than one occasion, that they two must inevitably feel for each other all the love that he felt for both of them, she could not share her husband's blithe confidence. Sir Geoffrey, she had heard, was, above all, a man sensible of his family position, and she too well remembered her first unhappy meeting with another such, his own godson and pupil.

So when the gentleman himself was announced, her courage all but deserted her. She started, and felt herself color, but collected her wits directly as she went to greet her guest. Darcy had already stepped forward to salute his oldest and most revered friend, and was delighted to make the introductions.

"My good Henry," said Sir Geoffrey, addressing him with the name that he alone had used since Darcy's childhood. "What pleasure to see you again at last. And this would be Mrs. Darcy," watching Elizabeth who just then approached them. "I can comprehend your fascination," he continued in a low tone.

Elizabeth was properly grateful for the greeting he extended, thanked him graciously, and though wishing to say more, fell silent. It took some minutes before she was able to regain her composure. Only then could she remark to Sir Geoffrey upon the early approach of the spring weather, and say all that was proper to inquire after his comfort, and admire his country.

His responses were gallant, yet the scrutiny in his eyes, affixed so firmly upon her person, displaced her usual ease of manner, making for an embarrassment difficult to overcome. She was relieved at last to have the duties of hostess call her away to the newest arrivals, and turned from him as soon as civility permitted.

Sir Geoffrey, left alone, continued to study her. But, he did so without the appearance of it, and it was not until the arrival of Lady Catherine and her daughter some moments later, that he allowed his impressions of the new Mrs. Darcy to be quizzed.

That good lady, having herself made her salutations to her nephew and his bride as brief as was possible, turned quickly to her demand for Sir Geoffrey's disinterested opinion. "Has not my nephew lost all sense of decorum?" she demanded. "Is he not bewitched, Sir? Surely, you can now see it," she added in agitation. "An ambitious upstart of inferior birth and little breeding, the mistress of Pemberley! Intolerable, surely. And her gown, while not unbecoming, has been out of fashion for this year past."

Sir Geoffrey, still deliberating, would acknowledge as yet no actual cause for discomfort. "Her demeanor is acceptable, if something lively," said he. "And her eyes are as fine as Henry has described."

Lady Catherine bridled at his words, and moved away from him, confirmed in the folly of the male sex. Ever vacillating and unreliable they were, and wretchedly susceptible to her own sex's superior wiles. Even a man so usually discerning as Sir Geoffrey could, she perceived, be taken in, and by a gown out-moded a full twelve months. She turned immediately to her daughter, exhorting her towards the delights of the dance.

CHAPTER 7

THE HALL NOW entertained a good number. Georgiana Darcy, having graciously greeted her guests, could be seen leading the dancers in a longaways, as the musicians played an energetic air. Often she glanced sweetly towards the Stantons, the Brooks, and the Middletons, all of whose approval of the cut of her gown, the arrangements of the ribbons in her hair, down to the very points of her slippers, was to be read in their countenances.

Sir Edward Stanton, an elderly gentleman of courtly manner, long in the neighborhood, and an intimate of her father's, observed her in pleasure. "Has not Pemberley come to life again?" said he. "Sadly silent it has been these many years. Now, what a joy it is to see!"

Indeed, Georgiana's was a radiant figure among the young dancers; even the most diligent observer could find no fault with her. Veritably, she was flawless. A more favorable prospect opened when the talk turned towards the host and hostess, now welcoming their guests on the other side of the room; *there*, agreement was unanimous too, if somewhat less commendatory. Mrs. Middleton, known for her benevolence, pronounced firmly upon the folly of an unequal match while her friends nodded their heads in unison. No one could be so simple as to challenge this sagacity.

Fortunate it was that just then the large Bingley party made its arrival, and Elizabeth could hasten towards her loving sister Jane to offer her warmest greetings. Mrs. Bingley's husband joined in the delight of the pair, who seemed, and indeed felt, as those seeing each other after an inordinately long absence, though it had been but a matter of days since they last met.

Jane admired all she saw in the ballroom, praising her sister's achievement and wondering at her calm in the midst of the whirl.

"Indeed, my dearest Lizzy," said she, "you are a picture of composure, and I do believe your table would do even my mother credit!"

Elizabeth would have turned to her sister to confide the unease she felt, but just at Jane's heels came Caroline Bingley, eager to join in the compliment to her hostess.

"I cannot fail to agree with you, Mrs. Bingley," she observed, directly after saluting the lady of the house. "How well Mrs. Darcy has accepted the duties of her new life does her credit, and it must be seen as a particular achievement, considering how little practice she has had. And here are the Misses Kitty and Mary Bennet come with us from Pelham Hall to partake of the evening's entertainments and to seek out for the family all the advantages that such superior society may afford."

Elizabeth, although taken somewhat aback, determined to be gracious still.

Said she, "My dear Miss Bingley, I hope you might be entertained at least as well as they. My husband has always considered you as almost a sister; and Georgiana will ever rely upon your greater experience of the world. You were well acquainted with Pemberley before I even met Mr. Darcy; *I* have only known it since I became its mistress."

With that, she left a perplexed Miss Bingley and went forward to greet her younger sisters, listening, with an affection that lasted fully into the fourth or fifth repetition, as they recounted the distressing news of their mother's illness, and of her disappointment at missing the festivities.

Kitty could hardly contain her excitement. But, after a short while even she became awed at the grandeur of the setting and went so far as to lower her voice as she spoke.

"Lizzy, what finery is here, what elegance," she exclaimed, "and so very many gentlemen."

It was good fortune, thought Elizabeth, that at this ball at least, there was no scarcity of young men. Kitty and Mary could dance to contentment and never be without partners. Glancing over the room to catch the eye of her husband, she was able to convey to him that she was in need of his help. He, alerted to his own duties as a host, and seeing the two eldest Brook boys at large, immediately brought them forward to be presented. It was to the delight of the sisters that the young men escorted them to the floor for the dance that had just begun.

Elizabeth, watching her sisters and the merriment of the other guests, began to see that the evening was progressing happily. She even believed she might enjoy herself.

Suddenly, for one moment, it seemed as though a quiet had descended upon the room. Captain Thomas Heywood had entered. He was becomingly attired in his naval uniform, a graceful figure in every respect, and all eyes turned to him, as he sought out his host and hostess to announce his presence.

"Mrs. Darcy," said he, directing himself as quickly as possible to the lady, "I was particularly eager to make your acquaintance, having learned of your recent arrival at Pemberley. I, too, am new to the county, new, I sometimes fear, even to my native England, having only now returned from a long and arduous engagement at sea."

Elizabeth was a little surprised by the familiarity of his address, but nevertheless, she extended to him all the compassion she felt due to one who had but just fought for his country.

"My good sir," responded she warmly, "you are indeed welcome. His Majesty's Navy has carried itself magnificently during these difficult times, and every gratification must by all means be enjoyed by such members of it as yourself. We are assured at least of your finding our food and drink acceptable, since your palate has already withstood the rigors of your noble calling, in the form of salt pork and biscuits. As for our small distractions here in Derbyshire, I cannot speak with as much certainty. After all that you must have seen in the world, we can only hope that we do not seem to you too dull."

"Impossible, upon my word," exclaimed the officer. "A mere glance around this room reduces the ballrooms of Malta and Gibraltar to veritable tedium."

Elizabeth, seeing her sister Georgiana approach, presented the officer. Captain Heywood's gallantries were sufficient to the occasion, if not excessive. He declared himself dazzled. He was unaccustomed, he protested, to the vision of so much beauty, so close at hand. And once again indulging his fondness for poetry, he sang out, to a captivated Georgiana, the very latest verse from his admirable Lord Byron:

> *She walks in Beauty like the night*
> *Of cloudless climes and starry skies;*
> *And all that's best of dark and bright*
> *Meet in her aspect and her eyes:*
> *Thus mellowed to that tender light*
> *Which Heaven to gaudy day denies.*

Thereupon, hearing the musicians again striking up, Captain Heywood could see no reason to delay. He bowed, offered her his hand, and, to the astonishment of her spoken partner, the eldest Middleton, he whisked her away to the dance.

CHAPTER 8

T HEY MADE A splendid couple, who commanded the
attention of the entire company. All eyes were upon
them, and many a hand went up in the air to shield the
whisperers. "Who was this bold young officer?" It was a
question that most of the assembly were intrigued to ask.

Only Anne de Bourgh, dancing with another gentleman,
had scarcely taken notice of what had passed. But, Lady
Catherine, ever vigilant of her family's station, and alert to
any possible trespass against it, rose from her chair in silent
displeasure. She now took it upon herself to secure her
daughter's prior claim upon the jaunty young officer.

Stepping forward to where her nephew stood, she con-
fronted him. "Mr. Darcy," said she, "I commend your warm
welcome for my husband's cousin Heywood. Doubtless you
do not so much as recall meeting him at Rosings as a child?
He is grown into a truly worthy fellow, and this moreover
without benefit of parental guidance. He, like you, lost them
at an early age. Yet *his* sufferings have been heroic. Only
lately has he been reprieved from the trials of the naval
battles in the Mediterranean. We are honored to have him
coming to call upon our dear Anne. And, I dare say that
though his fortune is not today what it may have been when
his good people were alive, it remains still perfectly acceptable. Anne is delighted with his attentions, I assure you."

An inquisitive Caroline Bingley now approached. She, too,
took a lively interest in the scene, and, addressing herself
urgently to Mr. Darcy, cried, "Is not Lady Catherine's cousin,

Mr. Darcy, connected to the Heywoods of Northumberland, well-acquainted with the Bingleys of old? You must present him to me, for we shall have a good deal to say to each other."

And, immediately upon the Captain's having surrendered Georgiana to one of the many gallants awaiting her, he was brought forward to lavish his attentions upon this newest captivator.

Miss Bingley could only wonder at their not having met before. Surely, the best families must necessarily encounter each other somewhere, whether it be in the Captain's native Hereford, here in Derbyshire, in London or in Bath.

Alas, explained Heywood in somber tones, he had so sadly misspent his youth as to pass more time among the seasick ships than in the company of superior society. However, he assured her, growing more confidential with each word he spoke, he meant to make up for the lack as promptly as possible by seeking such charming associates as he now saw before him.

Caroline colored, but was able to recover her composure in time to suggest that there were in the vicinity sufficient diversions to delight any such man of feeling and sensibility as he plainly was. The pair immediately fixed upon his calling at Pelham Hall on the morrow to plan a delightful excursion. Only moments later Lady Catherine appeared to reclaim her mariner.

The good Captain, casting a long glance at Miss Bingley, then dutifully escorted his cousin Anne back to the floor and gracefully danced to the country rhythms in play. Upon his manners, the entire company was in agreement: they were impeccable.

CHAPTER 9

T HE NEXT MORNING Georgiana took her accustomed ramble within Pemberley park. Always fond of her walks, she had, since the arrival of her sister-in-law often sought Elizabeth's companionship in her exercise. Both thought alike about the nature of such excursions, understanding that there was little need for conversation. Nature could provide so extravagantly for the pleasure of each that any exchange seemed an intrusion. Their outings, if silent, were sisterly and warm.

Today, however, she had chosen solitude. The events of the previous evening had left her mind in a such a flutter that she must be alone with her contemplations. She, who had determined so strongly in herself to remain unmoved and unmoveable, found her thoughts flying more often than was altogether comfortable to the recollection of Captain Thomas Heywood.

To the charms of the young Stantons, the elder Middleton and Richard Brook she had long prided herself on remaining impervious: but the Captain had taken her unawares. His surprising appearance, his romantic figure, the adventures he had hinted at, the sufferings he must surely have undergone—every circumstance about him seemed to capture her fancy. And when he had spoken to her in such a tone the words of Lord Byron, she had felt herself imperiled in a way she no longer thought possible. Variable creature she must be! Could her unsusceptibility be so frail after all?

The brisk spring air brought a high color to her cheeks as she walked along the muddy gravel lanes amid the shrubbery, climbed the hillocks, and wended her way through the coppices and the groves. In no time, her youth and the perfection of the morning had their effect. Her spirits rose and she set herself to search for such of the earliest and most tender of shoots as were then beginning to show themselves. But, as she bent upon this task, she was alarmed by a rustling in the syringa bushes just behind her. She turned abruptly to see what bird or animal might be burrowing there, when to her surprise she saw instead the figure of a young man emerge.

He was tall and gentlemanlike of appearance, and seemed himself startled at the sight of her. However, he quickly recovered, addressing her with a civil air:"I do not mean to intrude, Miss Darcy," said he."I did not expect anyone to be abroad so early in the morning."

Georgiana was astonished. A stranger at Pemberley, and to accost her with such familiarity! "You have the advantage of me, Sir," she replied coldly, "I cannot recollect that we have had the pleasure of being introduced."

At this he only laughed. "Your candor is admirable, Miss Darcy," said he, "and even your absent-mindedness may be excused. I counted no less than half-a-dozen admirers all about you for every single minute of last night. But, we were indeed introduced then, and by Mr. Darcy himself. I am James Leigh-Cooper."

Georgiana's discomfiture was great. *Now*, she was reminded of their meeting, and looking at the architect's lively countenance, she wondered how she could have overlooked him at all. Such a breach of civility would ordinarily have mortified her. But there was a self-assurance in the young man's address which, despite his agreeable appearance, agitated her.

"I assure you, Mr. Leigh-Cooper, I intended no slight," she conceded, "I was much distracted throughout the evening."

"I should not wonder at it," said he with a bow. "I observed every eye upon you and enjoyed the picture far too much to spoil it by my own intrusion. My charms, I consider, are adequate to most occasions, but even I would not venture to engage with one whose artillery includes Lord Byron himself."

Georgiana smiled at his playful manner. Had he, too, then, noticed the Captain's attentions to her?

"You refer to Captain Thomas Heywood," she said. "Does he not speak verse excellently?"

"He does indeed," agreed he. "So very well does the Captain recite, that one may almost overlook that the work is particularly addressed to a lady of dark coloring, while *you*, Madam, are strikingly fair."

Her cheeks warmed at this sally. It was nothing less than presumptuous of this stranger to gainsay one such as Captain Heywood, so heroic a figure and cousin by marriage to Lady Catherine. And, to turn his cavil upon the works of Lord Byron! Almost, she asked if he had had the leisure to read verse while the Captain was busy serving his country, but recollected herself instead, and diverted the conversation towards Pemberley.

"My brother has complete confidence in you, Mr. Leigh-Cooper," she began. "He considers you one of the few artists in England to whose skills he could entrust his beloved estate."

He smiled at the condescension in her tone, but replied gravely. "It is a trust I do not take lightly. And I pray you, Miss Darcy, not to concern yourself that I might in any way tamper with the grace that is already Pemberley's. Might I explain myself more particularly?"

He proffered his arm and, too surprised to refuse, she took it. He led her down the south avenue and across the lawn towards the river where there was a rise from which the two could survey the vista. At the top of this considerable eminence, they stood admiring the scene.

"This," said he, with a sweep of his arm, "is your Pemberley. Look at its handsome stone; see how nobly it stands against its woods. *That* is the character which I intend to preserve; to consult as Alexander Pope advised, 'the genius of the place in all.' Let others adorn their houses out of all harmony with whatever age built them and terrain surrounds them, I shall continue to see Pemberley as it is."

He proceeded in this vein, discussing animatedly the persistent influences from Italy, the great Palladian villas whose designs, though perhaps well-suited to the abundant sunshine of the Plain of Lombardy, seemed to him less happy among the English hedgerows.

"For myself," he concluded, "I do not profess to follow any one school; but in selecting beauties from the style of each, to adopt so much of grandeur as may accord with a palace, and so much of grace as may call forth the charms of the natural landscape. Simply a new bridge there, you see, and the south avenue widened to open up the view. *Then,* indeed, you might enjoy a greater prospect of that handsome stone of your house, without artificial interference."

There was true feeling in his voice although he seemed almost to have forgotten her presence. Georgiana found herself touched by the passion which informed his words. Following his gaze, she saw Pemberley as she had never seen it before. And with that, she found herself looking more agreeably upon the gentleman himself.

CHAPTER 10

T HE PAIR HAD already turned back towards the house
when they saw, approaching them from a distance, the
figure of Mrs. Darcy escorted by another, a smartly uni-
formed naval officer. Georgiana, who had not considered the
lateness of the hour as she became engrossed in the young
architect's discourse, was suddenly aware of the impropriety
of having lingered so long with him. *She*, unattended, and
roaming about with a perfect stranger! Her embarrassment
was considerable.

That Captain Heywood had come to call upon her at all was
gratifying. But for him to encounter her in this fashion, wind-
blown and disordered, and furthermore in the company of
another gentleman, was something less felicitous.

The Captain had indeed called early, protesting to Mrs.
Darcy that to stay long away from either of Pemberley's
beguiling ladies was beyond his powers. Having learned from
Elizabeth that the younger of those ladies was taking her
morning walk, he had insisted upon awaiting her in the
drawing room. Mrs. Darcy's assurances that Georgiana would
soon return, together with her own pleasant conversation,
had passed a comfortable hour. But when Georgiana did
not appear, and Captain Heywood—though having earlier
spoken of other appointments that morning—yet made no
move towards taking his leave, Elizabeth could but propose
that they set forth together to seek her.

While effusive in his greeting, the Captain had clearly
grown impatient.

"My dear Miss Darcy," cried he, "What a pleasure it is to see you again, and with such charmingly healthful color. It was worth the waiting for you this hour and more."

Georgiana was speechless. How unfortunate that their meeting should happen thus.

Mrs. Darcy, noting her young friend's discomposure, hastily made the introductions, explaining Mr. Leigh-Cooper's assignment for the improvement of Pemberley.

"And indeed," concluded she, "we consider ourselves fortunate in having secured this gentleman, of whose recent triumph at Hardwycke Hall you must surely have heard."

"Dear Hardwycke Hall," observed the Captain."I well remember it from my childhood. But, what a noble task is an architect's! And what fine material for it is Pemberley! Its size can easily encompass all manner of modern comforts. Such an opportunity for an ambitious young man! Most certainly you are going to put in an aviary."

Leigh-Cooper, something surprised, replied that he had not previously considered doing so.

"What!" cried the Captain, "No aviary! Why, my dear friend the Lady Jennings has in hers Java sparrows, Loretta bluebirds and Virginia nightingales, not to mention her crownbirds and goons. All London talks of it. Surely, the fashion cannot have passed you by."

Leigh-Cooper, having listened with attention, if some reserve, only responded that on this estate, he could see no appropriate setting for so exotic a menagerie.

But the Captain was unabashed. "Why, my dear fellow," persisted he, "surely so skilled an artisan as yourself, if you but put your mind to it, could find a dozen such sites."

"But perhaps," replied Leigh-Cooper almost inaudibly, "the whole of Pemberley would fare better in your own fashionable hands."

Georgiana, hearing his words, was distressed for the Captain. The cordiality she had begun to entertain towards Leigh-Cooper vanished on the instant: he had revealed himself to be, after all, an ill-humored young man. What could have possessed him to be so disdainful, and to a man of twice his consequence? And that *he* should be the companion with whom Captain Heywood should discover her!

But the Captain, preferring not to have heard him, was all

graciousness. "I am assured that you can accomplish wonders," he said, and turning away quickly to Georgiana, "What a joy it is to see once again an English complexion. They may sing of the Italian and Spanish beauties, but to my mind, nothing can compare with the roses in a pair of our English cheeks." And without further ado, he led her boldly back towards the great house.

Mrs. Darcy, left standing with Leigh-Cooper, quickly recovered the situation.

"Mr. Darcy and I have already had the pleasure of admiring your artistry," said she, as they followed the others. "When we visited Lady Hardwycke not two months ago, we were struck by your achievements there. I had never seen Hardwycke Hall before, but Mr. Darcy assures me that it is improved beyond all expectations. I was especially pleased with what you had done in the library. To my mind, books, like the dearest friends, merit the most inviting room in the house, and *that* is what you have succeeded in giving them."

"*Your* taste does you credit, Madam," said he, pleased at her words. "Too many have cried up the more showy splendors of the portrait gallery and the great staircase. Although few have the discernment to notice them, *my* favorites among my works are always the simpler rooms."

Elizabeth could not but notice the certainty of his tone. This young man, it appeared, was not afflicted with excessive modesty; but she was the more inclined to forgive him since he not only was brilliant, but also included *her* among the discriminating few.

"Our tastes are similar then," said she. "And both Mr. Darcy and I have every trust that your work on Pemberley will not, like so many of the other modern renovations, improve it to the point where it is barely tolerable."

The two continued on their way, talking animatedly of the folly of too much improvement. Leigh-Cooper, warming to the subject, was reminded of a recent commission.

"You will hardly credit it," said he, "but I have only recently refused a request from a lady whose name would surely be familiar to you, to design a suitable home for her pet tiger, a gift from her husband living in Rangoon, India!"

"I do indeed credit it," she laughed, "Were I married to such a lady, I myself should take care to remain in Rangoon, India."

"How fortunate are the fashionable," continued he, "to be so lightly bound by the fetters of common sense. The modes that rule them grow ever more outlandish. In these days, as we have heard, it is the aviaries which are so admired in London. You would suppose our English countryside so lacking in birds that we needed to import them from Virginia or Java."

They were already nearing the house as he spoke and she would not betray her amusement. But she decided that, despite the bluntness in his character, Mr. James Leigh-Cooper was unquestionably a man to be considered. Moreover, she quite liked him.

PART II

CHAPTER 11

T HE MEANWHILE, CAPTAIN Heywood, walking ahead with Georgiana, was provided with a perfect oppor-tunity to expound upon his good fortune in having secured so happy an anchorage—having, in short, arrived in so congenial a company. He soon fell to reviewing the gaiety of their previous evening, exclaiming upon the pleasure he had taken in it.

"I myself am but a dull fellow," added he, "more at ease, I confess, facing the tempest at sea than in your drawing rooms. However, any fears I might have felt of polished society quickly vanished in the warmth of your sister's wel-come, and more particularly," with a bow, "of your own."

Georgiana, bewildered by such attention, could only blush.

"I knew then," continued he, "that I had been from dear England too long. Oh, Miss Darcy, only look about you at those sturdy oaks, and graceful birches, and pity me my long exile. How fair is Pemberley!"

And with such real pleasure did he smile at her, that the young lady at last felt emboldened to respond.

"Your appearance at the ball," ventured she, "took me altogether by surprise. Little idea had I that my Aunt num-bered in her family one engaged quite so heroically in our country's defense."

The Captain was much pleased by this effusion, inclined towards her, and appeared on the point of saying more. But at the same moment, both observed the approach of their two companions, and he drew back instead.

"So pleasant a morning," he cried heartily. "And"—abruptly changing his tone—"how inconvenient that circumstances forbid me to spend more of it here at Pemberley."

Mrs. Darcy, something startled at this, nevertheless offered refreshment before he left. This he energetically declined. Pemberley's hospitality, he was certain, was of the first order; its table, he knew, famous throughout the Midlands; but already he had over-stayed his leave. And so, with a glance at Georgiana, he speedily departed.

"What a precipitate young man," observed Elizabeth as they watched him hastening towards the stables, "but he is correct, in one particular, at least—it is a pleasant morning. This spring air is altogether delightful and can, I think, only be improved by our going immediately indoors to discuss it over cold meats and cake. Mr. Leigh-Cooper, you will join us, of course?"

The young man responded to the suggestion with readiness. His morning's rounds had been long, and some refreshment before he continued would be of the most welcome.

Elizabeth need hear no more. Mrs. Hedges had but that morning baked a pigeon pie—was that not a cloud she espied in the north?—and beyond a doubt, the more modish of his clients had already introduced him to the new fashion of taking luncheon? They must go indoors on the instant.

Laughing, he followed her into the house.

Georgiana could scarcely contain her vexation. She had been awaiting private converse with Elizabeth in no little anticipation. Always, she valued her sister's good opinion; today, fresh from her walk, her thoughts ordered, she was sure of a composure which the other could not but admire. How wise she would have shown herself to her this morning, how exquisitely prudent, how little her head turned by the romantic gallantries of a Captain Heywood!

But Mr. James Leigh-Cooper had overthrown all. By interrupting her in the garden, he had quite distracted her from her meditations; his manner towards Captain Heywood had been openly churlish. And now, here he was yet again intruding himself, and worst of all, doing it upon the invitation of Mrs. Darcy! She could quite have cried.

As the group approached the saloon, they were met by Mrs. Reynolds bearing a letter that had come from Longbourn. Elizabeth took it from her with some misgiving as to what news of ill it might contain. Although neither would have it generally known, both she and Jane had been made uneasy by their mother's failure to attend the recent festivities. With Mrs. Bennet's nerves, the sisters had long been on terms of cordial familiarity; but that they should compel her to miss a ball at Pemberley must betoken some ill circumstance indeed!

So sharp was her anxiety, in truth, that she found herself incapable of delaying her reading of the letter until a quieter moment. She begged her companions' indulgence—this was a matter that would admit of no delay—they must proceed without her—she was confident that Miss Darcy would attend to their guest. Thus having put poor Georgiana in charge, she took herself to a more private quarter.

CHAPTER 12

T HE SALOON, INTO which Georgiana led her charge, was agreed to be one of the finest rooms in the house. This morning, it was to be seen in its most favorable aspect, the light from the north touching the furniture and fittings-up, while beyond the high windows, the Spanish chestnuts on the lawn and the woody hills in the distance showed a faint touch of springtime green. Not a corner was unlit; not an angle unpleasing.

Still, Miss Darcy was so piqued as to remain impervious to the beauties of both light and surroundings. She was alone again with this perplexing young man, now standing altogether at his ease in front of the great stone fireplace; a poor exchange for Elizabeth, yet he must be endured with a good grace.

Her first business was to order refreshments, which she did with dispatch. But after the servants had been sent on their way, and Mr. Leigh-Cooper asked whether he did not find the fire too hot, and been permitted the privilege of responding that it was perfectly to his liking, a pause succeeded.

Georgiana waited for him to speak; but he appeared altogether content to meet her gaze without words, until it seemed that the silence must engulf them both forever.

At last, reflecting with some exasperation that one of them at least might now introduce some innocuous topic of conversation, she availed herself of the well-bred schoolgirl's most elementary axiom: that everyone in proper society must by all means be related to everyone else.

"Pray, Mr. Leigh-Cooper," said she, "are you by chance connected with the Leighs of Devonshire? Mr. George Leigh is, although I have not yet met him, a close friend of our godfather, Sir Geoffrey Portland."

"I wonder that you should ask," said he. "Leigh is a common enough name. Our families *may* be connected; but I cannot think why you should so readily assume that they might."

Despite herself, Georgiana was nettled by his tone. "Depend upon it," said she, "if you *were* connected to the family, you would most certainly be aware of it. Mr. Leigh is first cousin to the Duke of Norfolk himself."

"Is he, indeed?" said he. "Do you then fancy everyone of merit to be in some way related to the aristocracy? I regret to disappoint you, my dear Miss Darcy, but *my* family does not, so far as I know, include a single baronet or viscount among us; and yet we count ourselves to be as estimable as most others and more so than many."

Georgiana knew not what to say. Mr. Leigh-Cooper's superciliousness was fully as evident here in the drawing room as it had shown itself outside in the park. And this from a young man, who, although already distinguished by considerable talents, was altogether without other connections in society! Brilliant Mr. Leigh-Cooper was, beyond a doubt; but there was that of the headstrong, of the too-assured in his temper. And yet, while contemplating Pemberley, they two had been in accord. What a lack was in him.

Distraction was happily provided by the arrival of the servants with refreshments. James Leigh-Cooper ate heartily of everything, his appetite in no way impaired by the exchange that had preceded. He gave no sign of consciousness that he had said anything at all untoward. She noted in surprise his progress through the tray of meats: he was not, it appeared, quite so proud as to disdain the joys of the table.

CHAPTER 13

T HE LETTER FROM Longbourn, perused by most, would have provided no other emotion than grateful relief. It conveyed the warmest of greetings from Mrs. Bennet to her sweetest Lizzy; it speculated with rapture upon the grandeurs of the ball, her dear Lizzy's dress, and her esteemed Fitzwilliam's liberality; it ended with the assurance of her own renewed health, and of the intention of both senior Bennets to visit Derbyshire within the fortnight. Anyone, receiving so sprightly a communication, must be heartened.

Not so, Elizabeth. She knew her mother's always careless hand too well not to note in it an agitation that others might have missed; moreover, the very suddenness of the Bennets' decision to join their daughters, as well as an allusion of her mother's to "some family difficulties that had arisen in recent weeks," signaled an urgency that belied the tone. Despite Mrs. Bennet's evasiveness concerning the source of the matter troubling her, her daughter was taken with foreboding. It was, after all, not so long ago that Lydia's indiscretion had nearly destroyed the family's reputation. Too well did Elizabeth recollect the agony of those long days, and sorely did she dread any new tribulations.

But the luxury of premature alarm was denied her by the exigencies of her present duty as mistress of Pemberley. Putting aside her thoughts, she hurried to the saloon.

There, she found the two young people sitting beside the much-depleted tray, deeply engaged in conversation, Georgiana's color high and countenance animated, their every aspect companionable. And yet her sister had seemed so little inclined towards the architect when Elizabeth had left her only moments before. Could her displeasure with the young man then have vanished so swiftly? With one such as James Leigh-Cooper, Elizabeth surmised, it might well be so. He had just such a way about him. About what he knew, he spoke well.

But, when she drew close enough to catch the substance of their speech, in what different light did it present itself.

"Surely Miss Darcy," he was saying, "you cannot mean that fashion could prove of so much consequence in your eyes that you would abandon your own tastes to answer to it?"

Indignant, Miss Darcy would reply, but noticing her sister's arrival, broke off. Both young people rose, and Georgiana offered such refreshment as remained.

But James Leigh-Cooper, still intent on their dispute, quickly turned his appeal to Mrs. Darcy.

"*You*, Madam, may be depended upon for good sense," cried he. "Miss Darcy and I have this minute been contesting the rival virtues of solid good taste and trifling modishness. Pray, will you not tell us where your own inclinations lie upon this matter?"

"Not upon my life," said Elizabeth smiling. "I would not for anything be an arbiter in such a contest—especially since your words leave so little room for doubt on your own convictions."

"You read me too clearly," said he, bowing his acquiescence. "I had some hope that I was presenting both views with tolerable impartiality. But, your understanding is too quick for such wiles as I may possess."

"Do not distress yourself," replied Elizabeth, now laughing outright. "Wiles are the proper weapons of *our* artful sex, and would sit ill upon so stalwart a fellow as yourself!"

Georgiana, watching their exchange, was all astonishment. *He*, to be complaisant, indeed playful! Why, he seemed with her sister positively at ease. And yet how altered he was when he spoke to *her*, how decided his tone, how unyielding his manner. Whatever could he mean by it?

"Indeed," she cried, "Mr. Leigh-Cooper need not fret unduly about his artfulness. He shows himself, on the whole, uncommonly candid—too much so, some might say, for the convenience of the rest of the world."

"My candor," said he, now smiling at her, "has served me well enough so far. However, propriety restrains me from giving such rein to it, as to remark, for example, on the admirable effects of a lively argument upon a young lady's complexion."

Georgiana was mortified to feel her color rise even the more. But turning to her sister, she observed her laughing too heartily by far to have noticed her discomfort, much less be inclined to alleviate it. Altogether, the effect that this young man had was singularly disturbing.

CHAPTER 14

J ANE RECEIVED HER own communication from Longbourn with emotions similar to those of her sister. She too saw unsteadiness in the hand, more than usual incoherence of expression. Something, she could not but fear, must be amiss.

Yet her husband remained untroubled by any such perception, and for his sake she would not betray her disquiet. Good nature was the virtue most often admired in Jane Bingley; but it was not her only quality. Growing up, as she had, her wits sharpened by the jibes of Mr. Bennet and her vision cleared by her sister Elizabeth's unrelenting eye for folly, she had developed more understanding than was commonly suspected of her. In short, she saw more than was supposed. But that very sweet nature too often kept her from giving utterance to her observations; she had, moreover, in her own early life, seen more nearly than had any of her younger sisters the unhappy results upon a marriage of too great a disparity of intellect, and had determined that no such disaster should befall her own union. Temptations were there, and, often, to point out to Bingley the foibles of one or another of their company; but always she would resist. She would not be wiser than her husband.

So she must perforce agree that the Bennets' arrival was the most splendid piece of news since the visit of Mr. Hurst's elderly mother shortly before Martinmas; that no time must be lost in spreading the glad tidings to their neighbors and friends; that three—no, rather, four—of those hens plumpest already must be fattened the more without delay.

"And the very best of it," concluded Bingley, "is that your parents have chosen rather to stay with us than at Pemberley. And this, despite their awareness of our already having our sisters with us. Oh, my dear Jane, what request we are in!"

"I would prefer to think so," responded his wife, "but cannot help suspecting that their choice arises less from the recognition of our own merits than from their dread of the alternative. You must remember that when last they stayed at Pemberley, my mother was veritably reduced by fear of her host."

"Yes, I have seen my friend Darcy affect others thus," said Bingley, "and yet I have known him only to be kind and courteous. But, I had hardly expected him so to daunt a Mrs. Bennet. I confess that I had thought *her* indomitable."

"Nonetheless," said Jane, "she will need feel no such discomfort with us here at Pelham. You, Mr. Bingley, are surely the best-natured man alive."

"And you, the most tender-hearted of women," responded he ardently. "My dear, what news! I can scarcely wait to tell Caroline and Louisa."

It may be easily supposed that the loving pair would have much to do, to make sure that their newest visitors could be welcomed and provided for in comfort. Jane would to the kitchen and the housekeeper, while her husband must needs rush the good news to the neighborhood.

Mrs. Randall's task, both she and her mistress agreed, was heavy. She must see to the white soup and the pigeon pies, the preserved ginger must be tasted and the black butter boiled to perfection; any number of plum cakes, pound cakes, fruit cakes, sweet rolls and jellies must be stocked. The good Mrs. Randall professed herself disappointed with the venison and apprehensive about such of the pork as remained; Mrs. Bingley lamented that it was too early for lamb. Both were altogether delighted by the exchange.

But Charles Bingley, before he had fully buttoned his greatcoat, was stayed by his sisters just returned from an excursion into the countryside. Caroline's approach and her manner were encouraging; there was today in her a warmth and animation of spirits not always visible to her brother. It was clear that she had something to say to him, and before he had advanced many steps, she addressed him in an eager tone.

"Why, dear brother, your park is pure wonder; we have been walking about in it hither and thither for hours. The place has fine capabilities; there is a curious collection of evergreen and flowering shrubs! But we have just now consulted upon the matter with another of our party, a most discerning observer, a man of fashion and taste, who has been so generous as to point to its shortcomings. Brother, the whole wants method. You must look to it, if you wish to be fully esteemed in your position as Master of Pelham Hall, to clear the wood and the clump of trees just near the stables. I assure you, you will need to present your lawns with greater care, arrange your groups of trees more exactly. Precision, my dear brother, we are informed by the truly knowledgeable, it is precision which is imperative to a man of fashion!"

Her brother was pleased by her attentions, although he had little idea of what her discourse could mean. Caroline, while rarely at a loss for advice on the arrrangement either of his houses or his life, had never before expressed so informed an opinion on any of his parklands. The counsel she urged upon him with such energy must come from some other acquaintance, one perhaps who had been lately in London.

"But my dear Caroline," cried he, "are we then to alter nature's own great gifts? Surely, they are more graceful just as they are. But, sisters," he continued in excitement, "there is news. I have only just learned that we shall be privileged with a visit from Jane's dear parents before the fortnight's end. Is that not capital? We shall entertain them as grandly as we can, perhaps even have our own ball at Pelham to present them to the country. Would you not think *this* a better means than pruning our trees for making our presence known here in Derbyshire?"

Mrs. Hurst was excessively stirred by this intelligence; so much so, indeed, that she was actually moved to a response. "Mr. and Mrs. Bennet to be shown off to the country? Surely, you jest, Charles."

Caroline could hardly contain her amusement. "My dear Charles, you would do better to keep them well to yourselves and hope that the neighborhood hears nothing of their visit."

As she spoke, the carriage approached, returning Kitty and Mary Bennet from their own morning's entertainment of a visit to Sophia Middleton, met last night at the Ball and, by morning, already pledged their closest friend and nearest confidante. Almost immediately they burst into the hall, sweeping with them their sister Jane.

"Oh! Brother," was Kitty's greeting. "Such a morning! What fun we had with Sophia, and how merry we were! Middleton Hall is larger, I fancy, than Pelham, but they have only the two barouches and their orchard is meaner. How we laughed! And here Jane tells us how Mama and Papa are to join us! I declare I long to present Sophia to them. Do you not agree, Mary, that Frank Middleton is prodigious handsome?"

"To some, perhaps," was Mary's response, "even perhaps indeed to the generality. But mere handsomeness has little charm for me. I seek rather the more substantial attractions of the intellect."

Kitty hardly listened. She never attended to Mary at all, confining her sisterly attentions merely to addressing her. "Lord, how we laughed. I vow, Sophia and me were ready to die of it. When she spilled the water over Watkin's livery— what an ugly fellow he is, I never saw so ugly a fellow. We laughed so loud you might have heard us here at Pelham."

Caroline Bingley had heard enough. She waited for a pause but finding none, spoke nevertheless.

"Your account of your morning's adventures gives assurance that your time here will be well spent," she began, "and with your parents' arrival the engagement of the entire neighborhood will be assured. We shall all look forward to the coming festivities with interest." And rising, she and Mrs. Hurst removed themselves to the library to consult the journals for news of landscape improvement.

CHAPTER 15

J ANE'S FEELINGS UPON the withdrawal of the Bingley
sisters were not unmixed: but for the most part they were
of relief. The cold composure of Louisa, the heartless
elegance of Caroline, served to bring to the entire company
an oppression that only departed when they did. For her own
sake, she would wish it not so; for the sake of her husband,
she would affect not to observe it so; but the reality, she
could not deny, was other. Wherever Charles's sisters went,
they cast a chill.

But barely had she time to reflect upon *their* deficiencies,
and her husband's thus the more remarkable benevolence,
when a footman entered bearing yet another letter, in a hand
which immediately she recognized to be that of her sister,
Lydia. In some dismay, she took it and read.

> *Brighton, Monday,*
> *April 22*
>
> *Dearest Jane,*
>
> *How delightful it is that Mama and Papa are to
> come to you directly. We too are, of course, eager, as
> Mama suggests, to join the family for the occasion,
> and since my dear Wickham has fortunately man-
> aged to secure a leave from the Regiment, we shall be
> able to do so without difficulty. I wish we might have
> arrived earlier, in time for the Ball. How we should
> have been merry! I long to see you all again, and
> living so grandly. Mama has talked so of the beauties*

*of your Pelham Hall and of the fine new quilt on your
bed. When Major Ainsley's wife learns where we are
going, she will be positively in a fit of envy. As to dear
Pemberley, my Wickham's childhood home, that I
feel I know already. I look eagerly, dear sister, to
week's end.*

*Yours,
Lydia*

These added tidings served further to increase the tumult
of Jane's mind. Not only were her parents to disturb the
already tenuous harmony existing now at Pelham Hall, but, it
appeared, were to be assisted in that endeavor by Lydia and
her husband as well. Even so generous a spirit as Jane's must
quail at the prospect! Nor could her own husband be of help
to her: one so patient and good-humored as he could serve
only to make matters worse. Help, if help there would be, was
not to be found at home.

Thinking upon it, she determined to go immediately to
visit Lizzy. Her thoughtful sister brought to any situation both
good sense, and—if that proved still inadequate to so dismay-
ing a circumstance—lively wit. The besetment did not exist
that was dire enough for Lizzy to fail to find sport in it: with
her, Jane could expect at least laughter. The more she considered, the more desirable her sister's company seemed to her.
She could not, must not wait; she would go to Pemberley
without delay.

Nor would she go alone. A visit to Elizabeth now would
provide her with a most fitting occasion to put into effect a
plan she had long contemplated. Kitty and Mary had so far
escaped the burden of family loyalty: going their own ignorant way they had until now delighted in proving themselves
ungovernable, accruing thus all the sweet privileges enjoyed
by those fully lacking in reliability. It was time, Jane had long
felt, that they awoke to good sense. She, while wishing whole-
heartedly for such a transformation, knew herself not equal
to effecting it. *That* arduous task, if to be achieved at all,
demanded no less than a Lizzy.

She would take her younger sisters with her.

CHAPTER 16

T WO DAYS AFTER the ball, Sir Geoffrey Portland awakened to discover that a fit of the gout had taken him in the foot. He passed the morning lying abed in some pain and greatly out of humor. Too much merriment, he was certain, had been the cause of his affliction. His was a quiet life, and to his way of thinking, the only life for a gentleman in the country. A morning's fishing, good sport at the hunt, the stimulating society of his beagles by day, and of an occasional evening a card table made up of his own small circle of friends; *that* was as much diversion as he deemed either necessitous or meet.

However, he was a devoted godfather, and for the sake of Georgiana, he had valiantly submitted himself to all the torments of unrelieved conviviality. He had danced with his ward, as was his duty and his pleasure; he had danced too with Lady Catherine and her daughter. He had talked; he had supped; he had even been civil to Celia Montague. In short, he had fulfilled every obligation which propriety demanded; and, at last feeling the benefits of these exertions, he moaned audibly.

He had now and then been prostrated by this very condition for the last ten years or more; but each attack he greeted with an indignation as fresh as if it were his first. To be gouty affronted his vanity: it was, in his estimation, the property of older men than he. Nor did it in any way improve the turn of his calf. Calling upon his manservant to bring him a primrose decoction, he surrendered himself to being cosseted until midday.

Lady Catherine too had arisen out of sorts this day; but hearing of her old friend's ill-health, she instantly rallied. "I suffer for you, dear Sir Geoffrey," she announced when she arrived in his room. "You must allow me to have Sally mix for you a remedy that all Kent favors. Nobody can contest the salutary effects of this powder: it derives from both oyster shell and egg shell, and, the most potent of all, no less than two ounces of soap. The mixture should cure you as quickly as you swallow. Is it not good fortune that I have brought my Sally to you?" she exclaimed while ringing for her servant.

Humbled as he was by his condition, Sir Geoffrey lacked the strength to resist the good lady's ministrations. Potent her mixture undoubtedly was, but whether its effects would prove preferable to the disease itself, remained in question. Still, he welcomed her solicitude, and as she sat down at his bedside, her talk served, if nothing further, to divert his attentions from the anguishing pain in his swollen big toe.

Besides, the conversation to which she very soon turned—her own meticulously refined version of their evening at Pemberley—was consoling to him for having in the last two days achieved all the sweet comfort of the reposeful familiar.

"Was not Anne's appearance noted especially by all in the festivities?" she asked immediately; and, without troubling to await a response, "Surely a gown of such elegance has not been seen in Derbyshire this season, or for many another either. You know, Sir Geoffrey, that I have long been praised for my sincerity. I do not dissemble and cannot withhold from you that I have never thought my dear child in finer complexion. It was quite plain that all judged her the most adorable of creatures. I delighted in the admiration she inspired."

Sir Geoffrey, gallant and laid low, would not differ. "Indeed," responded he instead, "nor has our neighborhood witnessed such an evening at Pemberley since young Henry's parents lived." Truth to tell, Sir Geoffrey's prime had been but brief, and such unshadowed happiness as he had known had come to an end when his Lady Arabella had departed this world. "Were those not happy days, Lady Catherine?" he continued, "were we not handsome and did we not have manner? You and your Lewis, I and my dear Arabella, and of course, Fitzwilliam and Susan. And now," sighing, "here are only you and I left, and I unable to stir."

Lady Catherine was pensive for a full moment, but mere fond memories were powerless in the face of her present purpose, which was to pursue the improprieties she had but two evenings before observed all about her. This was a subject near to her heart: one upon which she fancied her judgment incontestable, and the effects of her reproofs upon those guilty altogether remedial, no matter to whom her denunciations were presently addressed.

"And did you, dear friend, not observe the spectacle of the younger among the Bennet sisters?" she insisted. "A display worthy only of *her* ill-bred family." For thus she always referred to Elizabeth, since it defied her fortitude to name her a Darcy. "I have witnessed such vulgarity in their demeanor from the start, but *this* young woman is flagrant in her behavior. Parading herself as she did before the Middleton boy. Indelicate girl! She is altogether heedless. And, I assure you, dear Sir Geoffrey, you have not yet seen the half of it. Is my nephew thus ever to be plagued amongst his intimates?"

"Dear Madam," responded Sir Geoffrey, "you need not concern yourself on behalf of Henry. He is above all else a gentleman bred to his responsibilities. Let us not forget, Lady Catherine, that he is both *your* nephew and *my* godson. There is no doubt in my mind that he knows the limits of such triflings as we have witnessed, and will permit no real impropriety in his house. Depend upon it, if any of the Bennets truly affronts his sensibilities, he will be straightaway rid of the lot of them."

Lady Catherine, contemplating this pleasant prospect, was somewhat heartened. But, almost immediately, Sir Geoffrey proceeded with a eulogy which displayed the bad taste to include her daughter not at all.

"May we not console ourselves, dear Lady Catherine," said the rash gentleman, "with the development of our Georgiana? How well she looked that night, did she not? Such a pretty height and size! Such a firm and upright figure. *She* at least comports herself in a fashion that need disgrace neither herself nor her family. And how esteemed she was for it. Did she not take all eyes?"

"Indeed," replied Lady Catherine with energy, "no one can dispute that she cut a figure. As to *everyone's* admiration—there, I cannot applaud her. There was *one* eye which my niece would have done well to have left to cast its glance elsewhere."

Poor Sir Geoffrey, his toe still painful and her meaning eluding him entirely, could but nod his grave assent. Happily, this gave Lady Catherine immediate relief and she fell to instructing Sally upon the dosage of her celebrated remedy.

CHAPTER 17

NO SOONER HAD Jane conceived the scheme for the improvement of her younger sisters, and accorded to herself sufficient time for the congratulations due upon its felicity, than she had begun to put it into effect. Bingley's blessing applied for and received, the carriage was ordered, and a note dispatched to Elizabeth to inform her of their coming. But this morning, when she sought out the younger Bennets for the trip, they were less come-at-able even than she could have imagined.

Kitty awaited the visit staunchly promised her by Frank Middleton, who but the day before had roundly assevered that he might very well find himself passing Pelham Hall on his way from Eaton, if the hour were not too late. Mary was as ever absorbed in her true life of the mind; the wind was surely changing to a harsher quarter; they had promised Bingley to make up a card table that evening. Anyone would think they did not want to see Elizabeth.

"My one consolation," said Mary when they finally were in the carriage and on their way, "is that I may at last be able to avail myself of the pleasures of Pemberley's library. Never before have I had the leisure to enjoy its riches, although our brother Darcy has more than once suggested that I might spend several profitable hours there."

"Indeed you shall," said her sister heartily, although adding to herself, "and if *you* might be persuaded to read less, and your sister, to read at all, there might be an easier task for Elizabeth."

Thus encouraged, Mary turned her attention to the surrounding countryside. Her course of studies that winter had included the botanical, and she saw now the opportunity to apply her lately acquired erudition. "Are we, dear sister," said she, settling herself into the protection of the sheepskin, "to travel all the way with carriage closed? I cannot see why we must submit entirely to such caution. Can you not know that Derbyshire abounds in bearberry, cloudberry and lesser twayblade? I should better wish that we risk the weather and look full at the fields. What sense can there be in traveling by landaulette if we are to keep the roof drawn as in any ordinary chaise?"

To this Kitty replied with some animation that she for one had little intention of exposing herself needlessly to the ravages of the wind and the dust. If they must voyage so far, *she* would not arrive at Pemberley in wild and disreputable fashion. At which Mary wondered disagreeably whether Kitty had ever in her life cared for anything so much as for her curls. So the sisters continued their cavil, the one scorning all but the labors of the intellect, the other heedless of anything but the figure she cut.

Jane, altogether overwhelmed, listened in silence as the coach moved slowly over what, for all its many crevices and obstacles, was considered generally to be ten miles of good road. Despite Mary's urgings, the wind was indeed chill and the sky threatening. There was little to be seen outside the window; even had Mary's specimens been in bloom—which seemed, to Jane if not to her learned sister, unlikely so early in the season—they could hardly have been visible through the encroaching mist. Jane resigned herself to a journey that would provide her with neither the pleasures of stimulating conversation nor the solace of silence.

The clatter of her sisters' talk continued until they were approaching Lambton, where Jane at last thought she saw the opportunity to distract them from it. On a hill above the town stood the Church of All Saints, its octagonal tower dominating the view. She had grown accustomed to have her visitors exclaim upon its beauty; and like many of the finer English buildings, it was seen to its best advantage against a lowering sky. Kitty and Mary had not yet passed upon that road in daylight, and it would be a pity if they were to miss the sight for the sake of contentiousness.

"Oh, my dear sisters," she cried, "do but look ahead! Here is the most celebrated church in this country. Do you not think it splendid against that group of clouds?"

But she was barely attended to. "Just so," said Kitty fretfully. "A great, dark arrangement of clouds. And yet my sister would have us ride with open carriage for the sake of her floral studies."

"Just so, indeed," thought Jane, "and how foolish of me to have expected either one of you to be moved by so paltry a thing as an object of beauty and a monument to piety." Happily, it was then that another sight presented itself, one perhaps that would prove more worthy of her sisters' discriminating attention. "And it is here," she added aloud, pointing to the inn they were just now passing, "that our own Lizzy first entertained Mr. Darcy and his sister, Georgiana, nearly two years ago."

This at last engaged the young ladies' interest.

"Indeed," cried Kitty, craning to see better, "and how clever was my sister to have captivated such a man as he. To think that Lizzy is the richest woman in the county! Even though your husband, Jane, is so much more agreeable than Mr. Darcy, I should think that Lizzy's lace alone would make up for any inadequacies of temper. And then Mr. Darcy is so very tall. I admire a lofty figure; Frank Middleton is by far the tallest among his brothers. Dear Lizzy is to be congratulated upon her success: you and I, Mary, must study her closely from now on."

"Lizzy admittedly has done well for herself," responded Mary. "But the contrary question may also be put—how well has her husband fared? I think that he could have done not ill to look elsewhere for a wife, and that without leaving Hertfordshire."

"Whatever can you mean?" cried Kitty. "You are surely not suggesting that he might have chosen one of the Lucas girls over our Lizzy?"

"Certainly not," said she. "But since their marriage, I myself have had the opportunity to converse at length with our brother, and I have discovered him to be an uncommonly learned man. What a pity that such an one has been enticed by mere brilliance of wit into a marriage that time will only prove inadequate to his intellectual powers. Had he but thought," with a meaningful glance, "when making his choice, to look beyond pleasantries to someone who holds reason more dear than good humor, how happier might his situation be now!"

This speech drew even Jane and Kitty together in their astonishment. Kitty would reply, but Jane, glancing at her, was swift to interject.

"Do but look to your right," said she. "The tall building is the very mill that Mr. Bingley spoke of last night. Does it not grow colder? Well, we are sure at least of excellent fires at Pemberley. Are we not, Kitty?"

CHAPTER 18

THE HARMONY OF human intercourse may be said to be antithetical to the number three. A party of two or four may differ with reasonable expectations of balance; but when three tangle, there must be inequity. Amongst sisters, this maxim holds relentless: no matter how momentous or trivial the dispute, *their* divisions are fierce. The two of the triangle who chance to concur will glory in their alliance, while the third, left friendless and forlorn, may only forbear.

Happy the sisters were, therefore, with the first appearance of Pemberley woods. Their journey nearly over, the sight of the majestic stone house rising against the wooded hills, and the prospect of their being soon provided with a more happy number by Elizabeth, cheered them all. Even Kitty forgot herself so far as to speak for three minutes together without once referring to Frank Middleton.

As they crossed over the stream and approached the entrance, they could make out a group of people already standing near the door. There was Mr. Darcy deep in consultation with his bailiff, Samuel Merkin; Georgiana and Elizabeth; and with them a stalwart young man unknown to the sisters. The Pemberley curricle stood prepared to depart, and every so often Mr. Darcy would make a start towards it; but each time Merkin would detain him in further conversation. All looked towards the Pelham landaulette as it approached.

"You are here not a moment too soon," cried Elizabeth, after the warmest of greetings had been exchanged. "Mr. Darcy's godfather is taken ill, and he and Georgiana are this minute preparing to attend him. But a half hour's delay of your arrival and you would have missed them altogether."

"Not even so long," said her husband. "We should have been off these twenty-minutes since, had Merkin not hindered us with his talk."

"He is to be the more commended then," said Elizabeth playfully. "But for his solicitude, you should have had to endure until this evening before you saw my sisters."

"That is quite true," agreed he, bowing to the sisters, and hastily mounting the curricle. "Well, do whatever you can, Merkin. But the worst of this business, Leigh-Cooper," now addressing the young man, "is that you and I have not even begun our discussions for the course of the South Avenue as we had planned for this morning. No matter. Proceed as you think fit, and we shall settle it upon my return."

"Willingly," replied the young man, "I had already intended to devote the afternoon to the surroundings of the new parterre. Miss Darcy," turning towards her with a bow, "was kind enough to think well of our scheme as I explained it to her but yesterday morning."

"Upon my word, brother," said Miss Darcy, coloring, "Mr. Leigh-Cooper's vision of Pemberley is altogether inspiring. None, I imagine, could question his excellence," glancing at him, "with regard to his profession."

A close observer, witnessing this exchange, might have wondered whether Miss Darcy had not placed some particular emphasis upon the last words of her speech. But the younger Bennets were not attentive, and Elizabeth was too much occupied with her husband. As for Mr. Leigh-Cooper, he only smiled broadly and handed the young lady into the carriage. Final salutations made, Sir Geoffrey wished an early recovery, and the Darcys' departure lamented by all, the curricle made speedily off.

Mrs. Darcy led the remaining party into the house without further delay, her younger sisters talking the while around her. Between Kitty's immediate entreaties that Elizabeth reveal in all candor precisely what she thought about her new bonnet, and, following hard upon those, Mary's being so magnanimous as to provide lengthy discursions upon each and every portrait hanging in the long corridor, there was much chatter.

Soon enough, therefore, Mr. Leigh-Cooper excused himself, begging leave to undertake his remaining morning's work, and the Bennet sisters were left to their own devices. Elizabeth settled them comfortably in their chambers, and withdrew to the saloon to await them.

Jane was the first to rejoin her. Both had been impatient for the opportunity to talk privately about their mother's communications, and neither would waste needless time in approaching the matter.

"I can not, dear Lizzy, no matter how I try," began Jane, "erase from my mind the fear that my mother's visit this very week brings us some other intelligence than she has yet confessed. Her letter told little; yet were you not also concerned?"

"Deeply concerned," agreed her sister, yet with a half-smile, "and the more so that her letter was so signally lacking in complaint. Confess now, have you before this received a communication from my mother which neglected entirely to bemoan either her nerves or my father's latest equivocations? Her agues, I find entirely tolerable; it is her lack of them that leaves me perturbed."

"Ah, Lizzy, you will make sport," said Jane. "But perhaps you laugh too soon. There is that yet to tell that might check even *your* merriment."

"Oh, my dearest Jane," cried Elizabeth, "we have been apart too much of late, if you can so misread me. You cannot think me insensible to our family's interests; but surely, you, gentle Jane, will permit us some levity amongst these kinsmen of ours lest the very weight of them sink us altogether. My feelings towards them you know; but pray do not ask me to forego what diversions their eccentricities allow."

Jane smiled, but must now produce for her sister's perusal the letter she had received from Lydia the very day before. Elizabeth, reading it, was incensed no less by its contents than by the cheer in its tone.

"Insufferable girl," cried she, "how we should have been merry, indeed! She improves not a whit! But, in the company of her dear Wickham what shall we expect? Eager to join the family! Can she have forgotten what has passed between us? And to talk of dear Pemberley in so familiar a fashion! Dear Pemberley, indeed!"

"The letter is disappointing, I own," agreed Jane. "But do not, I entreat you, distress yourself too much. Lydia and her husband shall come to us at Pelham Hall and our brother Darcy need not suffer Wickham's presence for so much as an afternoon. Mr. Bingley and I have already arranged to provide amusement in plenty. The worst that you may expect is that Lydia alone could choose to accompany my mother and father when they visit Pemberley."

"So excessively formal, dear Jane?" said Elizabeth. "Recollect that it is of *dear* Pemberley that you speak. One would fancy that you, who have been so often a welcome guest here, knew it less well than Lydia, who has seen it never at all. Jane, Jane, you are too good, and I will have need of all your steadiness in the coming days."

For she could not long forget her own circumstance and especially her yet uncertain acquaintance with Sir Geoffrey Portland. He had been courtly at the ball, but reserved: try as she might, she could not estimate whether his stern carriage were merely peculiar to his character or whether it betokened real disapprobation. Darcy intended, when at Denby Park, to invite the elder gentleman to Pemberley as soon as his health permitted, and she already looked to the occasion with some apprehension. With what more reason did she so view it now. What should he make of her mother's pretensions, her father's eccentricities? And to have *that* prospect complicated by the possible appearance of Lydia! It was more than could be borne even to anticipate.

"Beyond question you shall have what help I can provide," said Jane with some hesitation. "But wait, Lizzy, we have not yet done. Still another matter hangs over us, and upon that *I* must ask for *your* assistance. It is not without intent that I have brought Mary and Kitty here to you today. They are still so little disciplined, so easily distracted, so heedless. Lamentable it would be if they, too, were to follow the example of Lydia. And yet at heart they are not ungovernable. It is not too late to improve them, though I confess the task to be far beyond my own powers. Not *your* abilities, however: you, Lizzy, if you put your mind to it, can help them if any one can."

"How extravagant is your view of my skills," said Elizabeth, "and for such flattery I suppose I should thank you, although I own, the task you commission me with is something heavy for excessive gratitude. But of course, you are altogether correct. Kitty and Mary *must* be taken in hand, and your own tender-heartedness prevents you from accomplishing that task. Jane, never have I wished you harsher of nature before, but I confess that I do now, and heartily."

Hard upon this, the door burst open and the subjects of discussion themselves appeared. Kitty was in the highest of spirits, having decided that her bedroom was larger than Mary's, and possessed a fairer prospect over the park. Mary, unmoved, insisted that it was her own quarters that were the more spacious, and that her view of the woods was conducive to philosophical study, with which, however, she could hardly expect Kitty to be acquainted.

Jane and Elizabeth exchanged a glance. Their task would be formidable indeed.

CHAPTER 19

L ADY CATHERINE, HAVING settled Sir Geoffrey's dosage to her satisfaction, straightaway turned her efforts to improving his domestic situation. But the task proved sadly unequal to her redoubtable skills; within the bare hour, she had effected profitable change in the needlewoman's system; uncovered carelessness in the newest footman's livery, and sent him packing to repair it; and checked the cook at the very moment she was about to commit the intolerable extravagance of baking a pie with a full half-dozen from the last but one bushel of apples. Anne, she had assigned to a brisk walk in the wind, in quest of a brilliant complexion; Captain Heywood had left earlier on another excursion. There remained little for her to do but examine the silver for tarnish and wait until Sir Geoffrey should show the good sense to respond to her medicine. Time, therefore, hung heavy on her hands and she greatly welcomed the appearance of Darcy and Georgiana.

"Nephew," she announced as quickly as Darcy had stepped from the carriage, "You come in good time, for Sir Geoffrey's agonies are great. You may take heart, however, for I myself have brought from Rosings an excellent remedy, known to have defeated the worst of such maladies, and we have only to await its effects. But, the illness has taken a sad toll upon his disposition: I could wish that he might bear his affliction with a better grace. It remains *your* task, Darcy, to see if you cannot improve his temper."

Darcy immediately reassured the good lady. He had found Sir Geoffrey thus before and knew his ways; he would go directly to his quarters, while Georgiana remained with her aunt to give her comfort.

"Pray, Madam," began she, "do not distress yourself excessively. My brother, as he says, has often attended Sir Geoffrey in these afflictions, and always his company has proved pleasing. He alone has more than once been able to raise my godfather's spirits, where others have despaired."

"That is curious," was Her Ladyship's gracious response, "since Darcy's own humor is so often ill. Yet, I suppose, his frequent distemper should at least serve to better his understanding of another's."

Georgiana bore for her aunt a great affection and but little less respect. Still, she would not hear Darcy so censured.

"Whatever you may say of my brother," said she, "he had but to learn of my godfather's illness and he was at his side. Perhaps, his address may at times be wanting, but be assured that his heart is always affectionate. And since his marriage, even his manner is greatly improved. All Derbyshire speaks of it. I am surprised that you yourself have not observed it."

Her Ladyship was incensed. "Upon my word," cried she. "Such boldness from one so young is unseemly. I wonder at it, and can but think that you have of late been exposed to a particularly unfortunate example. Even your celerity in attending your godfather when he is so in need cannot excuse your impertinence. That is what comes of it, you see. Young people are too little concerned these days with the health and comforts of their elders. They go about on their own account wholly without direction. *You*, I assure you, cannot be too attentive, whether it be to parents or to guardians. I myself have tutored Anne excellently in her filial obligations; she is at my service in all things, and most certainly will be at my side for ever. She is a dutiful daughter and you would do well to emulate her."

"I would hope, Aunt," was Georgiana's instant reply, "that it is affection and not duty that brings me here so promptly. The demands of duty may be easily satisfied; but since I so dearly love Sir Geoffrey, nothing should have kept me from him today. I should have come on foot if necessary. Compliance may serve for some; for myself I prefer to follow the dictates of a loving heart."

"Have a care, young lady," replied her aunt, affronted. "Your tone is not only sadly disrespectful, but, I may warn, hardly one that will serve you in your future. I have seen many another young woman with such a sharp tongue as yours who has regretted it at the end of a lonely life."

"Loneliness holds no terrors for me, Madam, I assure you."

"Indeed, Miss. And pray, where hope you, with such outlandish ideas as these, to encounter a suitable husband?"

"Why, Aunt," burst forth Georgiana, rising from her chair in some excitement, "*I* have but little inducement to marry at all. My fortune will come to me when I am one-and-twenty, and as for position, what could be more delightful than mine at Pemberley? Let other women seek consequence through the capture of a prominent husband; *I* shall rely upon the resources of a young woman of health, intelligence, and position in society!" For this was a subject that had been near to her this year and more. Eagerly she continued, "Look, dear Aunt, at my situation. My brother is forever adding volumes to our library: what advantage should they bring were I not to read them? My music master, you yourself brought down from London: should I then squander all those years of practice by neglecting now to play? And then, there is Pemberley. It is being splendidly restored by none other than James Leigh-Cooper himself. Shall I be gone from it before I may enjoy the fruits of his endeavor? Aunt, Aunt, a man need be superior indeed for me to change such a position as mine, and I assure you, *I* have never met such. You see," finishing with a smile, "I am quite proof."

Lady Catherine was readying her rebuke when a servant brought word from Sir Geoffrey. He felt himself somewhat relieved, and would, with the assistance of his godson, shortly make his appearance in the saloon. This message had a most happy effect on Her Ladyship, who, between expounding further upon the miracle of her cure and lamenting the ignorance of Derbyshire apothecaries, was quite distracted from her indignation. Indeed, when Sir Geoffrey, leaning heavily upon Darcy's arm, made his appearance, she had all but forgotten Georgiana in energetic scrutiny of her own proficiency.

"And to think," said she, "that only by my Sally's employing the store room's simplest ingredients, I have been able to effect this transformation. I declare, Sir Geoffrey, you look fitter than you did before your gout drew you down."

Sir Geoffrey assented with a polite inclination of his head, and would not by one look towards his godson let Her Ladyship know that between them they had disposed of the cordial in the vase of orchids along the stairs.

"My dear Georgiana," said he almost immediately, "how you grow beautiful like your mother. Lady Catherine, do you not agree that it is almost as if our dear Susan were returned to us?"

"Your memory, I fear, plays you false, Sir Geoffrey," replied her Ladyship. "Susan, while elegant, was sadly lacking in the figure and the complexion that accompany good health, and Georgiana must be said to enjoy both. However," she added quickly, "a high complexion is of small account when not attended by grace of manner. In *that* quarter, I have observed but today that my niece is sorely remiss."

Darcy, endeavoring to change the direction of his aunt's address, was driven so far as to comment upon the weather. "Do but look," said he, walking quickly to the window. "I believe it grows brighter. Perhaps, Sir, we might sit outdoors later on?"

But Lady Catherine would pursue her course. "I have seen it often," said she, "a woman of beauty, even of rank, cannot hope to excite approval without a proper demeanor. All women desire approval. Georgiana may suppose herself exceptional; but she is not. My niece would do well to look for example towards her cousin Anne. *She* is everything a young girl should be, demure, biddable, subdued. Never once have I heard her speak with such animation as your sister, Fitzwilliam."

Georgiana maintained her silence.

"Why, Aunt," said Darcy, "I cannot think what my sister has said to provoke you thus, but I assure you she meant no ill. She is only young yet and her spirits sometime escape her, do they not, Georgiana?" concluding with an affectionate smile.

"Anne's spirits never betray her," replied Her Ladyship. "I have taught her better. And, indeed," an idea occurring to her, "Georgiana herself is not yet quite beyond recovery. Send her to me when I return to Rosings and within weeks, I assure you, she will reflect the discipline I myself shall instill."

This enticing prospect suggested, further discussion was prevented by the appearance of Captain Heywood and

Anne, both back from their separate outings, and he in excellent humor.

"Only look," cried he, "at whom I chanced to encounter at the very gates of the house. Miss Anne de Bourgh herself, wrapped in her tippet and battling the wind. How I admire your vigor, Miss de Bourgh." Then, noticing for the first time the presence of Darcy and Georgiana, he immediately made his salutations.

"Mr. and Miss Darcy too," cried he with a zeal. "Both here: this is a pleasure indeed. And Sir Geoffrey quite recovered—but that is no surprise with so fair a visitor to attend him."

Georgiana's gratification at the Captain's sudden appearance was considerable; it was greater than she either had anticipated, or would, precisely, have chosen.

In some agitation, she replied, "You are mistaken, Sir, although I thank you. We must credit my godfather's recovery not to my ministrations but to my brother's and my Aunt's. My own contribution has been but to admire their skills."

"And a handsome contribution it is," cried he. "The greatest of men, I am convinced, would not have achieved one quarter of what they did without the appreciation of their fair associates. And, by that reckoning, *your* admiration, Miss Darcy, must be valued above most."

And the look he gave to Georgiana, no less than the one she returned, once again apprised Lady Catherine of her former anxieties.

"Anne is vigorous indeed," said she, taking the Captain's arm and settling him beside herself upon the sofa, "so often as her health allows. I am confident that were she less often indisposed, she would have become the most accomplished horsewoman in Kent. Perhaps when next she rides, you will accompany her? Would that not be delightful, Anne?"

Anne attended carefully, dissented in nothing, and at the end was heard by those closest to her to venture, "Yes, ma'am."

PART III

CHAPTER 20

S PRING IN THE country, all agreed, might prove capricious, but was never unlovely. In the weeks following the ball at Pemberley came a more temperate weather. Clouds which had been menacing, lifted; the sun shone; the youngest shoots emerged, and the tinges of color on the lawns became quite green. With the advance of the season, moreover, most felicitously came fresh matter for the country's discussion, in the arrival of the elder Bennets.

Sad contrast to the clime were the countenances of the Bingleys' latest visitors. Drawn, even haggard, as they were handed out from their carriage, Mr. and Mrs. Bennet admitted great fatigue. But with so many good friends to greet them, and no less than three footmen to carry in their belongings, they could at least take comfort in the good fortune of safe arrival and smart livery.

Jane Bingley and her solicitous husband saw their need, and allowed no delay in dispatching them to their rest. The morning, Jane gave assurance, would be time enough for whatever news they brought. Indeed, in that way, the entire family could hear it together; Mr. and Mrs. Darcy had been so gracious as to invite them to call at Pemberley upon the very next day. Soothed by the honor thus bestowed, Mrs. Bennet fell into a tranquil sleep.

On the morrow therefore, the larger group assembled early and made its way towards the great estate.

"Oh, my dearest Jane," began Mrs. Bennet, the first minute she observed no one else in attendance, "if you but knew how sorely put upon I am! The trials I have lately been subject to! Indeed, we should have been with you sooner but I forgot my newest sprigged lawn, and we were obliged to turn back for it at Bishop's Stortford. And Mr. Bennet was so unfeeling as to stay cross all the way! Was ever a woman so unhappy as I? I vow it has quite destroyed my complexion!"

Jane would have responded, but noting the approach of her husband, she thought it better to delay. She glanced at her mother instead, took her hand and pressed it gently, saying only, "We shall soon be together with my sister, Madam, and you shall, be assured, have every assistance we can call upon to give." And she quickly turned the conversation to happier issues.

Thus it was, that, even many hours later, after the journey was over, the warmest greetings had been exchanged, the fondest admiration of their second daughter's situation expressed, and all gathered in the great drawing room of Pemberley, the Bennets' ominous news remained still unspoken.

It was Mr. Bennet who at last revealed the ill-tidings. "We have these weeks," he began in somber tones, "been much distressed over the plight of your Aunt Philips. It is, I fear, almost too much to tell. But tell I must. Dearest daughters, she stands accused of having taken home unpaid for from our Meryton milliner's shop a length of precious lace: in short, of petty theft."

"Aunt Philips?" cried Elizabeth in the greatest agitation. "My dear Father, what can you mean by this? Absent-minded my aunt may be in trivial affairs," for indeed the limitations of Mrs. Philips' intellect surpassed even those of Mrs. Bennet's own, "but to be considered a thief, capable of stealing lace from a shop? Who has made such an accusation, and with what authority?"

"It is, I agree," responded he, sighing, "a circumstance perplexing in the extreme. Yet, there is no denying that such a claim has indeed been made against her, and more, she is already paying the price."

With these words, Mr. Bennet drew from his waistcoat an already frayed sheet from *The Hertfordshire Gazette* and handed it to his astonished daughters, where they read:

> *The Lady of a certain Gentleman of Meryton, possessed of a good fortune, and respected by a numerous*

circle of acquaintance, was committed on Thursday by G. Porter, Esq. the Mayor, to the County Gaol at Hertford, on a charge of privately stealing a card of lace from a haberdasher's shop.

Mrs. Bennet was now unable to remain silent one minute longer. She burst into tears, crying, "Lizzy, Jane, my dearest daughters, shall we ever live down the shame of it? What short of lunacy could have made my sister act so? My very own sister! To steal lace from Turner's! The disgrace of it—and my two elder daughters so rich and so great! One would think that Jane had not but this Christmas last sent her a full ell from Brussels itself! Depend upon it, it is talked about already in the neighborhood, there is no subject more upon everyone's lips. What is to become of us, dearest girls? Your unmarried sisters are ruined, I fear. They will never marry now—spinsters for life—and Mr. Bennet's estate so cruelly entailed away from them. What will become of me? I shall go distracted!" And looking at Kitty and Mary, she wept loudly.

"But Madam," interrupted Darcy, who until then had stood grave and silent as he observed the anguish which overtook Elizabeth, and watched Jane, almost overcome, grasp her husband's arm for support. "There must surely be some mistake. Mrs. Philips is certainly a woman of means: *that* should render so foolish an action unlikely on even her part."

"Without question, my sister is innocent," said Mr. Bennet. "Still, she *is* in prison."

"Then the matter must require further investigation: but, do not, I pray you, Madam, give way to despair. I myself shall look to it without delay. This is grievous news indeed."

"For your solicitousness," replied Mr. Bennet, "I do thank you, Sir. I felt secure in coming to you that you would offer your service with such quick generosity. Still, I for one see more in this than mere misunderstanding. I cannot remove from my mind the suspicion that my sister's tribulation goes beyond a mistake to some mischief, or even ill-will."

"What can you mean, good Sir?" cried Bingley, deeply distressed. "What ill-will is this? Can there be someone who would jeopardize the family's good name?"

Mr. Bennet, though himself betraying faintness of voice and gesture, continued, "I confess, I know of none such. Yet what other explanation can there be? The news of our family's recent rise in fortune has not gone unremarked in the neighborhood. Any villain might plan to disgrace us for his own profit. And this following so hard upon the deplorable event of Lydia's folly. Will our family never be free of reproach?"

"And what of my Uncle?" said Jane, recovering herself sufficiently to attend to her father. "How does he bear up?"

"Not well, I fear," replied Mr. Bennet. "He cannot tolerate the thought of your Aunt Philips incarcerated, and talks of nothing but freeing her and hushing the matter as soon as possible. He even suggests a settlement with the rogues, her accusers. I have not, in truth, known how best to counsel him. Though innocent she undoubtedly is, this affair stands to ruin her good standing entirely; and if money can indeed prevent such a scandal, perhaps my brother Philips is wise. I cannot say. I only know that while his wife is still held by the Law, he cannot rest."

At this, Mrs. Bennet once more raised an energetic lamentation while her elder daughters did what they could to comfort her. Kitty and Mary, hitherto silent and overcome by fear, now added to their mother's wails the stalwart support of their own younger voices.

While the gentlemen continued their discussion, Elizabeth could not but revel in the superiority her husband demonstrated in his every aspect. With what authority did he approach the situation, with what intelligence question her father, with what patience even did he attend to the uncontrolled demonstrations of her mother. And what a credit to him that *he*, who once had so slighted her family, should now treat them with such gentleness, such concern. How well his new-found compassion became him! Deplorable was the family's latest disaster, yet to see him thus, was gratifying indeed. Not for anything would Elizabeth have wished ill upon her Aunt Philips; but since the matter *was* so, in how pleasing a light had it cast her Darcy!

So occupied, she was startled by the knock of a footman bringing word that Sir Geoffrey Portland was below and wished to pay his respects. Elizabeth's spirits sank into oppression. Her so-feared second meeting with Sir Geoffrey had still not yet taken place; and with its delay—although *that*,

Darcy assured her, owed only to his illness and added affairs at Denby Park—had come an increase in apprehension. And now, here he was, and at the very moment when she could scarcely have been less desirous of his presence. To have him meet her family under such circumstances!

She glanced towards her husband, but failed to catch his eye; and after a mere moment's pause, she could but instruct the footman to send the visitor up.

Sir Geoffrey entered the room, a figure of such elegant deportment and gentlemanlike demeanor that the assembled party fell immediately into a hush. Even Mrs. Bennet and her younger daughters were silenced. Sir Geoffrey had been abroad since early that morning attending to the duties owing his estate, and looked fresh-faced and fully restored to health. Indeed, he had chosen this morning for his call particularly to make the early acquaintance of Mrs. Darcy's newly-arrived, and much advertised, parents. He greeted the company with all graciousness, having been well taught in the lessons of his station: to be unfailingly civil to his inferiors.

"I deeply regret, Mrs. Darcy," said he almost immediately, "the unconscionable time I have taken in coming to you to pay my compliments. As my godson has surely told you, I have been sorely indisposed of late and am but just recovered enough to go abroad." And turning to the elder Bennets, "Yet I see I am in most happy time to welcome you, Madam, Sir, to Derbyshire. I trust you are commodiously settled at Pelham Hall. These modern houses, some may complain to lack the grandeur of the older, but they often have the advantage in withstanding the weather."

"How truly you speak, Sir Geoffrey," cried Elizabeth. "As we at Pemberley know too well; our drafts are quite the envy of the neighbors."

Sir Geoffrey, inclining his head, acknowledged the pleasantry. "Pemberley's drafts are keen," agreed he, "but how grandly you are recompensed in the proportions of its rooms. For such magnificence, we willingly undertake some slight discomforts. But, I scarcely need to tutor a Mrs. Darcy in the appreciation of beauty. One need but look about Pemberley to see *that*."

Elizabeth was somewhat heartened. Drollery in Sir Geoffrey might be beyond expectation; but that he approved her eye spoke much for his own taste. There was hope between them yet.

"Indeed, Sir Geoffrey, your arrival is timely," said Darcy, "although not perhaps for the reasons you may think. We have but now been discussing a matter pertaining to the family, and your diversion is the more welcome for it." He knew his godfather wise in the ways of the world, and would dearly have valued Sir Geoffrey's advice on the incident. Yet he would say no more without Mr. Bennet's authority.

But Mr. Bennet, meeting his gaze, only shook his head and turned the conversation. "Welcome indeed, Sir Geoffrey" said he, heartily. "And we are, I thank you, Sir, most comfortably situated at Pelham. I, at least, am anticipating some fine fishing at Pemberley in the coming days. Are you yourself an angler?"

Sir Geoffrey, suspecting nothing, was pleased to recommend his own lake at Denby Park and to promise Mr. Bennet the use of his tackle whenever he should choose. All might yet have passed into sport and civilities had not Mrs. Bennet at that moment interposed:

"Indeed, dear Sir Geoffrey, your lake is renowned throughout the country, as is your own excellent eye for a fish. Why, I have heard it said that there are no finer fish in the land than the Denby Lake fish. No fatter of flesh, no brighter of hue—but as for *you*, Mr. Bennet, I cannot think, what can you have in mind. To talk of pleasure when the family remains in such distress."

Mr. Bennet and Elizabeth exchanged glances of mortification, but before either could speak, Mr. Darcy had replied. "It is at just such time, dear Mrs. Bennet," said he quickly, "that the simple pleasures of the countryside come to us as a most welcome—indeed, some would say a necessary—relief. And as to the particular sport in question, Sir, I well remember some capital fishing in your Hertfordshire. Do not you, Bingley?"

But Mrs. Bennet would not be deterred; and since she stood too much in awe of Darcy to reprove *him*, she affixed her wrath accordingly upon the latest recipient of his discourse. "I am disappointed in you, Mr. Bingley," said she. "Prittle-prattling with Mr. Bennet of fishing at such a time. Mr. Bennet, how can you vex me so? With my own sister languishing in gaol, and the family's name quite, quite ruined. Have you no compassion upon my poor nerves? My own sister, a thief!"

Elizabeth looked away, appalled. What must Sir Geoffrey think? Her mother's indelicacy had never, it seemed to her, been seen in such excess; and for her in *this* fashion to announce the family's shame! At last, she dared to steal a look at their visitor. What she saw in his face surpassed her greatest fears.

"I see," he said coldly, "that my arrival was untimely in the extreme. I apologize for intruding upon a family affair which had best be kept as closely among you as you can contrive. I shall take my leave now." And bowing, he left the room.

CHAPTER 21

G EORGIANA KNEW NOTHING of the events unfolding
at the opposite end of the house. The library at Pemberley was far removed from the receiving quarters,
and had, moreover been designed with a view to tranquility;
the room was quiet and the fire brisk; and she had been there
for some hours, lost in that perfect transport of the mind
which can only be achieved when every single need of the
body has been most assiduously addressed.

So complete, indeed, was her absorption in the poet Scott,
that she had quite overlooked the appointed hour for the
Pelham party's arrival. Nor was this uncommon with her: she
had learned long ago to take pleasure in her solitude by the
peopling of it with characters drawn from the pages of books.
Fashionable, it was not, for young ladies to reveal themselves
studious; her Aunt Catherine herself had more than once
cautioned her upon the perils it furnished to drawing room
conversation; but the truth was that Georgiana hardly knew a
sweeter morning than those spent in this calm, comfortable
room with the works of her favorite poets.

She was startled, therefore, when the heavy mahogany
door creaked open and decided footsteps announced the
arrival of another. So abruptly drawn back was she from her
preoccupation, that she actually gasped aloud. It was James
Leigh-Cooper.

"I seem always to be disquieting you, Miss Darcy," said he.
"I do assure you, I mean no harm. I came merely to consult
some early plans of the chapel which your brother showed

me upon my arrival, and will not, I promise, disturb your privacy a moment longer than is necessary."

Georgiana was surprised into cordiality. "It is rather I who should apologize to you," said she, before she could collect herself. "My attention was so fixed upon *Marmion* that I scarce knew where I was."

Smiling, he came closer to where she sat. "Do Scott's lines then have such an effect upon you?" said he. "Such sensibility speaks of a romantic nature. For myself, I admit him admirable, but rather choose to spend my leisure with his countryman, the poet Burns. Are you familiar with his works?"

"The poet Burns!" said Georgiana, blushing. "I could hardly expect my brother to introduce into the library a man of *his* unfortunate reputation."

"Mr. Darcy's scrupulousness does him credit," responded he immediately. "Yet if I may presume to put forward another consideration, it could be suggested that the man's poetry need not be subjected to the same censure as the man's character; and that in the *poetry* lies true genius." And then, warming to his subject, added, "Nor is that genius confined to his poems of love only. Were you to attempt some of his more consequential works—*A Man's A Man*, for instance—I would defy you not to be stirred. If you so admire Scott, Miss Darcy, how much more profoundly would Burns move you."

Georgiana was all amazement. That a Captain Heywood should quote Byron was both pleasing and proper; but *this* young man was proposing the works of a notorious rake— and doing so, moreover, with the air of a benefactor!

"It would seem, Sir, that you yourself have read very widely indeed," she countered. "I must wonder at the breadth of your erudition. Were you perhaps privy to some great library when you were growing up?"

He drew back straightaway. "None that might strike *you* so," said he. "My own father, although well respected, was far from rich. Still, he loved books as well as any man, and took care to impart to me all of his devotion. I did not receive my education, Miss Darcy, under the painted ceiling of Pemberley library; but as to what and how to read, *there*, there was never any lack of guidance." Then, rising and gathering up the large volume of sketches he had removed from the shelves, he turned abruptly towards the door.

Georgiana was taken aback. Her words, it seemed, had given him true offence: both tone and gesture betrayed it. Yet until this, he had greeted her sallies with good-nature or open amusement; and she had meant no more than a gentle rebuke to what appeared to be a too unfailing assurance, a certainty of superior understanding upon every subject available to conversation. Now, however, that she had put him out of humor, she began to be ashamed of her own presumption; and not least because she had, even while speaking, begun to hear in her own voice the awful tones of her aunt, Lady Catherine de Bourgh. *That* was not to be supported.

She therefore began in some confusion, "Mr. Leigh-Cooper, I pray you, do not take me amiss. I err perhaps only in betraying a curious nature. I meant you no affront. But, I am acquainted with you as an architect: to hear you speak with such authority upon so wide a range of subjects continues to bewilder me. Please let us walk out together, since I am already awaited by my dear sister's family, newly come from Hertfordshire."

Leigh-Cooper, regaining his own composure, could only consent to lead her towards the great hall. However, the oak stairway was descended and the landing crossed with but little speech; and the silence might have persisted for the entire length of the north corridor had the young man been able to countenance it. But since his good-nature was equalled only by his garrulity, he could not; and he began instead to offer his own observations upon what he knew to be a safer subject altogether: the perfect proportions of the Pemberley chapel, the excellent common sense of having quarried local alabaster for its altarpiece, and the fine hewings of its limewood carvings. For the which Georgiana, observing his improved humor, rewarded him with that most brilliant of womanly rejoinders: rapt attention.

So the pair continued until at last, reaching the far end of the house, they chanced upon Darcy and Sir Geoffrey just then leaving the drawing room. As they approached, Georgiana could see that both her brother and her godfather seemed troubled. She was immediately disquieted.

"Dear Uncle," cried she, "You cannot already be taking your leave while I have not so much as had the opportunity of greeting you? What can be the matter?" And she glanced at her brother, hoping from him to gain an explanation for the older man's displeasure.

But it was Sir Geoffrey who spoke first. "My child, do not alarm yourself," said he. "I have had the misfortune of calling to make the acquaintance of your brother's new family at a most inconvenient moment." And, fixing her eye, he continued emphatically, "Take heed, Georgiana, whom you choose to marry. A match outside your station can only result in unhappiness and, at last, shame."

"I must entreat you, dear Sir," broke in Darcy with some consternation, "not to take your leave in this fashion. Only consider that we are none of us proof against unjust accusations, no matter how blamelessly we may conduct our lives. Not I, nor even you, yourself."

Never before had Georgiana witnessed such an exchange between her brother and his old friend. Never had she seen Sir Geoffrey's features so grim, his bearing so aloof; nor her brother in his presence so discomfited. What could have caused it?

"Good heavens," cried she, now quite dismayed, "do tell me immediately what you are talking about. Who has been accused? What shame is this? Dear Uncle, why do you look so stern?"

Instead of replying, both men exchanged a glance, and Darcy cast his eye towards Leigh-Cooper. That young man instantly discovered some business left unattended about the parterre, and with the briefest of courtesies, took himself off.

"There is little to be gained, Georgiana," said Darcy as soon as Leigh-Cooper had gone, "by attempting to hide from you the unfortunate news that the Bennets bring us from Hertford-shire." Hastily, and in a low tone, he described to her the circumstance. "And I fear," concluded he, shaking his head, "that whatever the outcome—and I do believe Mrs. Philips to be innocent of crime—it cannot but unloose odious prattle in the neighborhood and thus mean wretchedness for Elizabeth. It is up to us, dear Georgiana, to solace her in this distress."

"Oh, my poor sister," cried Georgiana. "What must she not be feeling. I am grieved indeed for her. But tell me,

Brother, what can be done to recover the situation? We must act without delay!"

Sir Geoffrey had been growing incensed as he listened and must now intervene. "On the contrary, dear children," said he, his tone disdainful, "our one action must be to keep ourselves as distant as we may from this most deplorable source of scandal. Henry, your Aunt Catherine cautioned you against alliance with a family so unlike your own; and this, you see, is what comes of it! Such a breach of custom and propriety must bring grievous consequences. Georgiana, as your loving godfather, I must enjoin you for the sake of your own future to look upon this embarrassment and be governed by it."

And with that, the gentleman turned and swiftly took his leave.

CHAPTER 22

T
HE RECOLLECTION OF her own earlier misadventure—
her so nearly disastrous infatuation with the unprincipled Wickham—and the grief that that incident had
caused her brother, stayed with Georgiana. Now, that memory, scarcely faded, was renewed by this latest ill-fortune of
Elizabeth's. The very manner of Sir Geoffrey's departure from
Pemberley had quite discomposed her. Her godfather's open
distaste for the Bennet family's predicament, his stern manner,
his curt farewell, had filled her alike with perplexity and
alarm. Well she knew that her brother had kept her own
youthful imprudence a close secret even from this, his dearest friend. Had Sir Geoffrey guessed the desperate business in
which she herself had been involved, how might he not have
looked upon *her*!

The elder Bennets' visit, and the flurry created by it, afforded
little opportunity for private words between herself and
Elizabeth until some days had passed and the two found
themselves traveling together to Pelham to return the Bennets' call. Darcy, who was to have accompanied them, had
cried off, pleading business about Pemberley, and both had
accepted his apologies with private relief: Georgiana for the
chance of intimate conversation, and Elizabeth, knowing
that, warm as her husband's affections were, and loyal as was
his heart, he was, in the drawing room, little short of an
encumbrance. So, contentedly enough, they traveled alone.

Barely had they lost sight of Pemberley, when Georgiana
began: "I hardly dare say so, dear Elizabeth, you seem

so much yourself as always. But I cannot help suspecting that your appearance of good cheer arises more from self-command than from disposition, and it pains me, my dearest sister, to think of your family's plight. I would most earnestly wish to be of some use to you if I could, in however small a fashion. Is there nothing at all that I can do?"

Elizabeth, while wondering precisely by what means the young lady herself proposed to retrieve the situation, was nonetheless grateful for her constancy. "Only to keep up heart," said she, smiling, "that is all that either you or I can do. Mr. Darcy has already written to my Uncle Philips and prepares to journey to Hertfordshire so soon as he may and then on to London to confer with his solicitor. The rest lies in the future. What will be said of us in Derbyshire society, I cannot know. But say what our neighbors will—and they are, I do believe, disposed to say a great deal—I can but hope that you and I may continue to be of good courage. It is of your godfather's regard, which I had till now some hopes of engaging, that the affair may prove ruinous." And with that she broke off, as her courage failed her.

Georgiana, sensible now to Elizabeth's shaken spirits, drew up straight in her seat, displaying all the dignity and elegance of her figure. "I cannot," exclaimed she with an indignation Elizabeth had not seen in her before, "speak to any measures of my godfather. But, as to the opinions of our society here in Derbyshire, I do most heartily assure you, there is little to fear. We are, my dear Elizabeth, who we are, after all. You must not doubt the importance of *that* circumstance."

Elizabeth suppressed a smile. Never had she been made more aware of the difference in their two upbringings. Moreover, that pride, which now revealed itself for the first time, must remind her of her own early encounters with another unrelenting figure, Georgiana's brother. There was in them both that surety of address which nothing could overthrow, and no Bennet could shake with mere jocularity. Nor would she now try. Her only rejoinder, therefore, and with a tolerably grave air, was:

"You are wise indeed, my dear. I shall hold up my head knowing that I may safely entrust my perfect felicity to your family's good name." And, both cheered by this exchange, they observed at the same moment the tower of Pelham Hall ahead.

Mrs. Bingley already stood upon the threshold, and with her, her younger sisters, Kitty and Mary, in welcome. Their greetings were affectionate, and Jane rejoiced in Miss Darcy's having come to call upon her parents.

"Although," said she, "the circumstances are not happy at this time for our family, nevertheless, you, Georgiana, are as welcome here as always. Elizabeth, my mother and father attend you in the drawing room."

"Welcome, indeed," cried her husband, at that moment returning from the stables with his dogs. "Kitty and Mary, I feel sure, have suffered enough talk of serious matters for one day. Georgiana, you are obliged in charity to walk with them in the garden, and talk of inconsequential concerns. Surely, one at least of you plans to retrim a bonnet?"

Georgiana received the suggestion with no great pleasure. In that eagerness to be of assistance which had drawn her to Pelham this morning, she had imagined for herself a more heroic role than making comfortable chat with two girls of her own age: moreover, Kitty and Mary's forwardness alarmed her. The young Bennets, however, having seen no one but their immediate family for some fifteen hours, were overjoyed at the prospect of company and led her with a will through the park, talking the while.

"Oh, Miss Darcy," began Kitty without delay, "what an exceeding good ball was yours! I vow I scarce stopped dancing for five minutes together. Frank Middleton declared that I quite wore him out. Lord, he is droll! I have been to many balls, Miss Darcy—some six or eight indeed—and I can say with confidence that yours was quite splendid."

In spite of her discomfort, Georgiana was gratified by the compliment. That her dance had provided diversion, she had already guessed, but to have one so worldly as Elizabeth's sister approve it, gave substance to her satisfaction.

"Indeed," ventured she in response, "I am sure your own presence contributed heartily to its gaiety."

Kitty, laughing, tossed her head, "The success of any ball," said she, "depends largely upon the spirits of those attending. So long as *I* am of their number, Miss Darcy" (with an air) "you need fear no lifelessness."

There followed now a silence. Georgiana scarcely knew how to reply; and Mary, who had little to say on so insignificant a subject as good fellowship, remained mute. But Kitty would persist.

"Tell me, Miss Darcy," cried she, "what of your own beaux? With so many smart young men around, you must have prodigious many?" Georgiana said nothing and averted her face. "Oh, come, Miss Darcy, you can confide in us, for are we not almost sisters, after all?"

Georgiana murmured something indistinguishable; but if the words were spoken low, there was that yet in her tone which quieted even Kitty.

So they progressed around the park, each occupied with her own reflections, until, turning a corner, they were startled by the sudden appearance of Caroline Bingley, accompanied by none other than Captain Thomas Heywood himself.

The two were close in conversation and appeared to be laughing; but as soon as they recognized the others, they broke off, and Captain Heywood came immediately forward to greet them. "How very fortunate it is," said he, "to encounter such a charming group," and turning to his companion added with emphasis, "is it not, Miss Bingley?" Then, straightaway, with all his attention upon Miss Darcy, and his spirits high: "Miss Bingley has kindly been fulfilling her promise to introduce me to the splendors of the neighborhood. And how gloriously your Derbyshire can evoke a melancholy mood. The grottos summon the sweetest of woes, while the ruined cottages along the lane conjure a desolation I can hardly contain. But Miss Darcy, I warrant, you are familiar with every nook and cranny of such places, having been so fortunate as to have grown up here in Derbyshire."

Georgiana was in a flutter. If, indeed, the indifference she professed to the attentions of this young man were a true measure of her feelings, she could only wonder at the agitation she now experienced on seeing him so friendly in the company of another. Yet the Captain, lively as he was, was nevertheless visibly discountenanced; and Georgiana, observing this, was soon able to convince herself that any embarrassment she felt was for his sake rather than her own. She certainly had little intention of having her own affections attached once more, and thus must have little cause for jealousy. So, after a bare moment's pause, she was able to arrive at unaffected friendliness.

Said she, with hardly a blush, "I cannot boast of more than a passing acquaintance with the countryside hereabouts. I fear my education in the delights of Pelham has been sadly remiss."

Miss Bingley, who had herself found nothing to say until now, was moved to reply: "Miss Darcy I have known to prefer her world of books, and with Pemberley's renowned library at her disposal, I expect she seldom indulges herself with frivolous pleasures. Isn't that so, my dear Georgiana?"

"You flatter me, Miss Bingley," replied she. "And I would that it were true. But, I dearly love my morning walks and wanderings, and would scarcely dare regard my own reading as precisely serious in nature. I read, I confess, more for entertainment than for instruction."

"Nevertheless," persisted Miss Bingley, with a smile, "you do spend many hours with your books, and thus must be considered by the rest of us as a student."

Mary could contain herself no longer. "Serious study," cried she, "is altogether of a different character from what you discuss. Reading alone does not determine scholarship; *that* can only be demonstrated when one has engaged her mind enough to injure her eyesight. I myself am accustomed to devote my entire intellect when *I* read, and, as you can see, my eyes are quite ruined. No one with strong eyes can justly claim learning."

The group, having no answer to this at all, turned back towards Pelham Hall. Miss Bingley would take Captain Heywood's arm, but as they crossed the bridge over the river, he contrived to release himself, and take Georgiana to one side.

"A welcome surprise to find *you* here," said he in a low tone. "Had I known that I would, with what lighter a heart would I have come out this morning."

Georgiana, despite her resolve, felt her heart stir at his tone. But, she was proof; and besides, he had seemed so uncommonly cordial with Miss Bingley.

"Indeed," said she, coolly. "And yet you seemed, but a moment ago, to be enjoying yourself prodigiously."

"Oh, Miss Darcy," protested he, with a sigh. "If you but knew the real disposition behind my apparent ease of address. The truth is that many social situations fill me with alarm. But a man, especially one thrown so much into the company of strangers as myself, is not permitted the luxury of diffidence. My manner, perhaps suggests otherwise, but believe me, I am, by nature, so painfully ill-fitted to the delights of society, that. . . . But I have said too much."

They were already nearing the drive, and before Georgiana could calm herself sufficiently to reply, they saw a carriage rounding the gatepost and approaching the entry.

"How odd," cried Kitty, just then rejoining them. It looks just like Lydia's carriage—does it not, Mary? Yet it cannot be, for she is not to arrive until week's end."

But as they watched, the carriage came to a stop by the door and to Georgiana's complete mortification, out stepped Lydia herself, accompanied by her husband, Lieutenant George Wickham.

CHAPTER 23

WRETCHEDNESS OVERTOOK GEORGIANA. How ill-judged was her having come to Pelham Hall today! Already flustered by her encounter with Captain Heywood and Miss Bingley in the garden, she was now to be exposed to the anguish of a meeting with the very man who was the cause of her earlier folly and shame!

Her cheeks overspread with the deepest blush; she dared not lift her eyes lest her embarrassment become visible to the entire party. Had she not, after all, been given every assurance that Elizabeth's sister and her husband would not arrive for days, and that even when they did, *he* should never be in her presence? Now, to be forced to be civil, to exchange pleasantries, to pretend to any good will towards this arrant villain defied her remaining strength. Even with the certainty that none of their party could possibly be aware of their former relations, her vexation grew.

As Kitty and Mary Bennet hurried towards their sister's carriage, Georgiana stood quite still in the hope of recovering her command. Miss Bingley, on the contrary, was delighted by the sight of the latest arrivals. The presence of the notorious Wickhams, together with Mr. and Mrs. Bennet, would certainly provide her with the diversion that had to her mind been hitherto all too sadly lacking in her brother's amiable household.

Cried she: "*Here*, my dear Captain Heywood, you see a welcome addition. Now, we both may rejoice in the exquisite manners of my brother's new family, especially those of the Brighton branch just come to the door."

But Captain Heywood, observing the pallor that had over-taken Miss Darcy, was paying no heed. He offered his arm instead, and began to lead her towards the house.

"Are you unwell?" he asked, alarmed. "I must find Mrs. Bingley and Mrs. Darcy to assist you." And he hastened forward about that errand.

There was no escape for Georgiana, however. As, with slower footsteps, she neared the doorway, the Lieutenant and his wife were but a few paces away, and too soon, they had come face to face.

Mrs. Wickham's pleasure was unrestrained. "Oh, my dear Miss Darcy!" cried she, "for Georgiana Darcy you must surely be, so closely do you resemble my brother Darcy. I may call you Georgiana, may I not? Here we are come a full three days in advance. I would have waited, but Mr. Wickham would be off. 'I cannot,' said he 'abide a minute more away from Derbyshire'—and you see now that he was in the right. For here we appear and *you* are arrived to greet us. Come, my dear sister, give me your hand."

Georgiana shrank; but Mrs. Wickham's effusiveness was merely a beginning. There was more to come, and this time from the gentleman himself:

"It has been some years since we met, Miss Darcy," inter-rupted he, addressing her with all the warmth of close famil-iarity, "and I can only marvel at the development of so blooming a young woman from the frail child I remember. I must compliment you heartily upon your splendid pro-gress." And, gazing about the park with a satisfied air, he continued, "If you but knew how I longed to breathe the air of my native country. Wherever I journey, I vow, I do make haste, one gets on better that way. And there is, besides," he added slyly, "the pleasure of coming upon one's friends just a whit before one is expected."

Georgiana had succeeded in responding to Mrs. Wick-ham's greetings with a tolerable civility; she sought now with failing confidence to employ sufficient aplomb in resisting her husband's. Fortunately, at that very moment, she was joined by Captain Heywood, who had returned with a foot-man to assist her.

Relieved to see him, she was able to rally a little and would at least have tried to present the pair to him. But he interrupted

her words with a curt, "I have already had the pleasure of acquaintance with this gentleman. And, now if you will pardon us," he bowed to Mrs. Wickham and promptly led Georgiana away into the house and the comforts of the drawing room.

Her gratitude for the rescue knew no bounds. She would express it to the Captain even as, together with the footman, he supported her steps on their way.

"Captain Heywood, your good offices have put me in your debt. Though I could never intend a slight to any one of my dear brother and sister's family, I confess that I welcomed escape just then and thank you for effecting it."

"Your service is my pleasure," said he. "But you tremble; let us repair to the drawing room without further words."

In his solicitude, he seemed to Georgiana more heroic than ever before. How swift had been his action in her distress, how keen his understanding—nor even had any words need pass between them. It spoke to a sensitivity that pierced her resolution. Captain Heywood's countenance, his elegance of speech and polish of manner, had already established him as possessing every gallant grace; but in his tender attentions this morning there was something more, a chivalry that must command her deeper regard.

Elizabeth and Jane, seeing Georgiana thus accompanied and looking faint, directly seated her and attended her until she felt herself again.

"My dear sister, what can have occurred?" said Elizabeth. "You have quite lost your color. Has she not, dear Mother?"

But at that moment, the new arrivals were announced, and Georgiana's reduced state was no longer a mystery, at least to Mrs. Darcy.

"My dear," said she with most ready interposition, "I do believe you to be settled too near to the fireplace for your comfort. The closeness of the room can only disturb you further." And seeking out for her sister the airiest and most distant corner of the broad drawing room, she quickly secluded Miss Darcy from the larger company.

Captain Heywood, unwilling to leave her side, accompanied her. Thus they formed two distinct parties, with the Bennet family discussing their own travails, while the Captain engrossed the young lady in conversation of such abundant indifference as could not but restore her spirits.

Mr. and Mrs. Wickham bustled in with an easy assurance that spoke not a doubt in their minds of their welcome. Nor need they have had, for Mrs. Bennet's rapture at their appearance was unaffected, and Mr. Bennet, although grave, still concealed his feelings with a civil demeanor more than equal to deceiving two of so limited sensitivity.

Mrs. Wickham, Elizabeth saw, remained still felicitously untouched by either diminished bloom or improved discernment. She circled noisily about the room, greeting, laughing, demanding compliments. Had not Jane grown fat? Was not Papa solemn? And was it not droll that Kitty and Mary both remained yet unmarried while *she* was a matron of a year or more?

Elizabeth would turn away in disgust. But even in doing so, she caught the eye of Caroline Bingley, and the expression she read therein directed her attention back to Lydia forthwith. She looked expressively at her youngest sister, hoping, since she despaired of turning the conversation into more sensible channels, at least to stem its flow; but at that moment Mrs. Bennet herself began:

"Oh, my dearest child," said she, "what good fortune to have all my girls with me now at this time above all. Dearest Lydia, you have heard of our misfortune?"

"Lord, Mama, yes," responded she. "Kitty told me all in the vestibule. This is the worst news of all. I was so overcome, I near swooned." And addressing her eldest sister, in the most cheerful of tones: "Jane, what a fine gown, I declare! And do you not admire mine? See the lace upon it—my dear Wickham carried it from London."

"Lace," moaned Mrs. Bennet. "Do you talk to me of lace? It was lace, do not forget, that brought your Aunt Philips to this sorry pass. Lace, my dear girls, will be the undoing of our family." And a torrent of tears burst from her.

"Dear Aunt Philips," added Wickham, "how it grieves my heart to think of her in Hertford Gaol. And denounced as a thief! But I have heard that as a woman advances in age, her behaviour not seldom becomes odd and even eccentric. Poor dear lady," and he concluded with a sigh, and turned to admire the sheen of his boots in the long looking glass.

Mrs. Bingley, like her sister, was growing more uncomfortable to have family woes thus exposed to strangers. Captain Heywood, happily, had engaged Miss Darcy so completely that he hardly heard; but Caroline Bingley, her hostess could not but observe, was exhibiting more pleasure than she had yet displayed in her visit. The conversation must be turned at once.

"And how liked you your excursion this morning, Miss Bingley," said she. "Did you, as you planned, walk your way to the village?"

Miss Bingley, although loath to abandon so interesting a topic as the Bennet family's anguish, nevertheless recognized in the question an occasion to rejoin Captain Heywood which she could not neglect.

"Only so far as Drewsbury Farm," said she. And turning to a surprised Lieutenant Wickham, who chanced to stand nearby, "Come, Lieutenant, allow me to show you from the window." Engaging his arm, she led him the length of the room to where Captain Heywood and Miss Darcy sat in conversation.

"My dear Georgiana," said she, so soon as they drew close, "how I do hope you are recovered now from your malaise. It is not often that we see *you* thus ailing: but you are to be commended at least upon having been taken faint amid such attentive company. And the Captain indeed has effected an excellent cure. If anything, your complexion may have improved."

Miss Darcy, surprised at her tone, could but smile and look to Captain Heywood to introduce a more harmonious topic. This, however, brought a result even less happy, for the sweetness of her gaze moved the bold Lieutenant Wickham to renew his approach.

"Miss Darcy's fine complexion I am acquainted with of old," said he with meaning. "Likewise her other charms. We were always good friends, were we not, Georgiana?"

Georgiana was mortified, and knew not what to say. Was she to be subjected, on top of all else, to this insolent familiarity of address? But Captain Heywood, observing her chagrin, rose forthwith, and addressed the Lieutenant in the sternest of tones:

"You are impertinent, Sir," said he, and turning to Georgiana, "Your sister is correct: it *is* something close in here. Shall we take a turn outdoors?" And, with that, he led out a Georgiana whose confusion knew no bounds. For at that very moment, the idea came to her that Captain Heywood might indeed have engaged not only her attention but possibly her heart.

CHAPTER 24

E VEN AS MR. Darcy and his father-in-law prepared to depart for London to consult with the solicitors, Charles Bingley recollected his earlier promise to give a ball at Pelham. "And what a pity it would be, dear Jane," said he to his wife, "to dash the expectations of my sisters and yours, who count upon my word. Your family's circumstance may not be of the most appropriate for a ball; but in good conscience, I cannot deny them such pleasure, and especially now when Lydia has made our party complete. What think you, dear wife, upon the matter?"

Jane Bingley, while too aware that her mother's appetite for festivities would be scant, nevertheless could see no ill with that which her affable husband deemed mannerly. "There can be no harm in it, surely," cried she, "and how happy it should make Kitty and Mary! Dear Mr. Bingley, you *are* astute." There but remained to secure the assent of Mrs. Bennet.

Kitty and Mary, when sent about that errand, vouchsafed absolute sympathy with their mother's somber mood. The time, they decreed, was grievously inauspicious for dancing; the family's spirits too heavy by far for frivolity. And with what heavy hearts they were forced to acknowledge the pity of it: that the opportunity to meet so many eligible young men as Derbyshire afforded, should arise at precisely the moment when they could least turn it to advantage. Mrs. Bennet had heard enough. Rising from her *chaise*, she marshalled her resources instanter. "My poor girls," moaned she, "with your mother in torment, and your futures yet uncontracted. How should I oppose you in this? I fear there is nothing for it: I must submit to Bingley's kind offer."

So it was settled, and the courage of that lady applauded widely. Even Miss Bingley saw fit to reflect upon it. "A ball," said she to her eager brother, "will be the very thing to lift all our spirits. As for the neighbors, let them reproach as they please. I, for one, abhor gossip and shall have none of it."

By now the whole countryside was aware of the Bennets' latest adversity: it could no more be kept private than a change in the government or the whelping of Frank Middleton's pointer bitch. For if discretion within society is an unimpeachable ideal, it nevertheless, like the best of our aspirations, remains resolutely in the realm of fancy.

Elizabeth Darcy, all too sensible of this, looked to the ball with expectations less sanguine than those of her sister Jane. Days had passed since Sir Geoffrey Portland's visit to Pemberley, and the temper of his departure had power to oppress her still. Mr. Darcy himself had said nothing of it, yet she was certain that he, too, felt the uncordiality, and was saddened. Now, to meet Sir Geoffrey again, and under the diligent scrutiny of the neighborhood, could only add to her despondency.

Georgiana Darcy's sentiment was quite another. Once informed of the scheme, she could not but applaud it, both as an admirable defiance to the family's ill fortune, and for more particular reasons of her own. The troubling idea that had occurred to her that morning at Pelham Hall had as yet refused to quiet: not even the trustworthy remedies of a sleepless night and a morning spent reading Cowper had proved tonic. She well knew that she must not fall in love. Yet the Captain's face, and the remembrance of his mastery of the situation, would recur.

Any sensible young woman need shun a too-warm attachment; but should she discover herself nearing that perilous condition, the occasion demands that she at least appraise its origin at as close quarters as she may. To meet the Captain again, and upon the ballroom floor, must measure how dangerous was the extent of Georgiana's own partiality, and she looked to it with a staunch resolve. Indeed, when the day of the ball arrived, her animation was so high that even Kitty forswore her lifelong habit of indifference to any but herself so far as to remark upon it.

"And small wonder," added she, "for that rose color of your gown would cast a glow upon even the palest cheek. My own of that very hue, my dear Miss Darcy, caused a veritable sensation among the _____shire when last I wore it. Did it not, Mary?" And she turned to her sister as usual with no particular reply in mind.

But it was Elizabeth who answered. "You apply to Mary," said she, laughing. "And yet she would scarce distinguish a rose-colored gown from a sofa cover. Had you the deference to apply to your *elder* sister, I would have provided informed assurance that both gowns are particularly becoming. But, alas, the happy moment is forever gone."

Not for any thing would Elizabeth allow the company to suspect her heaviness of spirits. These were low indeed, and the more so since the absence of her husband and father left the family exposed alike to the negligence of Lieutenant Wickham and the protection of Mr. Bingley. Yet ever had she had about her a stubbornness which would not allow her to suffer intimidation. Could she now permit the assembled company to frighten her, especially when Mr. Darcy was at a distance? The pitiful picture of herself in so ignoble a state was quite enough to pique that obstinacy. Let happen what may, she resolved, none should see her falter.

Georgiana was cheered by her sister's warmth. Elizabeth's humor had been something lacking in their journey together from Pemberley; but now that it was restored, her sister felt sufficiently composed to look to her own concerns. She gazed around the room, and even as she did so, her heart swelled to see Captain Heywood arrive, accompanied by her Aunt Catherine, Sir Geoffrey, and her cousin Anne. He saw her, and started in her direction; but before he had advanced more than a step, his path was obstructed by Miss Caroline Bingley, who speedily engaged him in conversation of unyielding animation.

He halted; soon his demeanor took up such liveliness as would satisfy his interlocutor; civility must be served and Miss Bingley would not be dismissed. With resignation, Georgiana returned her attention to her immediate company.

"Where can Frank Middleton be?" cried Kitty, craning her head in all directions. "He promised me that he would almost certainly come early, if he had returned in time from bowls. Is not that Miss Anne de Bourgh? La! How pale she is. Only think, Mama, if one of your girls should look as she."

"Miss de Bourgh's meager appearance is one she can well afford," replied her mother. "But you, Kitty, and especially you, Mary, should do well to remember that such an extravagance is beyond your father's poor means. Were *we* as rich as the de Bourghs, you could look quite as ill as you chose. But here now comes Captain Heywood."

Disentangled from Miss Bingley, the Captain hastened to pay his respects to the party. So soon as greetings had been exchanged, he turned particularly to Georgiana. "I trust," said he, "that you are quite recovered from your indisposition of the other day?"

"Quite recovered, I thank you," she replied; yet to her annoyance she felt her color rise as she spoke. There was that, surely, of tenderness in his gaze, which must disturb her.

But the Captain persisted. "Well enough, therefore, to oblige me with the next dance?"

Georgiana could but assent. Was it not precisely upon the dance floor that she had planned the closest study of her emotions? So, smiling, she suffered herself to be led out.

Released from the charge of her young friend, Elizabeth could now address herself to the joyous task of approaching Lady Catherine and Sir Geoffrey, who stood in conversation with Mr. and Mrs. Bingley.

"Mr. Darcy regrets that he cannot attend," began she, "but he has accompanied my father to London on urgent business." Lady Catherine acknowledged that she had indeed already heard something of it, and added, "We shall instead, I presume, have the pleasure this evening of seeing your mother and your Brighton relatives only. Is not that your mother approaching now?"

Mrs. Bennet, joining the group, first turned the force of her attentions upon Sir Geoffrey.

"Your hasty departure from Pemberley, Sir Geoffrey," she lamented, "hardly permitted the moment to pay those respects owing to one of your consequence. Mr. Bennet has explicitly instructed me to do so in his stead, this evening." For so, she had stalwartly persuaded herself, he had. And turning next to Lady Catherine, "Is this not, dear lady, a charming house? My daughter Jane will surely come to rival her sister as one of the finest hostesses in Derbyshire. But then, in all modesty, I too am reputed to keep a good table on every occasion."

Sir Geoffrey said nothing. His silence rather pleased Mrs. Bennet than not, suited as it was to her estimation of his high importance; but to Elizabeth it could cause nothing but pain.

"My mother," interposed Jane, observing her sister's confusion, "is indeed a hostess of note in Hertfordshire, and what talents my sister or I may enjoy in that direction we must ascribe directly to her teaching."

Whereupon Lydia, who until then had been content to giggle with Kitty in harmless enough seclusion, saw fit to join them. Once the notion came across her, she naturally acted upon it without delay, since so happily unfettered was she by the burdens of polite society as to deem it unnecessary to wait until she was summoned.

"Lady Catherine," she cried, so soon as she had been presented, and before the surprised lady could herself speak, "We meet now for the first time, but you know, of course, my husband of old, having so often encountered him in his childhood at dear Pemberley." And, straightaway interrupting her own words to turn to her mother with a laugh, "Oh, Mama, can that be Frank Middleton? That lanky fright who has just come? What can Kitty be thinking of? He is positively oafish. Is he then very rich?"

Sir Geoffrey looked astonished at this want of breeding, and Jane had turned away in humiliation. It was left to Elizabeth to restore such harmony as she may.

"Mrs. Middleton, I hear to be a very good sort of woman," she said concisely, with a meaning look at her youngest sister. And addressing herself civilly to Lady Catherine, "Is not her eldest daughter Lucy a great favorite with Miss Anne de Bourgh?"

But the attempt was worse than none: Had she designed it, she could not have invoked a less fortunate name. "Miss de Bourgh," interrupted Lydia, all eager solicitousness. "I saw her but now in her chair, looking quite poorly. Is she long unwell, Lady Catherine? Have you considered the waters at Bath? I myself have never been but stout and strong, but I hear most encouraging reports of them from the invalid among the regimental wives."

Lady Catherine could scarce contain her choler. "Unwell,"
she cried. "My dear Mrs. Wickham, my Anne has never been
unwell a day in her life. If she should look pale, it is, I assure
you, only because she has caught a chill in her frequent
excursions of late, walking out in the countryside with her
particular friend, Captain Heywood." And turning to the floor
to seek out the happy couple, she observed instead her daughter sitting quietly upon a chair, while at the same time Captain
Heywood led through the dance a Georgiana who had never
appeared lovelier. Her decision was made immediately.

"As for Bath!" she continued, "It is a trumpery place at
best. We have waters of our own near Rosings. And it is
to Rosings that our party—I should say, our *entire* party—
returns, tomorrow, at first light." And with not another word,
she left them to seek her solace at the supper table.

PART IV

CHAPTER 25

WITH SUCH EXEMPLARY resolution did Lady Catherine adhere to her intent to quit Derbyshire as soon as she might, that on the morning after the ball, she roused Sir Geoffrey's entire household at dawn to make ready for her departure. No matter that Captain Heywood, extolling the beauties of spring in the Midlands, would linger, or that she herself had bidden the Middletons to Sir Geoffrey's table that very evening; no matter that Anne's looks, when deprived of sleep, suffered sufficiently for even her mother to notice; Lady Catherine would brook no delay. Nor did Sir Geoffrey, upon being awakened, attempt to forestall her with excessive vigor: rarely at his most benevolent before noon, he made his farewells as briefly as in civility he could, and valiantly endured the pain of their parting, fortified by the knowledge that after the rumbling of the carriage wheels had silenced, his bachelor routine would be restored to him, and his household his own again.

Lady Catherine, once reinstated within the familiar splendor of Rosings, her daughter dispatched to her rest, her pug Toby recalled to her side, found it meet to exclaim upon the manner of her old friend's leave-taking. "Sir Geoffrey," asseverated she, "is becoming in his years positively churlish. Had I not known better, I should have almost concluded from his behavior this morning that he preferred solitude. He is altogether too much alone. Men, Captain Heywood, do best in the company of women. They grow surly otherwise, and odd. Have a care, my dear Captain, not to end your days a bachelor: your sex is formed for marriage. Ours may seek it the more energetically; but it is the men who derive from it the greater advantage."

The Captain agreed with her most fervently. His own kind was poor indeed; pitiable left to its own devices; incapable of flourishing without fair assistance; whereas, for an example of the superiority of the frailer sex, one had but to look to Lady Catherine herself, who, left all alone, yet had managed these many years most skillfully to run this great estate, and, he had heard, much of the village of Hunsford besides?

So showing himself to be not without skills of his own, he contrived to divert her from a dear subject to her very dearest. While expositing upon the virtues of her sex, Her Ladyship was eloquent; when talking of herself, she approached the oratorical.

"And have done, dear Captain, since my widowhood!" concurred she. "No sooner had poor Sir Lewis left me prostrated by bereavement, than I set about looking to his property, examining each failing of government that had occurred during his lifetime, and righting it. Rosings prospers now more than ever it did while my unfortunate spouse provided his support. The greatest benefit he ever conferred upon his estate was in the leaving of it to me. A woman alone, unaided by a loving attachment, can accomplish almost anything."

Captain Heywood was pleased to attend this speech with every appearance of edification. He listened with an unfaltering gravity of countenance, and would have continued so until Her Ladyship should have spoken her full, but happily was spared that fate by the interruption of the footman announcing a visitor. The rector of Hunsford, Mr. William Collins, was come to present to her Ladyship the new curate, Mr. Samuel Beasley.

Mr. Collins had had the pleasure of making the Captain's acquaintance upon his first arrival, and, having discerned in him a man of sensibilities matching even to his own, the two were able to greet each other warmly, to exclaim upon the felicity of a second meeting so soon, and Mr. Collins to fall without further delay into a litany of all the ills endured by Hunsford in Her Ladyship's absence: the sow that had farrowed a litter all runts; the apple orchard that was destroyed by storm; the overturned carriage that had cost the best bell-ringer his right arm.

"And the last misfortune," concluded he, shaking his head dolefully, "has been the very worst of our woes: for pork, if overcooked, or apples, if underripe, may upset our digestion; but the tribulation of being denied the innocent pleasures of campanology is unmitigated."

Her Ladyship was much comforted to hear of her estate's distress. "A sorry circumstance," agreed she with energy. "You see, Captain Heywood, the havoc wrought by but two weeks of my absence. Sir Lewis was able to leave Rosings for months at a time with negligible effects." Exhilarated by this recollection, she turned her attention straightaway to her rector. "You yourself, Mr. Collins," declared she, "are looking but ill, I observe: can you have had your hair cut since we departed? It poorly becomes you."

Mr. Collins, indeed, had been all but shorn, and that in so curious a fashion that few could fail to notice, although most would be restrained by good manners from comment. This fresh evidence of the astuteness of his patroness threw him into raptures.

"These, Your Ladyship," joyously assented he, "are the hapless consequences of my own disregard of your advice. You will recall yourself cautioning me most solemnly against the employment of poor Peplow's son, his eyes, you observed, being set too close for a barber; but then, in your absence, my Charlotte so worked upon my compassion by urging me to pity his youth and the sad loss of his father, that I could not refuse; and here before you is the result. Never again will I select a barber without particular assessment of his eye-span."

Lady Catherine, appeased by both his deference of manner and the uncomeliness of his appearance, was able now to confer the bounty of her attention upon his companion, a young man of plain features but sensible aspect, who was listening to this exchange in some surprise.

"And this fellow will be my curate," said she, turning in her seat abruptly to inspect him. "Come forth, Sir, and do not skulk so in the corner. I cannot abide skulkers."

Without hesitation, the young man emerged. "Samuel Beasley, Ma'am," said he. "Arrived but a week ago, and

looking forward to being of service to both Your Ladyship
and the parish. And by no means skulking, for I fully share
your own aversion to that activity. I was merely waiting until
I should be properly presented, as common gentility dictates
I must."

Should an observer have cared to notice Mr. Collins' complexion during this speech, he might have charted in it an
uncommon fluctuation of color, progressing swiftly from the
vermilion to the very ghastly. Never before had the rector of
Hunsford heard Lady Catherine so addressed. But observer
there was none; for the gazes, open of Mr. Beasley, and
sidelong of the Captain, were fixed upon the lady, who in her
turn was staring at the young curate.

During the short silence which ensued, even the pug Toby
saw fit to seek shelter under the table.

But Her Ladyship, having studied the young man quite
exhaustively through her quizzing glass, merely observed,
"I detect in your speech, Mr. Beasley, an accent that is not
from here, and I never err in such matters. You are, I perceive,
from Ireland."

"Ireland!" exclaimed Beasley, indignant. "Certainly not.
You are right that I am not a southern Englishman. But Irish I
am not. I come from Yorkshire, where we believe in honest
dealings, and speech as plain as you may find it anywhere in
the civilized world."

Mr. Collins moaned aloud.

"I see, Mr. Collins," remarked Her Ladyship, turning from
Beasley towards her beleaguered parson, "that Mrs. Collins
persists in ignoring my counsel about your diet. Less roast
meat, I caution her, and a little warm wine before you retire,
and you will soon feel the benefit. You see, Mr. Beasley, I was
in the right of it: you are not one of us. As I warned you, I am
never mistaken." And rejoicing in the accuracy of a trivial
portion of her appraisal, while electing to disregard the
egregious error which informed the whole, she turned her
attentions to more important matters in the parish.

"I look to you, Mr. Beasley," continued she without delay,
"to assist Mr. Collins where your predecessor was sorely wanting. I refer, of course, to the deplorable situation of the dogs."

Mr. Beasley, a young man not short in understanding,
could nevertheless not hide his puzzlement.

"Dogs, Madam? How can they signify?"

"Dogs, Sirrah," responded she with impatience. "There is a veritable plague of them invading our church of a Sunday matins. Can you not have noticed? Yapping and whimpering without cease, disturbing the quietude, and positively upsetting my poor Toby. Your first duty, Mr. Beasley, will be to rid Hunsford parish church of its dogs."

A tall figure of a man, Beasley loomed above Lady Catherine. Nevertheless, at this curious speech, he merely bowed and expressed himself unpracticed in such a pursuit, but eager to serve Her Ladyship in any way he might.

"Let us hope so indeed," was the lady's gracious response. "You have at least the advantage of youth over old Woodthorpe. He had become so frail that he could barely lift the dog tongs to snatch the creatures up. *You*, by your look, will have small trouble there." And without pause she turned to her next demand. "Do you do well by music?"

"Hardly at all," replied the curate, frankly. "I had the best of masters, but even they could not improve my singularly tuneless ear."

Her Ladyship was outraged at this brazen admission of so grievous a lack in clerical talents.

"No ear," cried she. "Why, Collins, what manner of fellow is this you have brought to Hunsford? Can you have forgotten that the church orchestra particularly wants an oboeist? And here you bring us a deaf ear!"

So unconditional a rebuke would have reduced a lesser man; but Mr. Beasley remained composed.

"Madam," responded he coolly, "you look upon one whose calling it is to bring to his community every benefit he may. There is no dearer object of any clergyman than to serve. To that end, I will consent to wield the dog tongs; I will even sweep the church floor if it is required. But I advise you now, that any request for music from me will needs be but bootless, for it is a talent that I do not possess. If I could oblige you in this, I would; but I cannot, and there's an end to it."

Thunder could not have more menaced the room. Lady Catherine was not used to having her judgments controverted, and the open speech of this Yorkshireman manifested itself to her as little short of an affront. Others might be lulled by the sincerity that underlay the young man's directness of speech; others could overlook its lack of blandishment; Lady Catherine's was the burden of her too-perceptive nature. In short, she was insulted.

She rose to her full stature. Mr. Collins cowered, Captain Heywood observed with avid attention.

"As to service," said she, "we shall see. But be forewarned that I will not indulge indolence. I was once forced to send a parlor maid packing from here after but a week, for that very fault—and *she* was from York, itself."

And thus assured that she, and not he, had had the last word in this exchange, she was able to turn her attention away from this upstart, and towards her daughter, Anne, who, looking tolerably restored to the rest of the company, and altogether radiant to her mother, had just then entered the room.

CHAPTER 26

READINESS OF WIT may enchant; nobility of line command respect, even awe; but in times of adversity, when deeds are imperative, nothing surpasses the value of good sense. Upon his arrival in London, Mr. Darcy speedily sought out Elizabeth's Uncle Gardiner, having long recognized in that gentleman a stability of temperament, a dependability, that he could only admire. It was not the first time that Elizabeth's husband had had occasion to be of service to the Bennet family; and during the trying days of Lydia's elopement, Darcy had come to appreciate, in the older man, the weight of a judicious mind, free alike from the eccentricity of his wife's relatives and the vanity of his own.

Mr. Darcy and Mr. Gardiner, indeed, soon discerned that in the present circumstances they two would of necessity be the family's mainstay. Mr. Bennet, affected as he was, was sorely lacking in steadfastness and could hardly be counted upon for any energetic assistance; Mr. Philips himself, still in Hertfordshire with his wife, was little less distraught than she. Upon the remaining two men would fall the greater part of the family's burden.

"And how fortunate it is, Mr. Darcy," exclaimed Mrs. Gardiner upon Darcy's third evening in London, "that we have you here to aid us. My brother Bennet has grown still more reclusive since Lizzy's departure from Longbourn, and truth to tell, brother Philips has never had much to him of consequence. But to you, Sir, we may look with assurance once more."

"My dear Mrs. Gardiner," replied he affectionately, "let us but hope that your trust in my powers is not misplaced. My consultations with my solicitor, as I have said, have not been encouraging. But tell me, Uncle Gardiner," turning to him, "how came your sister to such a strait? Even supposing that through absentmindedness she had indeed carried the lace from the shop, can any one have supposed her to intend actual theft? Does not the milliner, Turner, know her now these many years?"

"Old Mr. Turner did," replied Mr. Gardiner, sighing. "But it is of young Turner we speak. Old Turner died but last autumn, and his son, raised in London, and knowing, and known to, no one in Longbourn, is shopkeeper now."

"Yet surely, dear Uncle, Mrs. Philips is well respected in the neighborhood. There must be many who would willingly speak to her character. Sir William Lucas, for example, who is but little less familiar with superior society than he is eager to remind us of the fact. Does not this young Turner have regard for the good opinion even of one who has visited St. James's? What manner of fellow could this be?"

Mr. Gardiner smiled, but quickly explained that, although many had spoken for his sister, the man had remained obdurate.

"Both reasonings and entreaties have been to no avail. He *will* bring the matter to trial, he says, unless my brother Philips pay him the sum he demands of £1000. Nothing short of an infamy; but since the alternative for Mrs. Philips, should she be found guilty, is possible death, or, at the very least, deportation to Botany Bay, my brother Philips is ready, despite my own advice, to oblige him."

"Then young Turner is a rogue, upon my word."

"As to that," interjected Mrs. Gardiner, "I confess myself puzzled. Mr. Gardiner and I were visiting Longbourn shortly before Christmas and, at the time, Mrs. Bennet and I chanced to have some dealings in the shop. I wondered then that he had sufficient intelligence to measure a ribbon, let alone devise and carry out a scheme of extortion. There must be more to the matter—he has an accomplice, perhaps."

Despite himself Mr. Gardiner laughed. "My love, my love," chuckled he. "How you women will feed your fancies with romances. From whence did you draw this notion of an accomplice? *The Mysteries of Udolpho?* or *The Castle of Otranto?*"

Mrs. Gardiner would have retorted, for dispute over the current fashion for novels was a pastime dear to them both, but Darcy must continue.

"Even so," said he, "Mrs. Philips' situation remains a sorry one. I need scarce mention that—for an honorable purpose—the sum might certainly be found. But that is not the matter: we cannot—nay, we shall not—accede to so knavish a demand as this. Since your sister is innocent, justice demands that she protest it."

"I am altogether of your mind, Sir," agreed Mr. Gardiner. "Mr. Philips shall not pay for a crime of which his wife is blameless. Justice cannot be bartered for pounds and pence." But then he added, sighing, "Let us only hope that the price my sister does pay is not dearer than money."

Heedful of Elizabeth's anxieties for her aunt, Mr. Darcy was scrupulous, when writing to her the next morning, to allude not at all to Mr. Gardiner's fears. But his wife too easily saw through the contrived cheer of his words to the genuine foreboding beneath.

Wretched had been her recent days. Her husband absent and herself of a sudden much in request, she had been obliged again and again to endure, unsupported, the full severity of the neighborhood's sympathy. Mrs. Montague, especially, was solicitous in her despair of the Bennet family's future; Lady Stanton most profitably appended the perception that a fresh scandal was scarcely surprising given that family's past; Sir Edward Stanton, practical as ever, proffered the benevolent advice that Mrs. Darcy must instantly detach herself from every association with so unfortunate an origin.

As for Sir Geoffrey, his judgment upon the incident clearly had not altered: despite Elizabeth's woe, his silence persisted. Nor was help to be sought from other quarters. Jane was unwell of late, and such small resources as her mother could offer all directed towards the safe delivery of an heir to Pelham and its most happily unentailed estates. Kitty and Mary remained at best unimproved; and the most that could be said in commendation of Lydia or her husband, was that they had departed. Georgiana held fast in Elizabeth's cause; but since her devotion proclaimed itself most fervently in incivility to the neighborhood, the benefit of this support was arguable. In effect, Elizabeth stood all alone.

Reading her husband's letter, she could not hold back her tears, and for several minutes allowed herself, in the welcome solitude of the drawing room, the indulgence of unrestrained emotion. Would there be no cease to the troubles her family could provoke?

It was then that she heard a tapping at the door. She raised her head, and immediately set to drying her eyes and recovering herself for whatever fresh visitation might be announced. But no servant appeared; instead, it was the architect, James Leigh-Cooper.

The young man, noting her distress, hesitated at the threshold, as if wondering whether to enter; but soon, his concern overcoming his uncertainty, he joined her.

"You are ill," said he, with great gentleness. "Let me call your maid; would you take a glass of wine? Or," suddenly drawing back as he recollected himself, "perhaps I am intruding."

"On the contrary, pray stay a little while," said she. "I am not ill, I thank you; but it can scarcely be a secret to you that my family has had misfortune. I have just now received a letter from Mr. Darcy and his news is not cheering in the least."

Whether or not Mr. Leigh-Cooper had already learned of the affair, his expression gave no indication. His demeanor was all consideration. "Are you quite sure?" pressed he. "You seem so pale."

"Quite sure," she responded, grateful to encounter genuine warmth of feeling at last; and without a pause fell to crying again. He watched her in silent compassion, and, when at last her tears had subsided, she found herself confiding to this singular young man the whole sorry tale.

He listened attentively, saying little. At the end of her recital, he shook his head, his countenance grave. "This young Turner," said he, "you say was reared in London? Then you must excuse my speaking frankly, but I cannot pretend to great surprise at your story. Do not mistake me, I do not suggest that your aunt has committed such a crime. On the contrary, I am sure she has not, for this is not the first time I have heard of such skulduggery. England, Mrs. Darcy, is altered; in my profession I see it everywhere about. And while much of the change is to be applauded, an equal measure sadly must be deplored. London, dear Madam, and not your aunt, is the culprit in this case. Avarice lurks there, and dishonor. More than once have I seen a simple country boy—just such a one, in all probability, as this young Turner—arrive on its streets only to fall in with loose companions and soon to abandon all considerations either religious or moral. And then, when he returns to so innocent a town as, for instance, Meryton, who knows what he might not attempt? Too often have I witnessed country folk fall victim to the wiles of the townsman's cunning."

Elizabeth was all wonderment at his words. "Can you mean, Sir, that such an accusation as my aunt's, you have heard leveled before? And pray tell, what resulted?"

"Twice, to my certain knowledge," replied he. "Once in Dorset, and once near Hardwycke Hall itself. The incidents were not at all unlike your aunt's, although the details, of course, differed. The Hardwycke case was resolved; but as for the Dorset affair, well . . . ," interrupting himself, "Mr. Darcy and your uncle will undoubtedly have the best solicitors in London."

His tone was kindness itself, but Elizabeth trembled at his words. "You mean," said she, "that in one case at least, the accused has paid with his life."

"Be comforted, Mrs. Darcy," said he swiftly. "Your husband, I feel certain, would never permit such an injustice in the Darcy family."

Elizabeth would draw cheer from his words, yet could not. Attempt to reassure her as he might, the truth was that just such another as her aunt had indeed been brought to the gallows. Still, his intelligence of similar outrages inflicted upon the innocent could not but engage her interest. Her aunt, then, was not alone in her disgrace, but one victim among others. Elizabeth had had no inkling, nor had the most worldly of her neighbors, that such enormities were prevalent. And it was Mr. Leigh-Cooper, a young man quite without pretenses, who had opened her eyes. Despite her worry, his worth grew in her estimation.

"What you have told me may well be of particular significance," said she, deciding quickly that with this companion, she need not stand on formality, "and I must inform Mr. Darcy without delay. You will pray excuse me."

But even as she rose to go, Georgiana burst upon them, her color high, and, without so much as a glance about her,

began: "Dear Elizabeth," cried she, "might you at all spare
me for a fortnight? I have been pondering this morning upon
my aunt's invitation to visit her at Rosings, and I have decided
it would fall little short of outright discourtesy in me if I
failed to accept her kind offer. Of course, dear sister, if my
service be altogether indispensable in this time, then nothing
shall tear me from your side. But, I would go, if you can bear
it, for Kent is so fair in the spring. Dear Elizabeth, please say I
may go."

Elizabeth had not been blind to the exchanges between
her young sister and the dashing Captain Heywood before
the latter's departure. Now, observing Georgiana's animation, she must wonder whether the particular charm of
Rosings rested in either the opportunity for civility to her
aunt, or the beauties of the Kent countryside; or whether it
might rather lie in the company she would find there. Diverted despite all, she glanced towards her new friend. But James
Leigh-Cooper had turned away and was engrossed in the
stonework of the fireplace, his half-averted face manifesting
unmistakeable displeasure.

CHAPTER 27

G EORGIANA'S PURPOSE IN visiting Rosings was not all of indulgence. It was true that Captain Heywood would be of the company there; nor was the prospect of being thrust again into his presence one she found precisely insupportable. Yet a more pressing errand preoccupied her. She had observed with anguish her sister's pain over the last weeks, and that morning, in the library, had come upon a plan to amend the circumstance. The Bennets' situation she knew she could not resolve; but it struck her that there was one way in which she might serve. Elizabeth, above all, wanted allies; Georgiana would undertake to win to her side none other than her aunt, Lady Catherine de Bourgh.

An ambitious scheme it was, and not least because she and Her Ladyship had of late years shared few exchanges that had not foundered swiftly in contention. But Georgiana, fired with heroic intent, remembered this not at all. Once at Rosings, she would plead Elizabeth's cause with an eloquence which would fell all opposition; Lady Catherine, her resistance quite undone, would declare herself instantly in the Bennet family's defense; and they two, conjoined in this happy accord (for Georgiana's flight of fancy knew no bounds), must surely win over Sir Geoffrey himself. All Derbyshire then would hasten to Elizabeth's support. And if, in the course of her quest, Miss Darcy should chance to be thrown into the society of a Captain Heywood, that was a condition she could meet with fortitude.

Our heroine arrived at Rosings in high spirits. Her aunt's greeting, too, was energetic, although she would lose no time in wondering at Georgiana's traveling attended with a full three servants.

"Surely, two at the most would have sufficed," said she so soon as her niece had removed her bonnet. "I myself never travel with any other than Sally; but then I am more than commonly resourceful. Even so, there can be no reason for more than two to accompany you. Extravagance, my dear child, can only lead to idle servants and squandered means. Has not the mistress of Pemberley advised you so? But perhaps she herself is unaware of such particulars."

Georgiana, mindful of her mission, quickly recognized her opportunity; she smiled and curtsied.

"Dear Aunt," said she, "already, I see, your most diligent tutelage begins. I am grateful for it, and shall endeavor to prove a creditable pupil."

Her Ladyship received this deference with perplexity. Always before, her admonitions to Georgiana had called forth responses that were spirited, if not insolent. What could this precipitate complaisance signify? She searched her niece's features for signs of ill-health, but there were none. Her complexion was as splendid as ever.

"I welcome your improved discernment," she announced therefore, "and I trust such obedience will continue throughout your visit. With application, you may yet not dishonor the Darcy name." And with a sidelong glance at this unfamiliar young person, she went about her business.

Georgiana, left alone within the grandeur of Rosings, wanting as it did in both comfort and real elegance, found small inducement to remain indoors. Her cousin Anne and Captain Heywood, she learned, were out riding together; there remained yet two hours of daylight; she determined to walk before dinner in the direction of the Collins parsonage, where Elizabeth had particularly directed her to carry her greetings to her old friend, Mrs. William Collins.

As soon as she had settled herself into her chamber, and made as little alteration as she could to her dress, she left the house and walked until she had passed the gates of Rosings. Both apple and cherry trees were in blossom and the air was sweeter even than in Derbyshire; Kent in the springtime, she observed with some pleasurable surprise, revealed itself altogether as exquisite as she had cried it up to Elizabeth.

It was not long before she discerned the green pales and the laurel hedge that surrounded the parsonage. Strolling down the walk from the house even as she approached, was a gentleman in clerical attire with a curiously close haircut, who, upon seeing her, hastened forward with eager gait, his hand outstretched.

"Miss Georgiana Darcy, as I live," cried he. "You do not know me? No, of course, the recollection of one such as yourself, I could scarce hope to encompass a lowly cleric. But I had the honor of being presented to you, and by none other than my gracious patron, your aunt, the Lady Catherine de Bourgh, upon the occasion of your brother's wedding to my cousin, the former Miss Eliza Bennet. An edifying service it was indeed, and His Lordship the Bishop, I may say, has rarely been in heartier voice. I own that I could scarcely have performed the ceremony louder myself."

Georgiana greeted the parson, whom she did not indeed recollect; and desiring to cover the slight, was prompted to compliment the flowering shrubs along the garden's gravel paths. This perfunctory observation moved the cleric to passion. The garden was of his own design: did she genuinely admire his handiwork? Surely, not! She could not condescend to praise the lilac bushes, now seen, Miss Darcy must observe, to particular advantage in the late afternoon light; although his modest efforts with the rhododendrons, he dared to flatter himself, were not completely unworthy of consideration; and were she to accompany him to the vegetable garden, *there* she would see such an array of turnips and peas as would veritably set her a-quiver.

"But then, Miss Darcy," said he, catching himself, "the splendors of the grounds at Pemberley must certainly overshadow any poor triumphs of my own. We at the Parsonage are careful never to exceed the appropriate display of our skills with greenery, lest it cause offense at Rosings." And with that he hastened to usher his guest indoors to greet his wife.

Georgiana, if something absent-minded at times, was nevertheless certain that she had not yet met Mrs. Collins, whom indisposition had kept from her brother's wedding; but she had heard Elizabeth speak of her often and with much warmth. The parson's wife was a woman of some nine and twenty, faded and thin, her bloom quite vanished. Yet there was an intelligence in her aspect, an understanding in her eyes, which must excite esteem.

"You see, my dear," cried her husband, not troubling himself with a formal presentation, "whom I have discovered outside our very own door. None other than Miss Georgiana Darcy, just arrived at Rosings and so discriminating as to appreciate the arrangements of my garden. I protested that they were hardly worthy of her praise, but she would insist. My laburnum took her particular fancy, did it not, Miss Darcy?"

Georgiana overcame her astonishment at Mr. Collins' want of courtesy, not only to herself, but to his wife. Surmising that no more proper introduction would be forthcoming, she addressed herself directly to the lady.

"Mrs. Collins," said she, "I pray you to forgive my appearance thus unannounced at your door, but I simply desired to convey to you the most tender greetings from my sister Elizabeth. She speaks so affectionately of your attachment that I longed to meet you myself." If Mrs. Collins had noted her husband's incivility, she gave no sign of it. She responded gravely but with unaffected warmth, "I too, Miss Darcy, have eagerly anticipated making your acquaintance. Dear Elizabeth has written of you often and with such admiration. Pray tell us the news. How does my dear friend? And your brother? How do the improvements get on at Pemberley?"

"Excellent well," returned Georgiana. "The architect in charge of them, Mr. James Leigh-Cooper, is as diligent as he is inventive, and has already achieved much, despite the absence of my brother these many days in town."

"In town?" questioned Mrs. Collins in some surprise. "Did not Elizabeth last write to me that he had but lately returned? What could take him back there so soon?" But descrying Georgiana's expression, and looking quickly aside towards her husband, she hurried on. "Well, with such men of affairs, who knows how often they must journey? I trust, Miss Darcy, that Mrs. Bingley fares well in her condition?"

Mr. Collins could not attend them a moment longer. "My love," interrupted he, ringing the bell, almost before his wife had finished speaking, "we are sadly remiss. We have yet to show Miss Darcy our own son. Miss Darcy, you must prepare to view the latest heir to Longbourn."

The nurse appeared promptly, carrying this fortunate beneficiary, a child of fifteen months, whose aspect so resembled his father's—even to the close cropping of his head—that there could be no mistaking the good fortune of his lineage.

The boy, on entering the room, looked immediately towards his mother; but Mr. Collins would take him up and dandle him.

"Young William," said he, "I do assure you, Miss Darcy, is destined for distinction in all he undertakes. Is that not your estimation as well, my dear Charlotte? He has set himself apart by the superiority of his intelligence. Only mark how he gurgles at Miss Darcy, already recognizing the honor of her appearance at our abode. Veritably, he is every inch a Collins."

He proceeded thus until even the child's proud mother was moved to remonstrate. "Mr. Collins, you will surely drive Miss Darcy from us if you persist." And turning to Georgiana, she added softly, "You must forgive a doting father's effusions. Young William is his joy."

Georgiana was quick both to reassure the mother and admire the son. Nevertheless, it was without too profound a disappointment that she recollected that she must leave forthwith if she wished to return to Rosings before dark.

CHAPTER 28

A S SHE MADE her way back to Rosings, Georgiana's thoughts would linger with her new acquaintances. How little felicity had she discerned between the parson of Hunsford and his wife, how mean a companionship. The dejection of the lady, her unease in the presence of her husband, suggested not the comforts of a loving union but, rather, resignation to a state of affairs unalterable. *He*, so enthralled with his own skills as both gardener and progenitor, as effectively to ignore his wife; while *she*, a woman of qualities, must direct all her energies to—the very best she might hope for—sparing him outright humiliation.

And how contrary a picture to that which presented itself to her each day at Pemberley. Elizabeth and her brother, even when at variance, were, she knew, never in disaccord. The tenderness of their attachment was beyond question; and it manifested itself most happily in an irreverence which had at first alarmed Georgiana but which she now comprehended, with the wisdom of ripening years, as the sweetest expression of amity. Their bond was fortunate indeed.

But few there were in England, she mused, to peer Fitzwilliam Darcy. The youth of Derbyshire offered little to a romantic disposition beyond talk of card games or feats in the hunt. A Harry Middleton, or Robert Stanton were nothing to rival a man such as her brother. And that brother too was fortunate. *He* had found a woman who, although inferior in fortune, was in every other way incomparable; while Georgiana's own sole venture outside the society she knew had resulted in so near a disaster that she trembled still to think of it. Darcy had found his equal: where might be such a match for Georgiana?

As she walked in the brisk evening air, her determination grew. A comfortable home, and increased station in society, might lure a Charlotte Collins to the overthrow of all contentment; but Georgiana need never sink to such wretchedness. Hers was a higher hope of matrimony; she would not marry else. Let the world say what it chose, she, a Darcy, and a Darcy moreover living in this second decade of the new century, would please herself alone. That her interests had been stirred by Captain Heywood was true; but the brave Captain must needs show himself outstanding to aspire to her more particular esteem.

By the time she had reached the steps of the hall, her ankles were weary, but her spirits quite restored; and it was with pleasure that she perceived the approach of her cousin Anne and Captain Heywood, just now returned from their excursion. The Captain's appearance was greatly in his favor, and upon horseback showed all the more elegant.

"My dear Miss Darcy," exclaimed he, so soon as greetings had been exchanged. "What a pity you could not have been with us this afternoon. Miss Anne has been all tolerance for the poor horsemanship of a mere seaman. In fact, I suspect that she gave particular attention *not* to outpace me. Could I but hope for such clemency from yourself, I should straightaway suggest we all three ride tomorrow."

Georgiana loved the pastime, and the manner of his address was as pleasing as she remembered it. Her recent contemplations, however, together with the consciousness of her own superior horsemanship, made her respond archly. "Your hopes would surely be dashed then with *me*," said she. "I warn you that when I ride it is for the pleasure of the exercise alone, rather than for the gratification of any companion."

"And a capital sight that must be," cried the Captain. "To my mind, nothing could be more bewitching than the sight of a young woman in the full bloom of health on horseback."

Georgiana was hard put to resist such flattery, so addressed herself instead to her cousin, standing silent by the great door.

"Is the Captain's modesty false?" she asked. "If he means to recommend himself by the appearance of humility in his speech, while excelling in the deed itself, then, dear Anne, our kinship demands that you expose him instantly. But if he truly rides as badly as he claims, it was little short of heroic in you to endure it for the whole of the afternoon."

"*I* have been taught," replied Anne in a cold tone, "that *my* wishes must come second to those of my family and companions. It is, I have understood, the better part of good breeding." And, forthwith, she turned aside from the Captain, to continue, speaking low, "I chance to know, as I believe my mother does not, that had you, too, learned that lesson in your own younger days, a *certain* near indiscretion might have been avoided altogether."

Never before had Georgiana heard so lengthy a speech issue from the lips of Lady Catherine's daughter, and her cousin's words quite gave her pause. Anne, she knew from childhood to be remarkable in but few things: in her silence, her steadfast obedience to her mother, and above all, in her insipidity. Now for the first time, she perceived that beneath the listlessness lay, not indifference, but ill will.

Captain Heywood, the meanwhile, sensible of the discord in the cousins' exchange, hastened to interrupt it. Stepping between the two ladies, he urged the hour, escorted them into the house, and promised to meet them afresh at dinner, towards which he looked in anticipation for the pleasures of both the famed de Bourgh table, and the fairest of companies. Then all three removed to their separate quarters to dress. Her Ladyship, they well knew, dined at half-past six, and would brook nothing less than the strictest punctuality from any but Toby.

Georgiana was alert to her aunt's insistence upon promptness, and determined to seize the opportunity to be in the drawing room several minutes early. Her maid was quiet and quick; there remained time enough yet, she rejoiced, even to begin a note to Elizabeth assuring her of her safe arrival. But once she was seated and the paper before her, the events of the afternoon, and the beauties of Hunsford parish, so crowded in upon her thoughts that before she was aware, it was past six and Hannah not yet summoned. She made all haste; nevertheless, it was beyond the half-hour when, breathless and her gown barely tied, she made her entrance.

Her Ladyship was pacing the drawing room. Barely pausing to grasp at the bell and order "dinner to be on table *immediately!*" she turned upon her niece. "What is deemed meet at Pemberley in these days," said she, "I cannot say. But, here at Rosings, we extend the courtesy of regularity. Civility is the custom *here*; and *we* are never kept waiting. I trust this is a lesson you will learn before you leave."

She waited impatiently for her niece's response, but it was all meekness.

"Dear Aunt, I pray you forgive me, and be assured I will give my every endeavor to learning. Never would I wish to risk your disapprobation; but the truth is that my temper is sadly inattentive. I merely was taking the opportunity of the few quiet minutes to apprise Mrs. Darcy of my safe arrival—as that very civility demands I must—and mistook the time."

At this, Anne de Bourgh coughed, while the Captain looked on in amusement. Lady Catherine's disappointment was sore. Hardly had she been able to reacquaint herself with the sweet comfort of exasperation with her niece; and now, worsted by so humble an apology, she could do no other than accept it, and console herself by observing, on their way to the dining room, that certain ribbons might be better tied by a better directed maid.

Nor did her disgruntlement abate once they were at table. Her niece's manners continued impeccable; Her Ladyship's every stricture was greeted with respect. In desperation, she was reduced at last to broaching the scandal so newly attached to the Bennet family.

"I learn little from Sir Geoffrey," began she, "since he, of course, can hardly consider it a fit subject for his contemplation; yet it cannot be dismissed. That a Darcy should have married one who counts among her near relations a common thief! Never did I believe myself capable of rejoicing at your parents' death, Georgiana. But I confess that at this moment I do."

Georgiana was dumbfounded. In the face of cavils against herself she could maintain her fortitude; censure of blameless Elizabeth was impossible to bear. She felt her color rising, and struggled to compose herself. She *must not* undo her purpose so early in her visit by angering her aunt. Yet how could she maintain the appearance of complacency?

While she wrestled in desperation with such thoughts, it was Captain Heywood who, just as once before, plunged forward to her rescue.

"Your Ladyship will, I am sure, indulge the intervention of a a mere servant of His Majesty's Navy," began he. "And of you, as well, Miss Darcy, I ask forbearance, for I cannot pretend to be wholly ignorant of the matter to which you refer. I must speak out, for it remains my duty, good ladies, to remind you that one of the glories of the great country in which we live is that our English law does not connive against man or woman. I who have been in lands where it is not so, must attest it: but *here*, at least, a person accused may await, with tolerable security of reputation, a fair trial before being judged innocent or guilty."

Georgiana, much stirred by his protestation, was emboldened to take her aunt up.

"Dear Madam," cried she, "your abhorrence for any crime is well advertised and justly praised. But I beg you to hear the Captain's defense. He has traveled widely and may be expected to know much. Both the clarity of reason, and the weight of experience, inform his words. Do they not, Captain?"

"I know not of that," said he, pleased. "But like the poet Wordsworth, I too have 'traveled among unknown men in lands beyond the sea.' Happily have I now reached dear England's shore, and can this evening reflect that ' 'tis past, that melancholy dream,' and rejoice the more."

Rarely able to resist the Captain's amiability of address, and never when that alluring quality was fortified by his display of poetic erudition, Her Ladyship was diverted despite herself; and was able summarily to direct the conversation to its natural sequitur of her daughter's skills as a horsewoman. And almost immediately afterwards, realizing that their ride itself would have exhibited to its best Miss de Bourgh's prowess in the outdoors, it fell to her mother to wax eloquent in extolling her wit in the drawing room. She continued thus, rhapsodic, even to the point where her daughter was moved to words of her own:

"Captain Heywood," ventured she, her speech untainted by either truth or relevancy, "has, I can assure you, shown himself as honorably upon horseback as he has triumphantly at sea."

In the silence which followed, the courtly gentleman bowed to the young lady.

Soon they repaired to the drawing room. It so chanced that the young man placed himself next to Georgiana and was able to speak to her unattended by his hostess or her daughter. He quickly began in almost a whisper.

"Your precipitate appearance at Rosings is nothing short of a delight, although I confess it does not altogether surprise me. You must forgive my presumption if I suggest that I might comprehend its purpose."

Though something startled, Georgiana was affected by the quickness of his intelligence. Could he already have surmised her intent to save the reputation of the Bennets? How clever was he to understand her so well.

But there was no moment to reply, for Lady Catherine was upon them and demanded all of the Captain's attention until the coffee was served, at which time she condescended to recognize her niece with the command that she sit down directly to the pianoforte and perform for her.

Said she, "You are of course aware of my perfect enjoyment of music; I count myself among the few in England whose appreciation of it can be so regarded. Often have I lamented the grievous loss, and many with me, and those not undistinguished: how proficient I might have become, if I had ever learnt."

She endured the best part of a song, before being compelled to interrupt with her own observations. Georgiana's progress, she must acknowledge, was fair; she was not dissatisfied to see that her niece had taken to heart her urgings upon the necessity for practice; now she need only admonish her to practice the more if she wished to become as excellent as Her Ladyship might have been. Then, not to neglect for another minute her daughter's accomplishments, she returned to the praises of her achievements in purse netting and screen covering.

The Captain warmly acknowleded these wonders, favoring his hostess with admiration for herself as well as her daughter. So went the festivities. Georgiana was often innocent of her aunt's wiles; but even she, before the evening was out, must sense that this young gallant had been properly marked out, was in the process of being readied, and would soon be claimed for her cousin Anne.

Curiously, and despite all resolution, this comprehension proved vexatious; it sat, in fact, so ill with Georgiana Darcy that those there are who might even have mistaken it for jealousy.

CHAPTER 29

T HE WEEKS FOLLOWING at Rosings afforded Georgiana
emotions of no less confusion than did her first day.
The balmy weather, and the variety of delightful walks
around Hunsford, had contributed greatly to the improvement of her acquaintance with Captain Thomas Heywood. In
their excursions together, always in the company of her silent
cousin Anne, the Captain's attentions were unmistakeable,
although whatever he said, he said with such grace as to give
each lady the pleasure of his favor.

The young officer's talk turned often to his days at sea, to
exotic ports and to moments of danger in battle. To his
enthralled listeners, such narratives seemed the most romantic of tales from an unknown world.

"We arrived off the Rock of Gibraltar," he would begin,
"where our fleet was in want of assistance to repair their
damages. The wind was fine at first, fresh from the east to run
through the Straits, but before we were out of sight of the
garrison it chopped round to the westward, directly in our
teeth, and there came on to blow a very heavy gale, which
effectively prevented our proceeding."

And as the two gasped, he continued solemnly, "Who
could have been but ill prepared to encounter such a severe
storm? Indeed, I hardly expected to learn that our friends
could have escaped, so crippled were their masts." Then, his
delicacy forbidding more, he would check himself, passing
over such horrors as he had seen to the calming effect of their
being doubled in the young ladies' imaginations. "But those
days are most happily past and here am I in fair company!"

In short, his air, his walk, his countenance were beguiling, and his readiness to talk could but encourage them to listen and admire. He had become for Georgiana the most amiable man of her acquaintance.

Less happy was her campaign to influence Lady Catherine for Elizabeth's sake, since the mistress of Rosings proved a far more elusive adversary than she had at first imagined. The great lady, a most active arbitrator in her parish, was much occupied with the ills of the village. Tireless she was, in search of her tenants' differences, their injuries, their complaints.

"I cannot tolerate," she would boast, "squabbling among the cottagers. Ill-bred folk, I do assure you, if left to themselves, do little else. It is I who am burdened with the responsibility of maintaining their harmony, and I am too sensible of my duty to be lenient upon them. Let it invade my peace as it may, they *shall* enjoy good spirits, or answer to me."

Thus it was at the dinner table only that her niece might plead Elizabeth's cause. And though she did this faithfully, and with an ally able and ever more affectionate in Captain Heywood, the results were at best inconclusive. Her Ladyship was immovable.

Furthermore, it seemed likely to Georgiana that her aunt's recalcitrance arose not merely from her natural and reasonable disdain for the entire Bennet family, but from her own proprietorial demands upon Captain Heywood. Georgiana may have herself decided that a particular interest in any young man was not for her; yet when Lady Catherine turned to the Captain, or he, gallantly smiling, to Anne, she discovered herself able to bear it only with a tolerable grace.

News of distraction therefore must be welcome. In the fourth week of Georgiana's stay, she learned that Charlotte Collins was to be visited by her sister Maria, accompanied by her friend Kitty Bennet. Maria, Georgiana had not yet met, and Elizabeth's lively sister quite alarmed her; even so, the presence of other young people among them could only, she was sure, help to dispel the growing, and not always agreeable, intimacy between herself, the Captain, and Anne.

On the morning after the Hertfordshire party's arrival, she went to Hunsford to pay her respects, finding, however, no one within but Charlotte Collins. Maria and Kitty were abroad exploring the village under the able supervision of Master William, and Mr. Collins was about his duty of promoting peace among the neighboring families, a feat accomplished today by his acceptance from one of them of a hind quarter of pork.

Since that first uncomfortable evening, Georgiana had been reluctant to visit Hunsford Parsonage again, and now, alone with its mistress for the first time, she recollected the force of this slight. But the warmth of Mrs. Collins' welcome was unaffected, and, before long, they two were sitting in the backwards drawing room over sherry and a biscuit.

"Elizabeth," began Charlotte Collins so soon as both had concluded what was proper, "has written to me of her family's misfortune, and I know her spirits to be low. I can but be grateful that in this difficult time she may turn with such confidence to her new family, to her husband and yourself."

Georgiana felt the compliment, but must protest.

"You are kind, indeed," said she. "Too kind, for *I* can do but little for Elizabeth; and certainly in no measure begin to repay what Elizabeth has given to me. It is my brother whose efforts are unceasing in her behalf. He cannot abide the slightest unhappiness to touch her. I do believe he feels more deeply for her than for himself."

"He does, in truth," said Mrs. Collins with a sigh. "Their mutual affection is uncommon. I should be jealous, did my love for Elizabeth fall just a little short. Marriage has brought her what she merits. Nor would she settle for less."

"Settle for less!" cried Georgiana Darcy. "Why in heaven's name should she? A woman of Elizabeth's parts—why would she not seek out the single most harmonious attachment that England might offer her?" Even as she said it, she regretted having spoken at all, for Charlotte Collins' color rose as she turned from her.

"My dear," was all she said, however, after a moment, "you are yet young. And if you will forgive my mentioning it, your position in life sets you in a rather different circumstance from that of many ladies—your sister-in-law not excepted."

"Elizabeth," protested Georgiana, "would not marry but for love. To do so is base, and I believe her incapable of such an act."

"She may well be," countered the other. Mrs. Collins had
little intention of offending her young visitor, but her views
upon the matter she must own. Marriage, she had come
bitterly to understand to be as unnecessarily related to affairs
of the heart as the letting of a house or the selection of a table
for quadrille. Long since, she had given up the romantic
notion of its signifying either more or less than a provision for
ladies such as herself, blessed with neither looks nor fortunes
of consequence.

"The truth is," continued she, sighing, "that chance
smiled upon Elizabeth, as, in another fashion, has it on
you, too. Your sister happened to meet the one man who
might make her happy; and you, if you so choose, may
marry or may not. Not all are so comfortably situated. For
myself, the case was different; I was not always as you find
me today."

She paused, doubting whether to proceed, but after a
moment, as Georgiana sat silent, continued. "I, too, when
young, hoped—nay, expected—to meet and one day marry
the young man with whom I might fully engage my heart
and share the best of myself. And indeed, in my twentieth
summer, such a one there was. A music master brought from
London to instruct my sister Maria upon the harp, a young
person of upright character and the most agreeable bearing.
Our mutual esteem was immediate; within the month, our
affections were engaged as well. He asked my troth; I pledged
it. But, poor soul, good and gracious as he was, he was
without prospects, and when we applied to my dear father
for his blessing, he chose to decline the young man's
suit. Such a match, he believed, would disgrace the ennobled
name of Lucas. His rank, his position, his important ties with
St. James's, he explained, must all dictate against it. Young
I was and dutiful. I have ever desired to trust in the wisdom
of my good parents, and would not disobey them. And so
we parted. Yet, Miss Darcy, I have loved no other since,
and know surely now that I shall never love another so
well. But then, my dear," she sighed, "all of that was
long ago."

Much chastened at these words, Georgiana listened while
Mrs. Collins continued in some emotion. "Had I my youth
to live again, Miss Darcy, nothing—not duty, not even my

father's vanity—could prevent my following my heart. For a loveless life, however graced by respectability or establishment, is little more than wretchedness."

Georgiana felt her distress, but knew not how to comfort her. She grew absolutely ashamed of herself. That *she*, not only beautiful in the bloom of her youth, but also favored with the inestimable bounty of independent means, should have presumed to judge Charlotte Collins! It was a mortification to recall it. Now, knowing her sad history, she could but pity and admire her.

Happily, at that moment there came the sounds of the young people returning from their excursion; the girls bustled noisily into the room, the lusty young heir presumptive to Longbourn in Maria's arms. Kitty's delight at once again seeing Miss Darcy was effusively expressed, although her friend Maria was immediately silenced in the presence of so elevated a personage.

"My dear Miss Darcy," began Kitty in familiar tones, "how you would have been entertained in the village. Such queer, unfashionable dress as we saw upon the villagers. I said to Miss Lucas—did I not, Maria?—'Lord, Maria,' I said, 'if Miss Darcy could but be with us to enjoy the sight.' But perhaps you *will* join us tomorrow, for we are starved for want of clever conversation."

Georgiana was spared the necessity of reply by young William, whose resounding demands at that moment to be let down by his aunt must be obeyed instantly; as he made directly for his mother, all gazes were admiringly fixed upon him, for, for all his father's crying up of his merits, he was nevertheless a winning enough lad.

Mrs. Collins, regaining that composure which gave most others assurance that she was content in a household of love and piety, took up the child, kissed him, and was her firm self again. The servant recalled, and more refreshment requested, the group willingly mirrored the child's mirth.

It was not long before all were joined by the parson of Hunsford himself, breathless from his errands of good will about the parish, and following after him at a slower pace, his curate, Mr. Beasley.

"My dear Mrs. Collins," exclaimed the former in some excitement, "such a piece of pork as I have now delivered to Bridget, she had not seen before. Old Martin was resolved to give it to me, and I was obliged in all Christian charity to serve him. Ungraciousness, I need hardly remind you, my dear, is the property of the heathen, and it was an uncommonly fine sow."

And turning to the assembled company, he made his effusive greetings to Miss Darcy and his son; and only shortly afterwards hastened to present Mr. Beasley to his guests.

"Could the picture be prettier?" exulted he. "My infant babe; Miss Georgiana Darcy; two fair charmers in the bloom of their youth, and that is not to mention," he added hastily, after a moment, "the woman who has made me the happiest of men. Matrimony, Beasley, matrimony. Lady Catherine herself was so condescending as to importune it for me; I can but follow her example in recommending it to you. You can do no better in the world."

Mr. Beasley gave a perfunctory bow and quickly turned with a smile towards the parson's wife. "Could I find a one the like of Mrs. Collins, I should undertake it without hesitation. But I fear that no sensible woman would choose a man such as myself."

"How little you know your own worth," said Mrs. Collins, smiling. "A forthright fellow like yourself is worth one hundred fair-spoken gallants."

"In my own bachelor days," broke in Mr. Collins, with some ceremony, "I flattered myself upon having an especial way with the fair sex. Those days, my dear," he made haste to reassure his wife, "are quite gone. Still, I could advise you, Beasley, the way to any fine woman's heart is by deference. Depend upon it, Beasley, no matter what Mrs. Collins may say of it; a woman cannot be too much agreed with."

"Then I am in a sorry situation," said the curate, "for I cannot *seem* to agree where I *do* not. I must speak my mind."

"Good lord, Sir," cried Kitty, who could not receive in silence so outlandish a notion. "How can you mean what you say? Suppose that what is in your mind is not for any person's ears. I, for one, am often visited by thoughts which charity alone would prevent my speaking of aloud. How can a clergyman, of all men, be uncharitable?"

The young man, standing to his full height, looked down at her for the first time, in some interest, his eyes staring.

"Uncharitable?" queried he. "Surely, Miss, the affirmation of what is true can serve but for the good. It is only in the ideas of frivolous people that the harm may thrive."

Kitty bit her lip and was silenced. But later that afternoon, she confided to Maria. "Do you not find," she asked, "that these trifling handsome fellows like Frank Middleton are something dull? A pleasing countenance is well enough, but I have ever protested that that which is infinitely more appealing in a young man is substantiality of character."

Maria, quite taken aback by this novel claim from her friend, could make no answer.

Chapter 30

A HAPPY EVENT PROVED most heartening to the sunken spirits of the Bennet family. Jane Bingley was brought to bed and safely delivered of a healthy baby girl.

Mrs. Bennet, whose attendance to her daughter's comforts had been unceasing, was satisfaction itself; and her husband's pleasure over his first grandchild was almost equal to her own.

"Although, my dear Mrs. Bennet," began he, once they had retired to their own quarters, having admired the new-born to even Mrs. Bennet's fill, "*you* will prove a sore perplexity to the neighbors: there are few who shall willingly believe it possible for one so handsome as yourself to be the recipient of yet another generation of offspring. How they shall wonder at it! Mrs. Bennet, a grandmother, they will exclaim, why, that cannot be!"

"Mr. Bennet, you *will* try my patience," she protested, although his observation was well taken. "Lady Lucas, assuredly, is rather better suited to that position than my own, she is so wrinkled and thin. How she does stroll about in Meryton with her young heir, Master William Collins! An unfortunate looking child: it pains me to see him. To think that he shall have our Longbourn one day is positively irksome. But, I take comfort in the thought, Mr. Bennet, that this new child, this innocent baby girl, will see none of the distress of our own daughters in *her* coming of age. Mr. Bingley and Jane will quite properly see to that. Charles Bingley is not a man to allow their Pelham Park to succumb to the barbarity of entailment, depend upon it."

The triumphant parents themselves had early determined that if their child should be a daughter, her inevitable perfection in every particular should be heralded by their christening her after her Aunt Darcy. A daughter she was, and fulfilling of every expectation, to the extent, indeed, that Mr. Bingley, having himself suggested the name of Elizabeth, would still ever hold in his heart that she was in beauty and amiability her sweet mother alone. These considerations he kept secret from Mrs. Bingley, who already detected in little Eliza's eyes a foreshadowing of her aunt's wit, particularly when she was awake. As for Mrs. Darcy, her own joy for her sister's new state was boundless. Observing Jane together with her infant, she well remembered Mrs. Gardiner's praise of that young lady given so long ago, "If ever there had been a woman made for motherhood, Jane Bennet was she."

Elizabeth, herself, had borne these weeks with courage, while the neighborhood continued assiduously in its scrutiny of the Bennet family's misfortune, and the contemplation of the shame thus brought upon the Darcys. Fitzwilliam Darcy did his best to dispel her gloom, but he was seldom there to comfort her. Both her Aunt Philips' case, and business affairs of his own, took him frequently to London, and he was once more in town when the joyous announcement came from the Bingleys. He and the Gardiners themselves wrote frequently of every development; the matters were in the best legal hands, and Mr. Gardiner was at the service of his sister almost constantly, sustaining and supporting her to make her situation as tolerable as might be. Elizabeth could not doubt that all that could be, *was* being done for Mrs. Philips. Yet the outcome remained to be seen, and to the burden of local speculation, was added the too-real dread for her Aunt's life.

These affairs weighed heavily on her mind, when one evening she at last yielded to the persistent demands of Celia Montague to join a party at cards. Ill-inclined were Elizabeth's spirits for games—who could know when her sister Jane might require her?—moreover, she was sure she was catching a cold. But Mrs. Montague, a relentless hostess, would hear none of it. The evening was fine—could not injure even an invalid—what could better lift the spirits than a quiet evening among dear friends? Thus importuned, Elizabeth could only accept.

At the door of Montague Hall, she was surprised and not a little displeased to observe ahead of hers a veritable string of carriages, and those including that of Sir Geoffrey Portland. She and Sir Geoffrey, without a word spoken, had over these weeks arrived at an agreement of a rare and admirable perfection; that they should contrive to be in each other's presence as little as was possible, and when thrust together, should snub each other to the furthest extreme approved by polite society. She supposed that her partner in this understanding must have been unaware that she was to be of the company tonight. Whatever his qualities, he was seldom careless, and the lapse disappointed her.

Montague Hall was lit up and quite full of company. Elizabeth, who had been led to anticipate a quieter evening, if nothing more, ascended the stairs, was announced, and greeted her hostess with all the civility that she could compose. The room was insufferably hot; and friendly faces were few. She mingled for some time in the crowd, said what she must, and took comfort, at least, in the consideration that she might, with care, pass the whole evening without once encountering her adversary full on.

Several tables of cards were set up in the drawing room, and after she had satisfied the obligations of affability, she moved thither in the hope of wresting some slight diversion from the evening by a table of casino. At the door, she drew back. Sir Geoffrey, happily with his back to her, was sitting at the nearest table and holding the attention of the entire company with his speech. Elizabeth would have left instantly, but a knot of people beside the door prevented her. Like it or not, she must hear him.

"I do confess," the gentleman was saying, "that I would wish the situation other. But since no alteration is possible, I myself must keep as distant as I may, at least until the unpleasant business is concluded. I cannot in all good conscience condone the drawing down of so noble a name as my young friend's."

There was hardly a question to whom or to what he referred. Elizabeth, casting her eyes around in silent agony, found fixed upon her the quizzical gaze of Lady Stanton. Too oppressed even for tears, she made her adieus and departed.

She spoke of the incident to no one, but continued distraught. Her only consolation at Pemberley during that time came from a surprising source, Mr. James Leigh-Cooper. After she had confided in him that earlier day, and he had seen the depth of the pain she felt for her family, his concern for her had never waned. His solicitude, indeed, seemed altogether extraordinary.

"I am sorry to see, Madam," began he, the next morning, "that your commonly good spirits continue to be low. Has not your newborn niece at least the power to raise them?"

"Not altogether," replied Elizabeth, smiling despite herself. "The very perfection of infanthood she may be—nay, incontestably is—but—breathe not a word of this to my sister or brother—even *her* smiles have not the power to silence the neighbors."

"Oh, my dear Madam," replied he earnestly, "pray take comfort. Could you but see the aspect of our great families that is exposed to an humble architect, how much less would you regard their disapprobation. Lady Stanton, herself, for whom I designed a ceiling some years ago, demonstrated what tact compels me to dub a most curious eye. This exquisite work, for instance," pointing to a likeness of Georgiana Darcy that hung above the fireplace, "she would have relegated to a dark corner, and replaced with her favorite horse, as depicted by Mr. Stubbs, whose work, in her view, has never been surpassed. Yet what a portrait this is! How magnificently has Sir Henry Raeburn captured the brilliance of Miss Darcy's eyes."

He fell silent and—satisfied in both comfort well given, and the proper disparagement of England's greater families for their deficiency of aesthetic appreciation—allowed himself to stand for some little while absorbed in the painting. Observing him so engrossed, quite distracted by the sight of Georgiana, Mrs. Darcy was struck anew by a notion she had until now resisted as fancy. The young artist had taken of late to asking odd, unconnected questions about her husband's sister—about her childhood, her love of books, her pleasure in the open air. He had even begun asking impatiently when she would return from Rosings, and, although he himself, Elizabeth knew, had business to attend to in London, had put off his departure to town, on one pretext or another, for more than a fortnight. His partiality towards her young sister was unmistakeable; now she understood that he was in love with her.

The more Elizabeth considered this circumstance, the greater was her sense of foreboding for it. True, Mr. Leigh-Cooper was possessed of every admirable quality, both in steadfastness of temper and in quickness of understanding. Surely his eminence in the artistic world was remarkable in one so young. Elizabeth herself estimated it an excellent match. But the Darcys would ever be who they were; Pemberley, as she knew too well, rose above the rest of England. An architect, genius though he may prove in his profession, remained for them, even in this new age, yet a tradesman. While she yearned to encourage her young friend, she would not raise expectations which might only end in disappointment. Well therefore it was, that Pemberley would see nothing of Georgiana for some weeks, as a letter but that morning had brought word.

My dearest Elizabeth, the communication had begun, *you will be astonished I am sure at my writing to you from London, since my last letter found me still so comfortably situated at Rosings. In effect, I consider myself banished from those pleasant surroundings, and it is my good Aunt, herself, who has imposed my exile. But of that, more later.*

It is perhaps best, dear sister, that I begin at the beginning. My stay in Kent opened peacefully enough. I had observed your wish, and called promptly upon your old friend Mrs. Collins, whose good sense and guidance has, I believe, already profited me much. Of her husband, your cousin, I can say little, except perhaps that he seems a great favorite of my Aunt, and thrives in even her minutest condescension.

Her Ladyship, I own, was most eager to tutor me upon the proprieties, and I hope I was a willing student. I tried. My aim in going thither was above all to win her approval. But she took no pleasure in my obedience; seemed almost at times to suspect it. I pity her in that she must know she is doing me a wrong.

I need not explain myself further, but her anxiety for my cousin Anne must account for her tormenting me as she did. In truth, Elizabeth, her welcome was but cold, and she made small secret of her dissatisfaction in my friendship with one whom I swiftly perceived to be her prospective son-in-law. Captain Heywood is a young man, I confess, of some attraction. We have, these weeks, become amicable companions, walking and riding together with my cousin Anne. The Captain unites openness and vivacity in his speech, and our tastes in both books and music are strikingly alike. I do believe we could talk forever. Anne continued also among us.

Yesterday morning, I chanced to call upon Mrs. Collins, and she confided to me certain matters to which I do not doubt that you are privy. It seems cruelty itself that such a woman as she needs must choose so ill a lifetime partner. On my way from the Parsonage, deep in thought over those weighty matters of life and love we had so frankly talked of, I unexpectedly met the Captain—indeed, I did in truth run into and near topple him, so profound were my musings. He was his merry self and we laughed heartily at my foolishness. Offering me his arm, he engaged to lead me back to Rosings, supposing, said he, that a nymph wrapped in aerial contemplation might deign to recall so earthly a concern as Mrs. Eldridge's game pie.

It was then that the carriage wheels rumbling down the lane announced my Aunt. She was returning from affairs about Hunsford, and I need scarce describe to you, dear sister, the extent of her indignation at so cheerful a scene.

"You look positively wild, Miss," said she with her customary graciousness. "Did not Hannah attend to your hair before you went abroad?"

Her tone was far from friendly. But I made my response with all deference and grace. "Indeed she did, Madam," said I, "but I fear the wind has redone her work for her. I do regret if I fail to do Your Ladyship credit in the countryside."

But my dear Aunt was not to be appeased. "Young persons have no business abroad at this hour," continued she. "Anne is known to make better use of the morning hours at her study. She would not be found roaming like a gypsy with her hair blown and mud on her petticoats."

I confess, Elizabeth, that the last was more than I could support. Patient had I been until this—Griselda herself—but to hear her reproaches at every turn was insufferable.

"Anne may be at her studies," said I, "or for all I know she may be fast asleep. It could matter little to me. I will walk out when I choose."

I spoke no more than the truth. Had Her Ladyship more command of herself, I should not have been constrained so to speak to her at all. Yet she was more incensed than even I have ever seen her.

"Headstrong girl!" cried she, quite purple with rage. "Either mend your tone, or leave Rosings on the instant."

"Willingly," was my reply. "I need only instruct Hannah to ready my departure. You shall see me gone within the hour. Good day to you, Aunt."

"You must own, dear Elizabeth, that she was very wrong to treat so grievously one whose only purpose was to please. My consolation is that I am now removed to London to join my good brother, who feels in this, my hour of anguish, all the compassion for me, and indignation against his Aunt, of which his tender heart is capable. Or, at least, he will, as soon as he returns from his appointment in Chancery Lane, and I am able to relate these affairs to him.

Yours, very affectionately,
Georgiana

PART V

CHAPTER 31

"DEAREST LOUISA," BEGAN Caroline Bingley a few days after these events, "you cannot know my mortification. I had set off from Grosvenor Street immediately I had finished breakfast, and when I reached Crook & Besford's was still in tolerable good humor. But what a scene there was when I entered the shop. The counter was thronged; I was obliged to wait a full fifteen minutes before I was attended; and in that time, I espied no fewer than three ladies more modishly attired than I!"

Quite undone by so harrowing an experience, she sank to the sofa. "I cannot bear to consider how out of fashion we have become, dear sister. You must see how little reliability of taste is to be discovered in the country, or even in Bath, despite its pretensions to grand shops. Had I guessed indeed the result of my being absent from town for so many months, I should have thought better of rendering you my services for so long in Wiltshire. I vow that I am become a positive bumpkin. The shade of my trimming is quite insupportable—and on me—whose eye for the season's colors is so celebrated. I shall have Mrs. Lamb here this very afternoon to alter it. There is nothing for it but to start afresh with bugle beads."

Of Caroline Bingley, it was necessarily agreed that she was a singularly handsome woman. Well-schooled, and with a considerable fortune of her own to bestow, she had, moreover, arrived, at the age of twenty-four, at that forefront of elegance which can only be achieved at the cost of almost every other virtue. Her person was perfection itself, her manner such that none could fault, except those few exacting enough to seek from her any true cordiality. She was, in short, the very exemplar of superior society.

Some disappointment she had known when Mr. Darcy had so capriciously elected to marry Elizabeth Bennet over herself. His choice indeed had at first scandalized—for was he not pledged to his cousin Anne?—and soon, when she discovered the object of his perfidy to be other than herself, outraged her. Her brother Charles, she had long recognized for a goose; but of Fitzwilliam Darcy she had hoped better. A man of so considerable a standing in society should be constrained at least to accommodate its expectations.

But ever undaunted, Caroline speedily turned her disillusionment to good account by devoting her energies the more exclusively to what she perceived to be her most profitable employment in life: to attain precedence in all affairs no matter what or to whom the cost; to consort only with people of her own station, and snub those below; to marry, when marry she did, with the most scrupulous adherence to her own rank, or that a little above. Darcy may have discredited himself; Miss Bingley, at all events, would continue constant to her ideal. Nor, did the charge of fulfilling this obligation cause her anxiety. Her fortune undiminished, and her bloom hardly less so, she could look forward with little apprehension to being solicited by excellent blood before the years of danger assailed her.

Meanwhile, she remained at leisure to enjoy to its fullest the esteem of both her circle and her own discriminating self as an arbiter of good taste. In this capacity, she had most generously assented to spend the winter months at Mr. Hurst's conspicuously grand estate, lately inherited, in Wiltshire, conferring upon her fortunate sister the benefit of her judgments over fittings up in the house, and taking for her pains nothing but profuse praise and the finest hospitality the country had to offer. From there she had accompanied the Hursts to their brother Charles at Pelham Hall.

Their return to London had been arranged as promptly after their young niece's birth as civility decreed, Mrs. Hurst having intimated that she "could not endure a single instant longer in the presence of *that* woman." It was, of course, to the Bingley's other guest, Mrs. Bennet, that she referred, and, indeed at whose recollection she still now chafed. "I could, dear sister," said she, "tolerate her vulgarity of mind, her excesses with her grandchild, even her inquisitiveness about our brother's estate. But her presumption of intimacy with ourselves was not to be endured!"

"And the more so, dear Louisa," agreed Miss Bingley, diverted at last by this felicitous subject, "in that we so early made plain our preference. Jane Bingley, we needs must suffer—for, with all her lack of breeding, she is pretty enough for Charles. But, to be obliged to sit at table with her mother is more than even filial obligations require."

The pair laughed together in an intimacy that was seldom more comfortable between them. Now that they had returned to London, the benevolent pastime of deriding country custom joined the two in the harmony that was the sweetest part of their sisterly affection.

"How brown and coarse some do grow in the country," continued Miss Bingley. "I vow I quite mistook the eldest Montague girl for a dairy maid. At the Academy, we would no sooner have walked abroad in the sun than play at cricket."

In her girlhood, Miss Bingley had attended one of the first private seminaries in town. Her sister, who lacked that advantage, having come of age a little before their father had attained the fullest extent of gentility his trade had been able to purchase, swiftly made her retort.

"My husband," began she, with emphasis, "always remarks that there is no bringing the two worlds together. Country folk are simple and he, for one, is unable to fathom them. But then, Mr. Hurst's standards are high; he was at Oxford."

Miss Bingley, as willing to abstain from the subject of matrimony as was her sister from that of education, was pleased to return to their London business.

"The more delightful then to be back in town," cried she with energy. "Surely, sister, you now begin to perceive how urgently is our presence wanted in London. It is not, Louisa, merely my wardrobe that needs attention; consider also your window curtains. To ensure them as the handsomest yet seen in Wiltshire, we must needs devote ourselves to the linendrapers."

Mrs. Hurst, satisfied by her sister's stoutness of purpose, expressed herself warmly. For her part, she assured Caroline, she would apply herself directly to securing their places at Drury Lane for the Saturday, lest they be left without a box. "It has become quite vexing in these days when Kean is so firmly the rage. Only last week, Lady Grafton could find no seat at all and was obliged to go instead to the other play at the Little Theatre. A trumpery piece—poor acting—and not another person of consequential birth in the theater."

With such an arduous round of engagements did the sisters preserve themselves from the desolation of being thrown upon their own resources. Caroline Bingley, besides, anticipated her own distraction, of which she had said nothing even to her sister. She had intelligence that the bold Captain Heywood had departed Sir Geoffrey's for Rosings and understood, moreover, that he would thence to London; news of some interest to her.

Mr. Hurst soon joined them and, having graciously accepted a cup of tea, exhibited such unwonted animation as to profess himself perplexed by an incident which had occurred at Mr. Darcy's house nearby in Grosvenor Square. He had called upon their neighbor and, on finding him abroad, had been surprised to discover Mrs. Annesley, the family's former governness, who now lodged there, in the highest of spirits. On his inquiring the reason for her jubilation, he could elicit none but that her former charge, Georgiana Darcy, had arrived unexpectedly at her brother's. This caused Mrs. Annesley, in his view, a joy out of all proportion: one would quite have thought, concluded he, that she had come into money.

"Miss Darcy, in London?" said Caroline. "How exceeding strange; I had been sure she was for many weeks yet in Kent. The girl positively grows restless within the week.

"I wonder at her want of decorum. Why can she not remain in the country, pursuing her proper studies or persisting with her music? Are there not enough heiresses in London already? I am afraid she grows frivolous, like many of her years, and thinks only of diversion."

Ruefully, Mrs. Hurst must append her own fears for the young lady. "I cannot but observe her lack of discipline. She has views upon far too many matters for so young a person, and is wont to express them wherever she be. One must not pretend that the latest influences in her family have not taken hold. Poor Georgiana; she was a comely enough child. Yet, encouraged by such associates, I do not wonder that she grows more willful. It can, I assure you, come to no good."

CHAPTER 32

Of MR. GARDINER'S good sense, Mr. Darcy was already mindful; now, thrown by the latest circumstances so much into the other gentleman's society, he discovered him, moreover, to possess a rare congeniality. Darcy was himself by nature reserved, and, outside his most intimate circle, little inclined to overcome this disposition, a quality which had too often earned for him a reputation of arrogance. But in the company of Mr. Gardiner, he found himself able to demonstrate his own warmth of emotions more easily than with many he had known for all of his life.

Elizabeth's uncle, apart from his shrewdness in business dealings, demonstrated himself in conversation to be a man of lively wit and no pretension, his judgments balanced, his manner as cordial with his lowliest clerk as it was with Fitzwilliam Darcy himself. Sir Geoffrey Portland, Darcy both loved and respected, but knew to be limited by his admiration of position; while in Edward Gardiner, he daily recognized true discrimination, judging on correctness not of lineage but of feeling and behavior. Add to that, the philanthropy of the man, albeit at the time unwitting, that it was *he* who had brought Elizabeth to Derbyshire and Darcy; strange it would have been indeed had the two not become fast friends.

They had fallen into the habit, on such days as had taken them to consult Darcy's attorney, of strolling together afterwards in a leisurely fashion down Chancery Lane and through the City, towards Mr. Gardiner's house in Gracechurch Street, discussing on the way, as best they might over the rumbling of the carriage wheels and the cries of the street hawkers, not only the development of the case, but all manner of subjects other.

On the evening, some days after Georgiana Darcy's arrival in London, upon which she herself was engaged to join them at dinner, they had much to occupy them: the latest folly of the government, the shocking proliferation of beggars in the City, the admirable progress of Mr. Nash's new architectural sweep in the West End of town. Their mutually satisfying converse sped their steps; when they arrived in Gracechurch Street, Bow Bells were barely pealing five.

"And indeed, Mr. Gardiner," cried his lady, so soon as their guest was made comfortable in the drawing room, "you come not a minute too soon. Frederick has been tormenting Mary to distraction, while Harriet forever chases about with Richard. It is time and more for their father's firm hand."

Mr. Gardiner, a parent too affectionate for false indulgence, while privately admiring his children's high spirits, nevertheless assumed a sterner countenance and forthwith went above to the nursery to restore order.

The moment allowed Mr. Darcy a few private words with his good friend, Mrs. Gardiner. Always a favorite with her nieces, she had long endeared herself to him too by her clarity of mind and delicacy of feeling.

Began she immediately, "Both Mr. Gardiner and I long to see Miss Darcy. The opportunity to know her until now has been but slight, although Elizabeth's letters praise her often. A lively creature, she describes her, with a quick mind, and best of all, an uncommon love of books, a quality which her own new sister admits she might have pursued with more dedication. She sounds altogether captivating."

"*That* she undoubtedly is," replied her brother with a sigh. "But you yourself, Mrs. Gardiner, having the charge of young minds, will know that neither charm nor intelligence must mean tractability. Her very manner of coming here, in fact, was unseemly. Her Aunt Catherine, a formidable woman, to be sure, had, it appears, spoken to her sternly. What should Miss Georgiana do but up and off to London—and, what is more, expect my blessings for her action. I do welcome her presence, but such behavior in a young person is indecorous and I will not nor cannot condone it."

"Propriety by all means must be observed," agreed Mrs. Gardiner. "But might I venture to suggest, Mr. Darcy, as one whose advanced years have already given her some experience with willful young ladies, that such delicate plants must be cultivated with care? Georgiana, Elizabeth assures me, has superior sensibilities and, do what you may, they must out."

"As indeed they have," said he, and, having ere now discovered himself able to confide in her more freely even than in her husband, he continued with some feeling. "I do confess to you, Madam, that I find myself in this situation quite baffled. The ways of ladies are foreign to me: my mother died when I was yet a boy, and Georgiana, dearly as I love her, was until lately too young to provide me any true companionship. In short, I spent my youth surrounded by my own sex; the other continues even today to be mysterious. My Elizabeth has taught me much, but daily do I discover how little I yet comprehend. Surely *that* study must require a lifetime. Nor is it myself alone whom my wife's influence has touched. The Georgiana I watched grow up was a timid creature in society: not two years ago, as you yourself will recollect, she was barely able to preside over the serving of a simple tea. In private, however, her habit of reading encouraged her from her earliest years towards passionate acts and dramatic gestures. And now that the encouragement of my spirited wife has emboldened her, she is becoming positively ungovernable. The situation was difficult at Pemberley; but here is she in London, with Elizabeth still in Derbyshire, and I, dear Mrs. Gardiner, at my wit's end to know what to do with her."

Mrs. Gardiner would have smiled to see him so uncheerful over mere youthful exuberance; but understanding that his whole heart was in the subject, she checked herself and replied gravely.

"Pray console yourself, dear Mr. Darcy," said she. "High spirits in the young may well prove a torment for their protectors, but, with proper management, they are the very stuff which engenders the finest in men and women. Georgiana, I suspect, means nothing but well, and if she ruffles an occasional temper, it is hardly her intent. No," concluded she, "I have small doubt that I shall admire the independence of your sister."

Before long, Mrs. Gardiner was accorded the opportunity to make a more immediate assessment: the young lady herself was announced. Miss Darcy, indeed, entered in so veritable a flurry of high complexion and good spirits—delighted to see Elizabeth's aunt once again—had not seen enough of her at Pemberley—was not London delightful in the spring?—that even her brother, despite himself, must rejoice at the sight of her.

As for Mrs. Gardiner, she was hard put to it to conceal her astonishment. Elizabeth had written of Georgiana's development; but *this* animated young person was as another from the shy girl she had last seen two summers ago. Her expression was open, her speech, while unassuming, equal to any address. Mr. Gardiner, joining them, was visibly charmed.

"Too long it has been since we met," cried he almost immediately, "and the years, if I may say so, Miss Darcy, have only served to fulfill in you what was already so delightfully promised. Since Elizabeth's marriage, Mrs. Gardiner and I have many times designed to return to Derbyshire, but always until now have my business affairs kept me away. I am determined," with a bow, "that they shall not do so again."

Georgiana, while blushing a little at his affectionate tone, replied with a smile. "I fear you will find but little difference *there*," replied she. "London, I see, has changed greatly in even two years; but in the country nothing alters but the crops. But, oh, my dear Mr. Gardiner," she continued, in a low voice and agitated tone. "What changes have occurred in *your* life since we last met. Pray tell me, how does your unfortunate sister?"

Darcy winced at her words. Discretion Georgiana had long disdained—for her brother, a license difficult to tolerate in a stranger, impossible in this his nearest relation. But there was that, too, of sweetness in her speech that must disarm all critics but those most savage, or those most lovingly tied by fraternal bonds.

Mr. Gardiner certainly was far from offence. "Do not disturb yourself, Darcy," said he. "Mrs. Gardiner and I make so bold as to consider your sister, as yourself, of the family. We may speak before her as frankly as before anyone. Mrs. Philips, I saw but yesterday, Miss Darcy, and, I thank you for your concern, she remains in tolerable health. Her jailer's lodgings are comfortable enough, if hardly sumptuous, and she is well fed, at least. As to her prospects, who can say? Her case comes not up for trial for many weeks, and Fordyce will make no predictions of its outcome. Mr. Philips talks yet of settling with the scoundrel Turner, and it is all that your brother and I can do to dissuade him. Mrs Philips, herself, poor lady, is in a state of high indignation. *She* to be deprived of her liberty, and her jailer, moreover, unable to play backgammon! But," sighing, "my sister was ever foolish, I fear, and her misfortune has not improved her mind."

The next remove was to the dining parlor. Mrs. Gardiner's food was both ample and elegant, and yet served with so little fret, that one would have imagined her modest establishment to possess as many French cooks as Pemberley itself. Conversation around so felicitous a table could not be but genial; and presently, Mrs. Gardiner cried, "We want only one other for perfect contentment. Dear Mr. Darcy, dear Miss Darcy, only think if Elizabeth were here tonight, how merry would our company be."

"Too little we see of our niece nowadays," agreed Mr. Gardiner. "Her happiness, as you know, is as our own, but I confess that Mrs. Gardiner and I have more than once lamented that she elected not to find it a hundred or so miles closer to London. Mrs. Gardiner was laid low with the fever last year, and *then* how we missed Lizzy's capable presence. Quite apart from the joy of her company, how convenient it was for us when she could be summoned at a day's notice."

"Wretched ingrate," laughed his wife, "was *that* your best purpose for our Elizabeth, that she should serve us as a nurse? No," becoming serious, "you speak lightly of companionship, Mr. Gardiner, and it is very well for men to hold it so; going, as they do, about the affairs of the world, they may pick and choose their fellows where they will. We women have but meager choice. Good fortune it is if our lot throws us amongst those who are not altogether repugnant to us; how much rarer for us to encounter one whose society provides not merely the comfort of virtue, but the tonic of wit—and how much more precious, therefore, when, as in Elizabeth, we find her."

Georgiana was stirred by these words. Too often had her own life pressed upon her the company of such an one as

Caroline Bingley or Anne de Bourgh. Lately, it was only with the entrance into it of that very Elizabeth, that the possibility had occurred to her of any better. Here, at last, in Mrs. Gardiner, was a lady who held superiority of wit fully as dear as did she.

"To be sure," cried she with sparkling eyes, "harmony of spirit is more valuable than anything to be found in the castle halls, and I, for one, like the lady in the ballad, would gladly give up my goose feather bed to be 'off with the tag and rag gypsies,' if I deemed their companionship preferable."

Darcy, having listened to this exchange with increasing amusement, could now contain himself no longer. "No doubt you would," said he, "presuming, of course, that you might bring with you not one, but both of your serving maids. Georgiana, my dear, your romantic inclinations are very well, but you might better spend your time towards the serious end of furthering your education than by filling your head with poetry."

"And would you rather, Sir," interrupted Mrs. Gardiner, "that your sister could recite by rote the principal rivers of Russia and China or any of those other shreds of useless knowledge that are nowadays so much the fashion? You speak of education, Mr. Darcy; but what I call education is not that which smothers a woman with incidental accomplishments, but that which instead encourages in her the power and habit of thinking. It is *that* which polishes taste, inculcates principle, and leads, at last, to its most beneficial end, the understanding of the self. And if Georgiana finds this in books, not of history but of poetry, then poetry she must read."

Georgiana wondered to hear her. This was a woman who dared to speak her mind, and did so, moreover, in the full expectation that even Mr. Darcy of Pemberley would attend her. More laudable still than her frankness was that the cause she espoused was Georgiana's own. *Here* was one with whom she might find friendship.

Darcy bowed a civil acknowledgment of her words; the fowl was brought; and the dinner proceeded in such a way as to gratify mind and palate alike.

CHAPTER 33

C APTAIN HEYWOOD HAD himself departed Rosings for London. Deplorable it was that the burdens of his business affairs would permit him to linger no longer, but he must be off.

He was in town by the next day, and had found lodgings in George Street, from whence, no sooner had he settled himself comfortably, than he was about his business. His first call on the morrow was in Grosvenor Square, where, however, he found Mr. and Miss Darcy abroad, and must be content to leave a note. More fortunate was he in the visit following. Mr. and Mrs. Hurst's house was but a short walk away; *that* family was within and ready to receive him, though, it must be confessed, in some surprise and with considerable flurry.

Mr. Hurst, already seated in the drawing room, and triumphant in the recollection of the Captain at Georgiana Darcy's ball, extended his greetings with all the warmth of which he was capable. "The ladies," said he, "will most certainly rejoice in your appearance; I, too, am in want of fellowship, for London is thin this season. Are you by chance, Sir, fond of gaming?"

"I have, in my time," replied the other, "stood at the tables and done my share. It is a diversion I willingly confess a partiality for, certainly when the company is estimable and the stakes are high enough."

This was a reply to engage even Mr. Hurst's interest. "Brook's, I find tolerable enough this year," he offered, "but I would not give you tuppence for White's. Excellent good cock-fighting though, at Gray's Inn. I won forty pounds last Tuesday, and there were, besides, the finest screeches I have heard since Michaelmas."

Having discharged himself of so varied and fastidious an introduction to the City's amusements, he fell silent, his hospitable duties at end. It was not long after this that they were joined by the two ladies. Miss Bingley emerged animated, in high color, and, had the affable officer but been able to descry it, with the trimming upon her cap of the very latest hue. Cold meats and cakes were offered and gratefully accepted; and conversation began to flow.

Miss Bingley rejoiced to see the Captain, carrying with him, as he did, a very breath of the sweet Kent air. She, too, had been much in the country of late, but with rather less benefit than he. Well it was for men in uniforms! But she, who must keep pace with the fashions, now found herself sorely outmoded. Captain Heywood knew as little as any young man of ladies' attire; but he knew his business, and was moved immediately to comment upon how well the shade of her gown became Miss Bingley's eyes.

She, lowering those in modesty, inquired of the appointments he had made for his stay in town. He found himself unable to answer with any great precision, having many purposes in view, but hoped (this, with a meaningful glance) that such plans as he would make must include those he had come to regard as friends. She, emboldened, wondered if he might be prevailed upon to dine with them this very evening. He, alas, was engaged elsewhere, but looked with the highest of anticipation to being once more in the company of both sisters before week's end.

All derived the profoundest satisfaction from this visit before the Captain went about his other calls.

Later that evening, Caroline Bingley opened her heart to her sister. Having endured her brother-in-law's company with tolerable good humor through dinner and cards, and having soon after that firmly seen the master of the house off to Brook's for the evening, she was able at last to engage her sister in the subject closest to her. "I am not disinclined, Louisa," said she, "to confess to you that I quite expected to see Captain Heywood in London ere long; nay, even knew in my heart that he would come, so attentive was he in Derbyshire.

My dear," concluded she with some complacency, "if he continues so, I must believe myself to be in some danger."

Mrs. Hurst, while listening to her with scrupulous attention, must nevertheless address herself to the more substantial issue of what a fine addition so smart an officer must make to their party at Drury Lane the following week.

"Think you *The Recruiting Officer* quite suitable for our seafaring friend, Caroline?" she asked. "Is not it concerned with the military, rather than the naval, force?" And lest her sister suppose that all who had not the benefit of the Academy were quite without learning, "What a pity it is that Mr. Keane is not engaged instead to appear in *The Tempest.*"

Captain Heywood, the while, returning to his new quarters, was further cheered to find awaiting him a note in the hand of Miss Darcy, who regretted having missed his earlier call, but entertained the hope that she and Mr. Darcy might have the privilege of his company at a musical interval the next evening in Grosvenor Square. Without hesitation, the gentleman sent his acceptance.

Georgiana's surprise at discovering the Captain's card on the table when she returned from her morning drive had been considerable. Had he not when she had left Rosings been firmly attached there, and with every appearance of remaining? And yet, here he was in London and his lodgings but minutes away. Had he, could he have, so far rebelled against Her Ladyship's authority as to bid farewell to both her and her daughter, and if that were the case, might the reason be not unrelated to herself? Her fresh self-command dismissed so foolish a notion. If Captain Heywood had come so suddenly to London, it must surely be about some business, of which she herself could not be aware, some matters of money or the Admiralty. But the truth remained that he was indeed in town; nor could she deny her joy at his presence.

The following evening, Georgiana was ready well before the appointed time. The young officer, too, was prompt; and, observing as he entered the drawing room the opportunity for private converse, quickly seized it. Her abrupt departure from Rosings, he said, had caused him more dejection than she could know. Riding out, as they had done together so often in Kent, had become more precious to him every day. After her going, there seemed poor pleasure left in it.

Georgiana scarcely knew what to say; quickly turning the conversation, she made bold to hope that the tidings which had brought him so suddenly to town might not be ill. But, this question altered his mood altogether.

"I hardly dare express to you, Miss Darcy," said he, "the business that I am about. It is of such a nature—that—" he stopped, and was silent for a full moment. Georgiana, watching him, was all bewilderment. Did she not know better, she might almost have thought him on the brink of a declaration! But soon he jumped from his seat and walked about the room, muttering in a tone barely audible, of *certain* matters that pressed upon him, and a sole resolution that might only be reached here in London. Georgiana's confusion grew.

But presently the Captain observed her perplexity; and immediately roused himself to divert her. "Nor was I, Miss Darcy, alone in my dismay at your so abrupt exit," said he in the liveliest of tones. 'Astonished and mightily shocked,' was how your esteemed Aunt repeatedly described herself, or for variety, 'shocked and mightily astonished!'"

Georgiana was not bred to find diversion at the expense of her elders, and was surprised at the frivolity of her companion's words. But she quickly remembered that Elizabeth herself was given on many occasions to sportiveness; besides, the mock ceremony of the young officer's manner caused her to smile, despite her unease.

Encouraged, he continued. "Such impropriety, it falls to me to assure you, Her Ladyship has never before encountered. To think that a niece of *hers* should presume to have a thought or idea of her own. Shame upon you, Miss Darcy, for such audacity!"

The picture of Lady Catherine this called up so entertained them both that they laughed together until Georgiana continued, sighing: "My dear Aunt. In truth, Sir, I fear that nothing I do ever pleases her, no matter what the occasion. Alas, merely to speak my mind, she thinks unwomanly. As proof of my obedience, she would have me seated with my needlework, silent and sullen the day long."

"I see small possibility of that, Miss Darcy," said he admiringly. And, now looking full at her, he continued with considerable warmth. "It strikes me, now, that we have met before only in the country, where Derbyshire and Kent alike enveloped us both in balmy air and greenery. Never have I seen you in fashionable London, thronged as it is with modish ladies; and if I may venture to say so, the comparison does you little harm. Only yesterday it was, when finding you and Mr. Darcy not at home, I felt compelled, for propriety's sake, to call upon your near neighbors, Mr. and Mrs. Hurst and their sister, Caroline Bingley. They are stylish, beyond question—and handsome, in their fashion—but *you*, Miss Darcy, how little occupied you appear with such inconsequentiality, and yet—" and now, seeming to study her more intimately, he added, "there is about you that lively ease; it accompanies you wherever you go, whether it be Bakewell or Grosvenor Square."

This last was interrupted by the appearance of Mr. Darcy. Though at first startled to find his sister already descended, and conversing with their distant cousin as familiarly as she might with a long-established acquaintance, he greeted their guest with civility; welcomed him to Grosvenor Square, and trusted he was not unduly discommoded by the proximity of his own lodgings to Mr. Nash's improvements.

The energetic Captain, however, was not to be deterred. "I have, Sir," he persisted in engaging tones, "been admiring your successful guardianship of this young person; she is a credit to your careful hand in her upbringing. Of her self-possession, I myself was made aware but the other day, when I was so fortunate as to witness a severe drubbing she inflicted upon her distinguished relative, Lady Catherine." He cast towards Georgiana a glance of laughing warmth. "When Miss Darcy takes up a cause, it is plain to see, she is not easily intimidated."

Unfortunately, the effect of this encomium upon Mr. Darcy, was not altogether that which the officer had been seeking.

"My Aunt," said Darcy coldly, "if unyielding, is a woman of many parts, and not to be taken lightly. To make sport of her is certainly not the place of her niece, whose improvement only she has in mind. Georgiana is nothing if she is not outspoken; but she is yet young and need not be encouraged in disrespect. I trust that you do not applaud her impetuous flight from Rosings."

The Captain was all concern. "Sir," he said in great earnestness, "You mistake my meaning. I offer to your sister no tuition at all. It seems to me, she is in need of none. As to our

Aunt, she has been my own benefactor and I am bound to think well of her." Then, repressing a smile as he turned towards her once again, "Miss Darcy and I," said he, "have merely indulged ourselves in a touch of raillery at Her Ladyship's particularity; not, you will agree, the most shameful breach of etiquette."

This casual dismissal, and the assuredness with which the officer delivered it, took Darcy aback. Here was a young man who considered his own judgments infinitely superior to the general standards of propriety, and thus saw little need for instruction, even from so eminent a source as Mr. Darcy.

Just then it was that the Gardiners were announced, followed soon after by the other guests, among them the Hursts and their sister, expediently putting an end to this exchange. The musicians now assembled and the young people were charmingly grouped to enjoy them, with Captain Heywood seated at ease between his hostess and her smartly attired, and most attentive friend, Caroline Bingley.

CHAPTER 34

EW ARE SO fortunate as to select with any high degree of nicety the company which sustains them. At Hunsford Parsonage, the continued presence of Maria Lucas and Kitty Bennet, if hardly providing Mrs. Collins with edification, yet sufficed as a respite from the unwavering attentions of her husband. Between Kitty's high spirits, and the glee displayed by Maria at young William's every prank, the clamor proved adequate almost to drown Mr. Collins entirely. If Charlotte took care to keep to her back parlor, she might elude him for a full afternoon.

Heavy were the vexations with which the good clergyman had to contend in these days. Not merely did the parishioners continue to show themselves so disobliging as to persevere in poverty; but he had now, more distressingly still, the bleak temper of his patroness to contain.

"How very untoward has been the recent behavior of Miss Georgiana Darcy," pronounced he gravely to his devoted wife, on a morning when he had succeeded in discovering her. "To affront her aunt by such disobedience as she has is an enormity. Lady Catherine's exquisite condescension is, Mrs. Collins, a gift to be cherished, a cherished gift, to be sure. Wretched ingrate as is this young person! And to think that I myself led her around the gardens of my own humble abode, presented her to my own helpmeet, even permitted her to dandle in her arms my own young olive branch. Depend upon it, Mrs. Collins, it shall not happen again. My principles, nay, my solemn office itself, must prevent my ever again

receiving into my house, and exposing the tender gaze of my family to one who is capable of such flagrant effrontery to her elders. My mind is fixed; not if the young lady beseeched, not if my very life itself, and yours also, depended upon it, would I be persuaded to alter it. Unless," concluded he, recollecting that Georgiana was indeed his benefactress's niece, "Lady Catherine herself saw fit to demand it of me."

Thus cautioned of the excesses of which even the highest-born young women were capable, he bethought himself, and with some alarm, of those less lofty. "I trust, my dear," he continued, "that both your kin and mine will better know their places. Of my sister Maria I am tolerably confident, but what of Miss Kitty Bennet? Has she shown herself properly sensible of the veneration owed to my eminent patroness?"

Mrs. Collins, happily, was able to respond with that sweet reassurance which would secure the speediest end to his discourse. "Pray take heart, Mr. Collins," said she. "Both young ladies remain so much awed by the mistress of Rosings, that in her presence they can scarce speak at all, much less saucily. Even in their walks, my sister and Kitty are lately loath to wander far from the parsonage for fear of encountering that lady. It has been our good fortune that Mr. Beasley has taken it upon himself to divert them. Lord knows, his leisure hours are few enough. What a godsend he is, to be sure."

Her words effected more of her purpose even than she had anticipated; her husband, after the most perfunctory agreement, discovered some business in the library, and was about it. In truth, Mr. Collins' estimation of the new curate was not a little less favorable than was his wife's. Well enough Beasley might be as a fellow; but in the pursuit of his calling as curate of Hunsford, he was most unfortunately given to expenditures of energy that could but be deemed prodigal. Mr. Collins was pleased to consider himself as a more than creditable example of a clergyman of the Church of England, being ready on all occasions to christen and marry his wealthy parishioners, and only slightly less so to minister to his poorer. Yet, *this* young man understood no limits! Running about the meaner cottages with a zeal that bordered on the evangelical, indiscriminately educating the children, and, worse, causing himself thus to be so much solicited among the parish that good reports of his doings must certainly be carried to the ears of

Lady Catherine. It was barely sufferable. But Mr. Collins was a
man blessed with fortitude; he had, besides, properly read
Dr. Gisborne's description of the duties of a curate and understood that such a young man, however extravagant his disposition, must nevertheless remain incomparable to his rector. A
small consolation that may be; but from sorry circumstances,
we wrest what comforts we may.

Less afflicted by Mr. Beasley, but more perplexed, was Miss
Kitty Bennet, so unlike was he to any other young man she
had encountered. The officers at Meryton, or indeed, Frank
Middleton himself, ready-witted and flirtatious, had never
required other of her than playful replies and arch glances.
Mr. Beasley, instead, chose to converse of more serious
matters, and would persist despite all her endeavors, in talking not of plays, balls or riddles, but rather of the travails of
the poor among whom he passed his days.

"It is a fine sight and an affecting," said he one night after
supper, "to observe the piety that is visible in even the most
modest of dwellings. Not seldom in the evenings do I chance
to call upon one or another cottager, and as often as not, I
will discover the group gathered about the fireplace while the
head of the family reads from the Bible. Truly, it is an edifying
custom, and could without disgrace be taken up within our
grander houses. But I confess to you, Miss Bennet, that when
it comes to more domestic ministrations—which in some
houses are sadly wanting—I find myself at a loss. Perhaps, you
and Miss Lucas might favor me with some advice, or even
wish to accompany me in my visits? I do assure you that our
families would think it an honor."

Kitty listened, but must of custom reply laughingly. Said
she, "If you mean to mock us as idle, Sir, you hit your mark.
Still, if Miss Lucas and I accomplish little in our days, we
nevertheless usually secure our modest purpose of staying
out of harm's way. As for visitations to the poor, in my family,
we were used to leaving those to my elder sisters. Surely,
so frivolous a creature as you appear to think *me* could be
of little service to you, a man of the cloth. Pray, Sir, tease me
no more."

Her sally did him injustice. So far from mocking her,
Mr. Beasley had spoken in full earnest; being quite without
the power of levity, he knew no other fashion.

"You see, Miss Bennet," he continued, "that well as I have come to know our parishioners and their spiritual needs, I find myself ill-equipped, bachelor as I am, to think upon what will best profit them in their daily lives. I feel confident that so lively a young woman as yourself could bring a most beneficial understanding to their wants. Tell me, for example—how keep you small boys from striking each other?" And turning confidently toward her, he quietly awaited her judgment upon the issue.

This was so new an attention for Kitty Bennet that she was reduced to the state, highly uncommon for her, of speechlessness. The young man's rectitude was so natural, his reliance upon herself so unaffected, that the lady was entirely possessed before she had realized it.

_____

..rcy, ...y ....ou not
yourself? You are pale, grieved. Allow me to escort
ou immediately from this place to Green Park. The chestnuts are uncommonly fine there this season. Come, I will accept no denial, we shall go now together."

He took her arm, and they proceeded, at a pace which in a ess gallant gentleman she would have deemed inordinate aste, towards the Park. The chestnuts were indeed in flower nd the sun shining fair, and once the three had left Jermyn treet well behind them, the Captain slowed his gait, and egan very agreeably to talk nonsense.

Chapter 35

NOT MORE THAN a mile from Grosvenor Square lived a woman who, in her younger years, had been engaged at Pemberley to teach Miss Georgiana Darcy the elements of music. The widow Mrs. Spencer had differed from her successors in that she had, by means of unrelenting discipline, and the attraction of the subject itself, constrained her small charge to apply herself in earnest. Now, her health undone by age and life's disappointments, she lived in a sadly humble way in the vicinity of Shepherd's Market.

Georgiana, hearing of this from Mrs. Annesley, was deeply grieved, and her affectionate nature bade her visit her former tutor that very morning.

"Poor lady," cried she, "to think of her, all alone and her circumstances so reduced. And oh, Mrs. Annesley, only to remember the joyous evenings we once spent at Pemberley, we three and my brother. What satisfaction it must give to the lady if Mr. Darcy too were to accompany us today. I shall ask him directly."

But Mr. Darcy, found in the library, must regretfully decline his company. His own memories of Mrs. Spencer were fond, his dismay at her present position acute, but his morning was so much occupied with both Mrs. Philips' case and his own affairs of business as to permit not even half an hour for so charitable an errand.

"This matter, dear sister," said he, "I entrust to your own hands. I am entirely confident that your presence will comfort Mrs. Spencer; and perhaps while you are there you might

seek the ... not very great, ... streets were so knotted with hawkers and vendors as to make them impassable by foot. At last, down a winding alley, the found what they were searching, a dwelling whose unsav... location and mean aspect grieved them both.

The visit paid, and such comfort afforded as mi... Georgiana descended the narrow stairs from the much sobered by her friend's cheerless circums... resolving both to relieve the other's sufferings might, and to appreciate the more, the triflin... own disappointments.

contrive some ingenious way to help relieve her distress. Alas, how different must she find lodgings in Jermyn Street from her quarters at Pemberley."

Mr. Darcy's thoughts turned often these days towards Derbyshire. Too long had he been away from his home and his beloved wife; his impatience to return to her increased every day. His business affairs had taken more time than either had anticipated, and he longed to see his Lizzy again.

But, bestowing his attention once more upon his sister, he continued in a livelier tone, "I hope that you are in the humor for company at tea, because we are this very afternoon expecting a visitor from Derbyshire."

"Are we so, dear brother? And who might that be? Not, I most sincerely trust, Mrs. Montague?"

"Such irreverence, Miss, were best held for the appropriate occasion," reproved her brother, but must add with a smile, "although, I confess to some relief in assuring you that it is not she. The person of whom I speak is more welcome by far."

"More welcome by far! Can it be she, my sister Elizabeth?"

"Not she, either," said he with a sigh. "Nevertheless, he will bring us news of her. It is James Leigh-Cooper, whom Mr. Nash himself has summoned to London to consult upon a matter relating to the new crescent. It seems that our young man grows more and more esteemed in the highest circles."

"Not so celebrated, I hope, that he will abandon us at Pemberley before its improvement is entirely to our taste. That such new acclaim might cause him to become arrogant, I do not fear; *that* feat is already accomplished. Is it agreeable to you, brother, if I have the barouche?"

So did the two ladies set out to Jermyn Street in order to their friend. The distance was not very ~~~~ but the

On reaching the street, the two discovered it so thronged with smartly dressed gentlemen hastening from a neighboring club and calling to one another of the night's winnings at whist and macao, that for several moments they were obliged to seek shelter in a nearby doorway.

At last the crowd dispersed and they were ready to move on. Their progress, however, was hindered by the sight of a familiar figure at the corner, a gentleman in naval uniform who stood as if awaiting another. Georgiana drew back in amazement. It was none other than Captain Thomas Heywood.

The Captain's surprise at seeing her was greater than Georgiana's own. His complexion changed, and agitation affected his every feature. "Miss Georgiana Darcy, as I live," cried he; and then quickly recollecting himself, added in a more tranquil tone, "How curious—although delightful—to find you in this part of the city. I myself venture here seldom. It is, I make so bold as to comment, a far cry, if not furlongs, from Bond Street or Grosvenor Square's attraction. Whatever can have brought you to so rough a quarter?"

And with such tender concern did he incline his head towards her, awaiting her reply, that she quite neglected to wonder what errand he himself had been about there.

"No happy undertaking, alas," said she. "I came to call upon a former teacher of mine now fallen into sickness and misfortune. I gave her what cheer I could, but I fear," with a sigh, "her days left upon this earth are not many."

"What credit your tenderness of heart does you," said the officer. "Many there are who care little." But of a sudden, his manner altered again, and he began in a hurried fashion. "My dear Miss Darcy, in your concern for others, do yo neglect

"Have you ever observed, Miss Darcy," said he, "how music, so lauded in the general for soothing the savage breast, possesses besides a quality less celebrated, that of eliciting affectation? At, for instance, your brother's altogether delightful evening in Grosvenor Square, you yourself merely sat and attended to the music, which was indeed excellent. Others, however, were so much occupied with the *appearance* of enjoyment—with rapturous sighs and eyes cast up in ecstasy—that one must wonder whether they heard a single note."

Georgiana, recognizing in this the behavior of Caroline Bingley, was entertained. "Quite so," she said playfully, "and you yourself, Sir, were clearly too absorbed in the music to notice any of it. Come, I defy you to name the tunes that were played."

The Captain only smiled, and they walked on, both talking with such animation, such mutual satisfaction, that Georgiana must wonder what her gallant might have added had Mrs. Annesley not been of the company. Too soon they reached the gates of the Park where the barouche had been bidden to expect them.

But by the gate itself, the Captain, starting, took her arm and would draw her quickly to one side. It was too late: there in front of them stood Lieutenant George Wickham. The shock was too great to be borne; Georgiana felt herself shudder. To encounter *him* yet again, and moreover, so unexpectedly in London. Were her mortifications from this man never to be at a cease?

The Lieutenant himself, however, showed no signs of perturbation. Rather, he seemed as much at ease, almost, as if he had designed the meeting. "Ah, there you are, Heywood," cried he, immediately, "I had thought you—but whom have we here? Is not this the estimable Mrs. Annesley and her young charge, Miss Georgiana Darcy of Pemberley?"

Turning to the two ladies, he saluted them in a courtly fashion, and would have attempted to engage them in discourse; but, as before, Captain Heywood exerted himself to come to Georgiana's succor.

"I had not known you to be in London, Sir," he said hastily, and with some emphasis. "You will forgive us if we do not linger for pleasantries. We are much occupied, and Miss

Darcy's barouche awaits us." And offering an arm to each lady, he led them swiftly away.

How different now was the company leaving the Park from that which had with such high spirits traversed it. Mrs. Annesley herself was shaken, having recognized the one who had so nearly caused her young mistress's ruin; and Georgiana, leaning gratefully upon the Captain's arm, was in so great a turmoil of spirits that she scarce knew what to think. In all of London to encounter by chance first Captain Heywood, and now Lieutenant Wickham? All of a morning!

Few words were exchanged until they reached the carriage, where Captain Heywood, perceiving Georgiana's distress, insisted upon accompanying them to Grosvenor Square, a kindness readily accepted by both of his companions. During the short journey, his attentions continued diligent, and soon Georgiana began to feel somewhat restored; so much so indeed that as they approached the house she could even wish the distance longer that she might rally enough to enjoy them.

"Yet again, Sir, you have saved me from unpleasantness," said she with emotion when they arrived at the door. "You will not leave us, surely, before accepting some refreshment."

The Captain was willing, and together they climbed the great stairway. Georgiana, all eager to acquaint her brother with the happenings of the morning, preceded him into the drawing room, crying as she entered: "Dear brother, only wait until I have told you what has befallen us. Near Shepherd's Market we chanced upon the Captain; and a blessing it turned out, for, not fifteen minutes later, he was able to see us safely home after a most upsetting encounter in the Park."

She broke off in confusion, for Mr. Darcy was not alone. There beside him—to the surprise of Georgiana, who had quite forgotten their earlier discourse—stood James Leigh-Cooper, accompanied by a young gentleman unknown to Georgiana.

All three stood as she entered, and Leigh-Cooper immediately advanced towards her, warmth so animating his countenance, that before she was aware of it, she had given him her hand, and welcomed him most cordially to London.

"Well, sister," said Mr. Darcy so soon as he might, "I observe that you too, like our Leigh-Cooper, have brought a companion. The Captain and he, I know to be already acquainted. But allow me further to present to you both, Mr. Leigh-Cooper's dear friend, Mr. Hugh Jones, newly returned from the Continent, where he has until lately served as a surgeon among our brave soldiers."

"Miss Darcy will surely recognize the name," broke in Leigh-Cooper, "if not the gentleman's appearance. Not only is my friend skilled at dressing wounds; he is adept besides at fashioning verse. As a reader of discrimination, Miss Darcy must be familiar with his poems, which are already spoken of in lettered circles."

"Leigh-Cooper will cry me up," said the other young man laughing. And then studying the lady with some intensity, "He has told me much, Miss Darcy, of your love for the finest poetry; I entreat you to overlook his inclusion of my own rhymes in that class, as the mere excesses of a loyal friend."

Georgiana was surprised, not less that Leigh-Cooper's intimate should be an admired poet, than that he should be of a modest temper.

"You do yourself wrong, Sir," said she eagerly. "I have indeed read and admired your work, *The Waterfall*, for instance, or *The Death of Glendower*. Captain Heywood, you must surely recall the passage from *The Flower Bride*, in which the husband finds the armful of flowers. Was it not moving?"

But upon turning to her companion, she saw a countenance altered. The Captain's brow was drawn, his aspect ill-humored to a degree; he spoke not a word, but silently observed the two gentlemen by the fireplace. Never before had she seen him thus. What could account for it? Could he even now remember, and with bitterness, that earlier slight which Leigh-Cooper had dealt him at Pemberley? Georgiana must deplore such rudeness as the young architect had then displayed; would reprehend it the more now, were she not appeased by the interesting suspicion that the officer's present anger was fed by not only wounded pride, but jealousy.

Hiding a smile, she addressed him again. "Come, Captain," she cried archly. "Many times have I heard you recite poetry with both elegance and pleasure. You cannot tell me that *you* are unfamiliar with so eminent an one as Mr. Hugh Jones?"

"Naturally, I am acquainted with the gentleman's verses," said he. "But Miss Darcy, I must take my leave immediately.

There is business I had quite forgotten which requires my attendance on the other side of town. You must forgive me."

And, scarcely pausing to make his farewells to the company, he took his leave.

Georgiana's disappointment was keen. To see the Captain's mien so transformed, and so brusque his departure! But she was able to take solace in the admiring companions who remained behind him, and the lavish food tray then appearing.

CHAPTER 36

GEORGIANA AWOKE THE next morning in the highest of
spirits. True, the events of the day before had brought
her some discomfiture; but how had that been turned,
how brought to happy issue, by the actions of Captain Heywood. And how noble, moreover, had been his aspect in the
doing. Here was a man with whom one might fall in love; nay,
with whom she now saw, despite every earlier vow, she had.

To some, such a realization must comprise, with all its joys,
the dread of tender feelings unreturned; to Miss Darcy, it
brought only satisfaction. Seldom until this had any wish of hers
gone ungranted; one so essential must perforce be fulfilled.
Besides, that earlier ordeal into which the passionate feelings of
her youth had led her was already some two winters gone; hers
now was the inestimable advantage of maturity of mind. She
was arrived at the age of eighteen years and could depend upon
bestowing her love with all wisdom and discrimination.

She went through her toilet and through breakfast in an
exquisite flutter of happiness that brought poetry to her lips.
The lines of Lord Byron, so frequently spoken by Captain
Heywood, came to her freely:

> *"How welcome is each gentle air*
> *That wakes and wafts the odors there. . . ."*

They still lingered in her mind when she descended from
her quarters in the late morning to find James Leigh-Cooper
once again in the drawing room awaiting her brother.

"Oh, Mr. Leigh-Cooper." said she gaily. "Is not our present age rich in poetry? To think that within the year we might read new works by both Lord Byron and Mr. Hugh Jones! Does not your heart exult to think upon it?"

"Nor in poetry alone, Miss Darcy," agreed the architect, smiling in delight at her animation. "I come this very day to present Mr. Darcy to an exponent of my own art, whose brilliance we have not seen this hundred years and more. I have promised to take him to Dover Street to present to him Mr. John Nash. Your brother, as you know, is a zealous admirer of the metropolitan improvements."

"A varied and illustrious circle is yours, Mr. Leigh-Cooper," cried Georgiana. "But yesterday the very one hailed as the Welsh heir to the crown of Mr. Walter Scott himself stood in this drawing room at your invitation! And now here you are about to call upon Mr. Nash, who, as my brother tells me, has summoned you to London for advice. What demand you are in!"

The young man colored and repressed a smile, but answered her with unaccustomed modesty. "There is little honor to myself for either," said he. "Jones, I have known from my apprentice years, when we lodged together in Theobalds Road. An excellent fellow, and as forthright as you will find. With Mr. Nash, I am hardly acquainted; it was his patron, the Prince Regent, who was so kind as to bring me to his attention."

Too gentle was Georgiana's breeding for her to express her surprise. But until this she had had little notion of the height of Mr. Leigh-Cooper's reputation.

"Mr. Nash then, has not been abreast," said she cordially. "All the world other talks of you. Only last Tuesday evening, Captain Heywood spoke to me admiringly of Blayse Hall, which I believe owes not a little to your skill."

But these words threw her companion into ill-humor. "The good Captain's admiration surprises me," was his cold response. "I well recall his inspired recommendations at Pemberley; what could such an observer as he contrive to admire in a garden that boasted not so much as an elephant pit?"

Rare was the mastery with which Mr. Leigh-Cooper could at first beguile, and then anger Georgiana. He had done so on almost every occasion upon which they had met; she had quite forgotten his genius for it, and was still pondering this singular skill when her brother entered the room and the two gentlemen took their leave.

But small inclination had Georgiana to squander attention upon the contemplation of Mr. James Leigh-Cooper. A happier task by far awaited her; the imparting of her news to her sister Elizabeth. Without delay, she returned to her quarters and took up her pen.

"My dear sister," she began, *"Your letter yesterday was valued as it ought, though I must own my surprise that Kitty chooses to prolong her stay in Kent, especially as the village is small and I understand her so to enjoy fashionable society. It only makes the more admirable her visits to the poor which you describe. I had not remembered her as so solicitous a benefactor. Of little Eliza's good health, I hear with joy.*

"Elizabeth, I have much to tell. Though I confess to having many a time asserted to you my resolution never to engage my affections again, that vow, dear sister, is—" but at that moment Mrs. Barber was at her door announcing visitors below—and Georgiana must break off.

In the drawing room awaited Mr. and Mrs. Hurst, the former seated, the latter walking about the room, her disappointment evident that the master of the house was without, and none left but her husband to admire her. Always Louisa Hurst's carriage was imposing, buoyed by a good figure and delight in who she was; today, veritably, she dazzled. Her bearing was so jaunty, indeed, and her color so high, that, had it been a gloomier day, she might quite have passed for a young woman.

"Miss Darcy," cried she, barely according her hostess the moment to attend to her comfort, "Such news as we bring! Scarcely will you credit it. Nay, you shall not, I am resolved you shall not. Shall she, my love? Yet you shall hear it, the whole of it, and this very instant!"

Georgiana, having with some reluctance left her letter, nevertheless found her interest piqued, and ringing immediately for tea, she cried, "Good heavens, pray tell me what can have occurred? Nothing, I trust, of ill?"

"Of ill! Good gracious, no! Hardly could the news be more felicitous, for my sister Caroline and for those who hold her happiness as dear as their own. Sweet Miss Darcy, my sister is to be married forthwith."

"Miss Bingley, to be married?" cried a startled Georgiana. "Pray forgive my candor, Mrs. Hurst, but I knew not of any particular attachment."

"Oh, did not you? How exceeding odd, since he has been courting her these many weeks. But you must agree, Miss Darcy, that a fine fellow he is. His family and connections, we know to be unexceptionable, his fortune, we are led to believe, not inconsiderable; his address is engaging, his mind superior, and his teeth as straight as I have seen. Are they not, my love? I dare say," with a satisfied air, "that my sister and the Captain will make a handsome couple, at least until the sea air turns his complexion to mahogany."

What felt Georgiana at that moment? Astonishment too painful for imagining, affliction too deep for expression. Could the one she spoke of, be *he*?

After a short pause, "Forgive me, Mrs. Hurst." ventured Georgiana, "but is this young man then of the naval service?"

"The very same Captain Heywood," agreed Mrs. Hurst. "I wonder that you observed it not when he had so audaciously pursued her to London. But how you shall laugh when I tell how 'twas. It was yesterday evening at about five of the clock—or was it six, Mr. Hurst? No, it was five, for you had but just left for the gaming, made late and quite cross by Mr. Darlington's having so unconscionably overstayed his visit with that tiresome affair of the blight in Wiltshire. You would think the villagers might fend for themselves. Well, it was five, when on a sudden came such a pounding at the door that I thought London was afire at the least, or Mrs. Partridge had spilled ink on my newest gown, as she did on Lady Sinclair's— nothing could save it—Her Ladyship had worn it but once— and that, to call upon her mother.

"Well, who should it be but Captain H. Through the hall he runs—not waiting so much as to be announced—and up the stairs to the forwards drawing room where Caroline is seated at her embroidery, wearing her pink ribbons, for which I myself do not greatly care, but they are her favorite, and as you must know, you can tell Caroline nothing where ribbons are at issue. I am about my own business in the backwards drawing room— the connecting door will never close securely, although we speak often of mending it—their discourse, besides, is so excited, one might almost say, noisy—how can I help but hear?

le violent love.
ge of passion.
e loveliest, the
no longer live
be his wife?
lishments? Cer-
try. You might
er at the Acad-
sent Mr. Hurst
I relented, did I
delicacy, I was
ine—for all her
y, 'yes.'
eptance affects
y. He will brook
a clergyman in
t and they shall
to agree to such
ding lace. But,

nd I bade each
creep from the
at any turn she
the games. But
return till cock
it is, that she is
Miss Darcy, of all
ed without lace.
rts of Yorkshire,
im all upon his
een of age, and
felicity need not

ngs-on? Did I not
und? But are you
hat a time your
."

CHAPTER 37

GEORGIANA COULD CONTAIN her emotions only until she was able to see her visitors away; then, misery overwhelmed her. She, who but half an hour ago had been been high of heart, could now not imagine being ever happy again. Captain Heywood, so lately by her side, so devoted in his attentions, had chosen another.

Mrs. Hurst's words sounded yet in her ears: "I wonder that you observed not," said she, "when the Captain so audaciously pursued Caroline to London." Pursued Caroline! And all the while Georgiana had supposed that it was *she* whom he had sought. Each reflection brought fresh humiliation and new pain. Could she have read the Captain's addresses altogether amiss? Was she, even yet, of so little understanding that she could wrongly fancy herself the object of his admiration?

Scrupulous she had been to school her affections, only to be again deceived! There had been a time when Georgiana was gullible, open to every advance. How *that* had led to near disaster, she could never forget. But with Captain Heywood, she had begun, once again, to trust in her own steadiness of purpose, to feel the sweet assurance that her affections had been bestowed in no wise but properly and well. The Captain's family and standing were commendable and, besides, his demeanor to herself had been so tender, so particular. And now, this. He had never intended to attach her. He had eloped, and with a Caroline Bingley. She knew not which pain was the greater, of his betrayal or of her misjudgment.

The tumult of Georgiana's mind was such as to bring on a headache, and she was about to retire to her quarters, when she heard her brother's carriage. Now, how she missed Elizabeth. If only her new sister were here to offer her ready ear and counsel. Fitzwilliam Darcy, she knew, loved her with all the warmth of his affectionate heart. But consoling words came not easily to him; and, besides, to reveal to him this new mortification was more than she could bear. Yet, before she might make her escape, he was at the door.

"Oh, my dear sister," cried he entering, unwontedly animated, "to encounter such a mind as Mr. Nash's is a privilege, indeed. Such brilliance he has, such vision. And in what regard does he hold our own friend, Leigh-Cooper. Well, you shall hear more of our meeting this very evening, for we are engaged to dine at the Gardiners' with him as well as his friend Jones. But, Georgiana, you are pale," observing for the first time her demeanor. "Surely you cannot be ill? Is something the matter?"

"Yes—no—yes," stammered poor Georgiana, distraught. "That is, I fear I am unwell, and must beg to be excused from dining in company tonight. I shall retire to my room presently."

"This is unlike you, dear sister," replied her brother, studying her more closely. "Might perhaps your indisposition have to do with a visit from Mrs. Hurst, whom I passed in her carriage at the corner, looking more pleased with herself than bodes well?"

"By no means," countered Georgiana hastily. "It has been vexing me all the morning. But, I confess, Mr. and Mrs. Hurst did indeed pay a call upon us, and brought with them some not uninteresting news. It seems that Miss Caroline Bingley has eloped. She is to be married and with none other than our Captain Thomas Heywood. Are you not amazed?"

"Run off? The Captain? Good God!" exclaimed Darcy. "Surely it cannot be. You must have been improperly informed."

Georgiana, now finding it ever more difficult to hold back her tears, could but assure him that it was so.

As Darcy looked upon her woeful countenance, he was suddenly made aware of her inclination. His sister had fallen in love with the Captain. Discerning it now, he could only wonder at his not having done so before. Too easily might

Captain Heywood have won her heart. He was young, and, Darcy believed, well-favored; his manner was precisely such as to beguile an impressionable young lady; and had he not, after all, called upon Georgiana immediately after he had arrived in London, closely attended her at their musical evening, and later, appeared, as if by necromancy, to rescue her from every city peril? And to act *thus* without soundness of purpose or respectful intention. A villain, beyond question.

Swiftly following Darcy's indignation came his remorse. He might, had he troubled to notice, have long ere now anticipated just such an eventuality. Knowing his obdurate sister as he did, he must concede that few words of his might have so influenced her as to avert her present sorrow; still, he could, had he but been more observant, have had at least the consolation of being apprehensive for many weeks now.

As much as his sister did he want Elizabeth. Had his wife been there, readily would the tender feelings of both have been given expression. But for Darcy himself, yearn though he did to soothe Georgiana's heavy-heartedness, he knew not how. A true English man, he could not cosset her, but only feel for her.

Yet, he did what he might. "The Captain," declared he, "is a scoundrel. Elegant as he may be in his person, expert in his recitations of poetry, he is nevertheless a reprobate. A man who engages himself at Rosings, and then, abandoning that, comes courting every pretty woman within his reach, can be deemed nothing more.

"Caroline Bingley, I might have imagined more attentive to proprieties, so often has she deplored their lack in others. More the fool is she. Such a man as she has married can bring her only unhappiness. I am sorry for her."

Then, recovering himself, he continued. "But enough of this paltry fellow, Georgiana. He rates no more of our consideration. Do you not think, sister, that if you should rest now, you might be restored in time for this evening with the Gardiners? All look forward to your presence, and *there* at least, we may be assured of company that is both lively in conversation and honorable in intent. Come, sister, bear up; remember that you are a Darcy, after all."

And so real was his concern for her, albeit brusquely spoken, that she could not but consent. In the privacy of her

own room, however, she must succumb to all the wretchedness she felt. She went again through each of her meetings
with the Captain, reviewed the particulars of their every
conversation, searching to find whether there had at any
moment been in his polished manner that which might have
served her as a warning. Still discovering none, she wept
herself at last to the easement of oblivion.

Sleep brought some relief; wakening, only renewed desolation. Still, in the evening, how heavy Georgiana's spirits
were, only her brother knew. She smiled dutifully upon the
Gardiners and their guests—brushing aside Mrs. Gardiner's
anxieties upon her pale appearance—and even exerted herself to inquire of Mr. Gardiner after Aunt Philips' case.

"Alas, how slowly moves the law," was that good gentleman's response. "And yet, when all is brought to conclusion,
we may be the worse still. My sister suffers hourly; indeed, I
fear for her reason."

Even Georgiana's own misery was pierced by this sad intelligence. "Ah, poor lady," said she. And then, the memory of
her own plight warming her sympathy. "How destroyed are
some lives, and how without warning. To think that a mere
hour before her arrest, Mrs. Philips was sitting in her drawing
room, knowing not a care. And then, all had gone to ruin."

"My dear friends," interceded her brother, with a caution-
ary glance at his sister, "there is not yet reason for despair.
Mr. Gardiner and I shall not rest until we see Mrs. Philips safely
at home again and peacefully at backgammon with her
husband."

And quickly addressing Mr. Leigh-Cooper and his friend, he
turned the discourse to happier matters. "Would not Mr.
Gardiner have been engaged by Mr. John Nash's converse this
morning? His idea, Sir, is to adorn London with parks and fine
boulevards rivaling those of Vienna or Paris itself. Some there
may be in London now who deplore the present inconve-
nience of the excavations; but if they could only see beyond
to the results!"

"As in time they shall, Mr. Darcy," responded Leigh-Cooper.
"Mr. Nash's mastery is not to be underestimated. London
becomes ever more beautiful in his hands. We architects must
consider ourselves fortunate indeed that we are alive now to
witness such a renewal. Nor are we proficients alone in our zeal

for construction. In these days, all fancy themselves to be expert on improvements, whether they be or no."

"In truth," Mr. Gardiner joined in laughing, "it would seem that the spirit of design has infected every family with claims to social grace. It has become positively ill-bred to turn, for work upon our houses, to those qualified to provide it."

"You are quite right, Sir," said Leigh-Cooper. "Improvers make a mockery of our profession. Why, only lately was I urged by a fashionable young man, a relative, if I am not mistaken, of your Aunt, Mr. Darcy, to build an aviary of exotic birds for you at Pemberly. I was assured that no Londoner lacked one."

"You refer to Captain Thomas Heywood, do you not?" cried Mrs. Gardiner, who had been listening with a lively interest. "What an elegant person he showed himself at your musical evening, Georgiana. Mr. Gardiner and I intend one of our own next week and shall look forward to his presence. Do you see him before then?"

No question could her young guest have less welcomed at that moment. She hung her head and replied only that she did not expect to see the Captain for some time.

"Not see him?" cried Mr. Gardiner. "That is curious, when he seemed so particularly warm towards your family and yourself. But these naval men are a restless band, ever roving about. I imagine he has left London upon business in Dover or Portsmouth."

Georgiana knew not where to look. For his part, Darcy would prefer not to speak of the morning's news, but now saw it too late to hold back.

"Some surprising intelligence reached us today," said he. "It appears that the Captain has indeed gone from town, but on another errand than you suppose, Sir. He has eloped, and with Miss Caroline Bingley, of whose acquaintance also, I believe, you have the privilege."

He would have ended his explanation there, but open-hearted Mrs. Gardiner was unable to contain herself.

"The Captain and Caroline Bingley?" cried she. "You do not mean it. I had thought . . . but no matter. When did this happen? And where can they have gone?"

"I know very little of the affair," replied Darcy coldly. "*When* they left, I believe, was last night. As for *where* they might have gone, perhaps to the Captain's native village, which I understand to be Wallingford in Herefordshire. More I know not, nor care."

The arrival of the game pie provided a relief welcome to the whole party. But a few moments later, Mr. Hugh Jones, who was sitting upon Darcy's right, quietly drew his attention.

"Forgive my liberty, Sir," said he in a low voice, "but do I understand you to say that this Captain Heywood—the very officer I encountered in your drawing room—is from Wallingford in Herefordshire?"

"So I believe," responded Darcy. "Although the gentleman is a relative of my Aunt's, I hardly know him, and this incident does not make me wish to further the acquaintance."

"You are undoubtedly wise in that," was the young poet's sombre reply; he said no more but fell into preoccupation.

The while, James Leigh-Cooper was observing with dismay Miss Darcy's oppression. How thoughtless, he now saw, had been his words, how ill-advised. Leigh-Cooper was a man whose character was formed upon frankness. Some, less fortunate than he in their abilities, might need to make their way by unction or amenity; *he*, confident in his brilliance, could ignore such inessentials. Fortunate for him that most of England shared his assessment of his own skills: often, his blunt address caused in others surprise, even vexation. He knew it in particular to have more than once piqued Miss Georgiana Darcy, nor had been above taking pleasure in such exchanges.

But *this* latest sally, given with no more thought than for the amusement of the company, and the pleasure of seeing a blush upon her cheek, had unexpectedly caused her real pain. To witness such in anyone, would have distressed him; in Georgiana, it was not to be borne.

The news he had so unexpectedly elicited—that Captain Heywood stood unmasked for the worthless fellow Leigh-Cooper had always suspected him—was, indeed, such as could not altogether displease; but let it stand as a measure of his devotion to Miss Darcy that in the very hour of his rival's discredit, he experienced only a trifling of elation, and that quickly worsted in his concern for her.

He turned towards her. Now, his end in addressing her was not to tease but to comfort, and he sought the gentlest phrases he could command.

"Does not London grow oppressive, Miss Darcy," said he in a voice unaccustomedly affable. "I expect you yearn to breathe again the cool air of Derbyshire. I drive to Pemberley early next week and would willingly offer my carriage to you and your party, should you wish to accompany me. My horses will have us there within the two days."

But Georgiana could bear no pity, and least of all his.

"I thank you, Sir," replied she swiftly, "but I mind the weather little wherever I am. When I choose to return to Pemberley, it shall be in the company of my own family, and in one of our carriages, which, I assure you, travel speedily enough for my inclination."

And such was the disdain with which she spoke that Leigh-Cooper turned away altogether crestfallen.

CHAPTER 38

THE LADIES SOON afterwards removed to the drawing room. Georgiana, too conscious that her unhappiness had betrayed her into behaving ill towards Mr. Leigh-Cooper, inclined not to distress herself the further by acknowledging her wrong; rather, she would retire to the more comfortable consideration of his own insufferability.

"Veritably, Mrs. Gardiner," burst out she, so soon as they had settled themselves, "if you but knew the trials I have had to put up with from that young man we have just left. His arrogance is intolerable; his opinions—although some perhaps not without interest—entrenched. He is expert upon every subject; and you yourself have been witness to the intrusive fashion with which he is in the habit of addressing me, the sister of his patron. I do believe he fancies himself irresistible! While I concede him high spirits and intelligence—some would say even genius—*they* scarcely excuse his insupportable manner."

She ceased, confident of Mrs. Gardiner's accord, but the other remained silent for several moments, her face grave. At last, she spoke. "I would not usually, dear Georgiana, address as openly as I am about to, a young person I have known for so short a period as I have yourself. But, since I believe our feelings towards each other to be nothing but cordial, and I know, moreover, Elizabeth to regard you as a sister born, you will allow my speaking candidly, secure in your goodness of heart. My dear, how could you so insolently rebuff that young man?"

Georgiana blushed, but would pass off her words with a pleasantry. "I assure you, dear Madam," said she, "you need have little fear for Mr. Leigh-Cooper's sensibilities. He is proof against all attacks. Consider how often, dear Mrs. Gardiner, we are reminded that 'full many a flower is born to blush unseen;' I can quite assure you, that *that* person, having attained the renown he has, can scarcely be in danger of embarrassment. If he noted my words at all, I daresay, he will have considered them mere banter."

"Take care, dear Georgiana," said the other, still unsmiling, "lest you place too great a significance upon position in society. I myself know of what I speak. In the family to which I was born, I chanced to enjoy a standing superior to my husband's. Merely for that reason, they have ever considered themselves to be above him, not solely in the one sense of their rank, for which they themselves can take little credit, but in every other particular as well. Too often have I watched him slighted by them: my own dear mother, even now, considers my union nothing but an unfortunate decline. Yet, never have I seen anyone to match Mr. Gardiner, nor can I imagine being more happy in marriage than I am, for all the land or titles England has to offer. I am, my dear, the most fortunate of beings. But that is by the way: it is of yourself that we now speak, and your demeanor towards Mr. Leigh-Cooper.

"This is an excellent young man. Born into obscurity, he has nevertheless, through uncommon abilities, supported by exemplary diligence, brought himself to a position where he is consulted—and his opinion held in the highest regard—by the most eminent in the land. And yet, unlike too many who have so risen, he remains unaffected, as eager to speak—as I chanced to observe this very evening before you arrived—of the daily round of his mother and sister in Northumberland, as of the feats of Mr. Nash here in London. For that alone, you—who have grown up to every advantage which society and education can provide—would do well to esteem him.

"But more important even than these qualities is his generosity. I acknowledge that his manner can on occasion disconcert; but this evening, when he addressed you, his intentions were none but the most solicitous. It was badly done of you to have dismissed him thus. So to speak to anyone, little behooves you, no matter who he be. And to

Mr. Leigh-Cooper, in particular, so distant from you in situation, and so sincerely wishing to bring you comfort!"

Georgiana's oppression was grievous. That Mrs. Gardiner should address her thus—more, that she should have every justification so to do. It was impossible for her to pronounce another word.

Mrs. Gardiner, observing her half-averted face, soon continued in a softer tone.

"My dear, I see you to be dispirited, and I am sure that it was only that that led you to behave so unfeelingly. But pray let an older woman assure you that time will heal most hurts, even that which—if I may continue to speak freely—I suspect yours to be. You will not now credit this to be so, but you too will discover its truth. One word more, Georgiana, and I have done. While you may not choose to bestow again your heart for some little while, still, when you *do*, you would do well to look for a man who exhibits the constancy of a James Leigh-Cooper, rather than one who can beguile with soft words and lines of poetry.

"But pray, my child," smiling at last, "do not look so woeful. If I seem to have spoken severely, it is only because I expect well of you, and know your brother does too. You will not, we are confident, disappoint us."

But Georgiana could not return her heartening glance. The truth of Mrs. Gardiner's strictures, there was no denying: betrayed in love, she had now offended others as well. She had behaved, she saw, harshly towards James Leigh-Cooper and, in doing so, had incurred the severity of one she valued so well as her new friend, Mrs. Gardiner. All day she had known misery; now, to that was added anger against herself.

Her head was throbbing again; she could think only of the moment when she should be out of company, and at home in the quiet of her own room. Mrs. Gardiner, observing with compassion her anguish, would try to chat of indifferent matters, but poor Georgiana, overcome, could not respond with more than the briefest of replies.

So soon as the gentlemen arrived, she approached Mr. Darcy.

"Dear brother," whispered she, "I pray you, may we not return home directly? You know that I have been indisposed since this morning, and would retire without delay."

"What is this?" cried good Mr. Gardiner, hearing her words. "Miss Darcy, too, leaving us thus early? Here are our two young men, but just bethought themselves of pressing business about town; and now you, Miss Darcy, would desert us. The young of today can scarce remain in one place above the hour, can they, dear Mrs. Gardiner?"

"I do believe," replied his wife quietly, with a kind glance towards Georgiana, "that our guest is ready to leave us. She has been unwell all the evening and we must be grateful that she has come to us at all. You had best send for the carriages."

The carriages once arrived, the company prepared to depart. It was with tolerable composure that Georgiana was able to bid her farewells to Mr. Hugh Jones and her host; with only a little less so, to her hostess. Then summoning her courage, she turned towards the remaining guest. Few there were in the world she less wished to face at that moment than he, the recipient of her ill-use; but justice demanded that she, at the very least, bestir herself to cordiality before they parted. She advanced towards him.

"A good evening to you, Mr. Leigh-Cooper," said she warmly. "Should we not meet again before your return to Pemberley, I trust your journey there will be an easy one. Mr. Nash will surely miss you, but *his* loss must be to *our* benefit."

But, he only bowed abruptly, and with the briefest of salutations, was gone.

CHAPTER 39

STALE APPEARED TO Georgiana the diversions of the city when she awoke the next morning. Until now, they had been nothing but a source for delight; the town's streets each an event to her, every impediment therein a part of its allure. Yet, in what different light did London display itself today. Its somber chimneys fell sorely upon eyes that had scarce closed all night; the idea of its crowded thoroughfares bespoke not amusement, but peril. Little wonder that her thoughts would fly now to Derbyshire. At Pemberley, she could seek solace in rambles within the spacious park and, afterwards, return to her new sister, whose sweet counsel had never before seemed so expedient. Here, danger was without; within, confinement in a solitude permitting no escape from anguished thoughts.

In the eventful life of this young person, few circumstances had brought such perturbation as those of the previous evening. Sadness Georgiana had known before, but rarely self-censure. But Mrs. Gardiner's words, of a severity with which none had dared before address her, had shaken her into sensibility. Foolish as she was, she had fancied herself heroine of some romance of Sir Walter Scott or, more lately perhaps, of the poetry of a Mr. Hugh Jones. *Now*, she saw—and saw, moreover, with the merciless clarity of one who had been heretofore blind—how headstrong had been her conduct through the years, and how selfish. Her easy disregard of her governesses' chastisements; the anxieties she had caused her brother; the disrespect in which she had held her aunt; even the deed upon which she had prided herself the most, her late defense of Elizabeth against their neighbors, had served only to cause rancor, a greater harm than good. Yet all that paled before the unconscionable treatment she had meted to Mr. Leigh-Cooper the previous evening. She, a heroine! She was but a willful girl, as vainglorious in her own way as was her oft-decried Aunt Catherine in hers.

Nor was exoneration any longer to be found in recalling her contentions with the young architect in the past. Presumptuous he may have shown himself, but *she* had been worse. To have questioned him upon his family connections, as she so boldly had done, to inquire so particularly upon how he might have come to his superior education and learning! It was unbeseeming. If she—with all her advantages of birth and station—could show herself so little civil, it was only correct in him to take umbrage.

But gentilities, be they hers or his own, were of small moment. James Leigh-Cooper might display himself more arrogant than she, or he might not; of greater consequence was what he *was*, a proper man, constant of heart, superior by far to Captain Heywood, for all the other's graces. He had deserved better from her than he had received. Right he had been so to snub her at his leavetaking. Indeed, there could be no blaming him if, from now, he chose to shun her altogether, if such encounters as were unavoidable in the hall at Pemberley, resulted not in the animated conversation of before, but in cold bows and silence. She sighed at the thought, and her tears flowed without check.

So engrossed had she been in her reflections that she had quite failed to hear when, earlier that morning, a carriage had drawn up in front of the house and footsteps had ascended to her brother's study. But when Hannah arrived with the eleven o'clock post, the open door brought voices from the landing— and one, in particular, which she least expected to hear so soon in this, her brother's house, that of James Leigh-Cooper himself. Her spirits rallied and she ran to the stairs; now, could she but greet him cordially, she might begin to make amends for her earlier unmannerliness.

But as soon as she saw him, leaving the study in the company of Mr. Hugh Jones, the visages of both men solemn, her courage failed her, and she waited quietly out of view until they had departed.

Only then did she come forward to address her brother. "Dear Fitzwilliam," began she, "I fear I find my headache so little recovered today, that I cannot but wonder whether the air of Derbyshire might profit me more than any London physician. Could we not return home soon?"

Darcy listened to her kindly, but his expression was preoccupied. "Georgiana," said he so soon as she had concluded, "I have had intelligence of particular import, and upon a matter which concerns you as much as it does Elizabeth and myself. You would do well to seat yourself in comfort before you allow me to communicate the whole of it to you, for I hardly know where to begin."

Alarmed by the gravity of his words, Georgiana permitted herself to be led to the sitting room. When she had settled herself, Darcy spoke:

"Georgiana, I have that to relate to you, and on a subject you will find less pleasant than either of us might choose. I cannot but be aware of the hurt you have suffered lately at the hands of a certain gentleman. It now falls to me to add to your understanding of this person, though it give you pain. I recognized Captain Heywood yesterday to be an unscrupulous fellow in search of fortune, but I could hardly then have imagined the full extent of his iniquity."

Bitter as it was to Georgiana to hear the Captain's very name, still, she would be just. "Brother," she exclaimed, "what can you mean? Captain Heywood's having chosen to elope with Miss Bingley may be considered surprising or even improper; still, it is hardly villainy. He is a man of the world, and quite able to determine his own actions. If anyone should stand in need of reproach, it is rather myself, who so mistakenly put my trust in him."

But Mr. Darcy shook his head in impatience.

"My child, you do not yet comprehend. Captain Heywood is indeed unprincipled—his behavior to you alone is testimony, despite your too clement words—but there is a greater charge by far to be laid to him than mere fickleness."

Georgiana remained silent, at a loss to understand.

"Do you remember, dear sister—perhaps in your own distress you took no notice—with what suddenness the young gentlemen quitted the Gardiners yesterday evening? It was unexpected—Mr. Gardiner, as you know, particularly counts upon a table of whist—but there was that that had been said at the dinner table which made their speedy departure of the greatest urgency. To tell the story plain, Georgiana, I must tell it from the start.

"Mr. Jones, it seems, had occasion during his duty in Belgium to minister to a certain Ensign Henry Burgess, a worthless enough fellow whose life Jones had saved by the expeditious removal of a leg. This Burgess is now living in London in a sadly poor way, reaping, I fear, the rewards of a lifetime's dissipation and extravagance. The doctor, whose heart is kind, is in the habit of attending him when he can, although he entertains small hope of either payment for his services, or inspiration in his company. He persists, nevertheless.

"It would seem that of late this fellow had been bragging to him when in liquor of some money he expected to come his way. Jones had listened with but half an ear, for a poet's attention will wander and he recognizes, moreover, Burgess to be a boaster, so often befuddled by drink that he can scarce distinguish the real from the fantastical. This, however, was his refrain. In his gaming, Burgess had gathered to himself two cronies in particular, each as base as he, accustomed to profligacy, eager to grasp at anything to quiet their creditors. One, a fellow of the militia, was lately connected with a family newly come to fortune and simple in the ways of the world, whom he scrupled not to harm. The third, and most enterprising of this engaging triumvirate, was happily able to propose a scheme to relieve the country innocents of some of their burden of newfound wealth. The plan, Georgiana, was falsely to accuse one family member of stealing lace from a local shop."

"Good God, brother," in the utmost amazement, "you surely cannot suggest. . . ."

"Be patient and hear me out. The business was quickly executed with the help of a young Hertfordshire shopkeeper corrupted by city life; the lady was apprehended, and her freedom, her very life, hung in balance until her husband should secure it with the sum of £1000. The author of this vilest of intrigues, as Burgess cried up, was a fair-spoken naval Captain, a friend of his from childhood—that childhood which he spent in the village of Wallingford in Herefordshire. Jones, in truth, knowing his man, had not believed above a tenth of this tale. Imagine, therefore, Georgiana, his emotions upon hearing from myself that our captivating Captain Thomas Heywood, of His Majesty's Navy, also hailed from that same Wallingford!

"As soon as Jones and Leigh-Cooper had quit the Gardiners, they hastened directly to Burgess' lodgings in Covent Garden. There they found the Ensign as full of wine as was his custom at that hour, and in the highest of spirits besides, having just learned the latest in a series of misfortunes which had befallen his oldest friend. Little encouragement was required for the whole story to out.

"It would seem that Captain Heywood was indeed well-known upon the Continent; not, as he so often led us to believe, as a hero, but as a ne'er-do-well. His vices were many—some, my dear Georgiana, which can hardly be spoken of to your tender ears—but most destructive of all for the Captain was his love of the table. Long ago, it had claimed all of his money; soon had followed his family estate; every subsequent year had added to his debts. Desperation brought him to England as soon as his naval duties permitted, to seek a rich wife, and so recover himself.

"Much diversion had the rascal Burgess in the telling of his companion's woes. An heiress in Kent had for a time seemed promising, and Captain Heywood's hopes had been high; until her mother, discovering somehow or other the full extent of his pecuniary embarrassment, had sent him packing—Aunt Catherine, say of her what you might, is proficient where her daughter's fortune is at issue. Here in London, this newest chicanery for the moment distracted him from too egregious fortune hunting—or had done so until two days ago.

"It was in this very room, dear Georgiana, that Captain Heywood saw himself revealed, his intent imperiled. Burgess, it would seem, had applauded himself often in the Captain's hearing upon having his ailments treated by the eminent poet-doctor, Hugh Jones; but little idea had either had that Jones had any acquaintance with the family they intended to wrong. To come face-to-face with him, and in their very house, appalled the Captain. Small hope would there be that Burgess might have exercised discretion in his conversations with the physician! His agitation, when he visited Burgess that evening, was extreme. He had resolved, now he saw his exposure so likely, to abandon their whole enterprise, and was for paying off the shopkeeper, declaring the lady's innocence, and so being quit of the matter altogether; but the Ensign, foolhardy by nature and emboldened by gin, certain, moreover, that the third of their party would countenance no such reversal, could but laugh, and most graciously agree to accept a more favorable division of the spoils.

"Heywood sat long there, complaining of his lot, which indeed seemed to both men ruinous, for his creditors were importunate, and without his share of the gains, he knew not where to turn. Then—for our Captain is nothing if not nimble-witted—he bethought himself of a fitting solution to his woes. There was yet in London, he said, an heiress, of no great understanding and fast fading bloom, of whose affections he was secure. If he made haste, he might obtain her hand before her family had had time to inquire too closely into his prospects. Upon the instant, he was gone about this errand. Caroline Bingley's future was thus quickly sealed, and, I fear, it will not be a happy one."

So many emotions felt Georgiana upon hearing his recitation that for many moments she scarce knew what to say. Only then could she speak. "I pity Miss Bingley," said she with a sigh. "I have been wronged by the Captain, but she, poor lady, far more. But brother," recollecting herself, "do you tell me—is it really true—that Mrs. Philips' name may now be cleared and her freedom restored? These horrid revelations then carry with them something of good."

"Dreadful they are," said he, "and might have been still worse had it not been for *one* in particular. . . . Georgiana, there remains more to be divulged which I had questioned whether or not to reveal to you, knowing there is pain in it. But you should know; you *shall* know the whole of it, for the third malfeasant, dear sister, is one with whom I fear that you yourself are already acquainted, and in sadly distressing fashion; for in the past he has injured you grievously. His name is Lieutenant George Wickham."

"Lieutenant Wickham!" cried Georgiana, gone quite white. "Oh, my dear brother! To be plagued by such a man! Has he not yet ill-used us enough?"

"Your disbelief is scarce to be wondered at," replied her brother. "But be assured, sister, and take from it what comfort you can, that his motive in all is not harm to *you*, but revenge upon myself. Patience, Georgiana, and you shall know all."

"It seems that Burgess' merriment only grew in the continuation of his tale, to which our young friends listened with growing horror. Not an hour before their arrival, Burgess had summoned Wickham to him to impart the risible tidings of Captain Heywood's withdrawal from their scheme. This, to his astonishment, evoked in the good Lieutenant not mirth but rage. Burgess was a fool, he railed, if he could not see that Jones' connection put paid to their scheming. And then, to Burgess' high amusement, his anger accelerated. The family in whose drawing room Jones had appeared was the very one which had done him the most heinous of injuries. A proud line, once connected with his in the closest manner, which was responsible for all his ills; which had wrested from him his living, withheld from him advantages which were rightfully his own, reduced him to a state of poverty, such as *he* had never been meant for. And now—at last—they had thwarted this—his latest intrigue! It was not to be borne.

"He continued thus, Burgess said, for some minutes. Never would he repose until he had done injury to them as they had to him. He would discredit their name over London; he would spread word—dear Georgiana, courage, for this will be, beyond question, the most distressing of all—of certain indiscretions he claimed to have been committed with his own self by a young woman of the family. No, he had continued, he would not rest until he had disgraced the name of Miss Georgiana Darcy."

Georgiana cried out, quite overcome. Her brother allowed her a moment to recover herself, and then continued.

"The excellent young man, Leigh-Cooper, had listened to Burgess' tale with indignation. But when he heard *your* name so used, sister, his fury knew no bounds. Indeed, he seized the wretch Burgess by the very throat and threatened more violence still, if he did not reveal the others' whereabouts—a request with which the terrified Burgess quickly complied.

"Never before, our poet said, had he seen his friend in such a passion. Straight from Burgess's lodgings he burst, and, without awaiting Jones, to Edward Street where Wickham had rooms. I will not describe to you, little sister, the scene which ensued. You know Wickham to be a hearty man, and he was desperate. Even so, he was no match for Leigh-Cooper. Without onerous explication, Wickham is now held at Bow Street prison, and justice has been dispatched to pursue his cohorts. Mr. Gardiner, whose joy can scarce be contained, has already left for Hertford to bring home his sister.

"You may imagine, dearest Georgiana, how reluctant were our young friends to recount to me certain portions of this intelligence. About Wickham, they could say not enough of ill: he was a liar born, monstrous in his falsehoods. Leigh-Cooper, in particular, was incensed even to repeat such an infamy. The debt is immeasurable which our family owes to young Jones and, most especially, to that brave and excellent Leigh-Cooper."

Georgiana was equal to no response. So soon as she might, she hurried away to her room, to the agitation of her own private reflections.

PART VII

CHAPTER 40

WITH IMPATIENCE HAD Elizabeth Darcy awaited her husband's each communication from London; but none did she welcome with such joy as that which came in the days following. This was comfort indeed! Her Aunt's freedom to be secured, the Bennet name restored, and, most immediate happiness of all, her husband at last returned to her. Here was redress and more for every ill she had suffered.

The preceding weeks had been onerous for Mrs. Darcy. The scrutiny of the neighborhood had continued no less close than heretofore, the family's plight being chronicled daily in all quarters, with admirable attentiveness to its minutest particulars, and but scant heed paid to such trifling matters as either charity or accuracy. The days fell heavily, and sorely she missed the loving strength of her husband.

Even Jane, usually so dependable a source of steadiness, could avail her little here, engrossed as she was in domestic upheavals. *Her* life had changed altogether with the arrival of little Eliza. The child, her mother could minister to with small exertion, being both maternal by temperament and blessed with a placid infant; it was in the full-grown relatives that her trials lay. Between her parents' industrious deliberations upon whether a finer baby had ever been seen, and Bingley's more modest demurrals that she was after all but an infant like any other, nothing out of the way at all, although uncommonly pretty, to be sure, and had they not noticed the altogether captivating vigor with which she wielded her rattle?—this felicitous exchange repeated many times during the course of any single morning—poor Jane was much beset.

"I regret, dear Elizabeth," said she, "how little comfort I have been able to give you these weeks. I know that your burden has been wearisome. But, oh sister, here is deliverance. My aunt is to be freed! Let us go immediately to my mother to tell her!"

"By and by," said Elizabeth. "There is yet that within the letter which Mr. Darcy desires that I speak of to no one. But from you, dear Jane, I can have no reserves. So strange is this latest turn that I can scarce hope you will credit it. Jane, it seems that among the authors of this odious scheme to ruin my aunt, was none other than our own brother Wickham."

"George Wickham, a thief?" cried Jane in horror. "Surely you are in error, Lizzy. Our brother may be—is—sadly deficient in many qualities, but I cannot believe him vicious. It must be some other officer of whom you speak, one in his company, perhaps, or someone bearing a similar name. The latter, more probably, there are many names similar to his."

"Sweet Jane, you make of me a true prophet; I foretold you would not believe me, and you see, you do not. But even you, sister, need sometimes countenance the reprehensible, for it is *he*, no other. Oh, Jane, how to be pitied is poor Lydia. She has been a thoughtless giddy girl, it is true; but nothing she has done has merited such shame as is now hers."

"Poor Lydia, indeed," sighed Jane. "How she must suffer. What shall become of her husband?"

"It seems that he is already in the hands of the law," sighed Elizabeth. "But let us not yet despair, sister. Mr. Darcy has redeemed the wretch from his deserts before, and will, I am sure, contrive to do so again. As for young Turner, I fear, nothing can avail him."

"Veritably, Mr. Darcy's kindnesses to our family are unexampled," said Jane. "How fortunate we are to have him as our champion. But, oh Elizabeth, what must not my mother feel to witness her favorite so reduced. And this, marring what might have been the happiest of news. Will our family never escape ill-repute?"

Elizabeth could but shake her head, understanding too well that the neighborhood, its conversation depleted by so disappointing a removal of the old scandal, would seize upon this new, with an avidity reasonable to all but those most fastidious, or most closely connected to it. And so the coming days confirmed.

Solace, however, arrived in time. Before the Bennet family might sink once again into complete desolation, it was able to take comfort in a letter which arrived for Mr. Bennet from the amiable quarter of their cousin Collins.

My Dear Sir,

Yet again, our intimate connection and my calling to minister to humankind, place me in the distressing position of condoling with you upon your family afflictions. I am joined by Mrs. Collins in lamenting your new disgrace, the more melancholy as it must be for you, in the recollection that it was your own early paternal indulgence which has brought your daughter Lydia to such a pass. I cannot, in my office as a clergyman, neglect to remind you that I predicted such a consequence even before her patched-up marriage; and now, with what sorrow do I learn that I was right.

How bitterly it grieves me to know that I am heir to a house and estate thus fallen. Lady Catherine, herself, was so condescending as to offer me her most profound sympathy when I related the affair to her in its entirety this very morning, having learned of it in a letter Mrs. Collins received from Hertfordshire. This was the more gracious of Her Ladyship in that a certain relation of her own was not uninvolved with the affair—delicacy, you will understand, prevents my saying more. My patroness' righteous outrage at the villainy of your son Wickham knew no bounds. Her advice to me was to detach myself altogether from so ignoble a connection as yours must be; the magnanimity of my calling only insists that I write to you now these heartfelt words of compassionate counsel.

To Miss Kitty Bennet, I have intimated that she might soon return to the bosom of her family, who must surely require her more than my wife or I, now in this their hour of tribulation and notoriety. But she, headstrong as your leniency has left her, declines to depart until called for by her mother. I am confident that you will send for her directly.

My burdens in this affair have been augmented by the suspicion of a partiality held towards her by my curate, Mr. Samuel Beasley, whom it has been my sorry charge to caution upon the dangers of such an attachment. This, I regret to say, was ill-received, for he is a surly fellow. But his prospects are not inconsiderable: how unfortunate for your daughter, Kitty, that her sister's calamitous match has destroyed her last hope of happiness, for after this latest, you will agree, she can have no other.

What pity I feel for you, dear Sir. And even as I write, my good patroness's advice appears to me ever more astute. I must therefore advise you, my dear Mr. Bennet, that I dissociate myself from you and your family, from the departure of Miss Kitty Bennet from Hunsford, until such time as I must assume the responsibilities of caring for Longbourn. I am, dear sir, etc., etc.

Mr. Bennet soon called upon his elder daughters to peruse this curious communication.

"What miracle have we here?" he asked. "I confess that I have wondered in reading Kitty's letters. It does appear that she has been about the charitable errands of the Hunsford parish of late with as much ardor as she more commonly devotes to the choosing of a new bonnet. I have been hard put to it to recognize in these recitations the silly, ignorant miss who has been the comfort of my age these many years. Can this sudden change of heart owe less to the Collins' superior society and more to this young Beasley? And, if indeed, he has contrived to reform such an one as Kitty, what exceptional manner of man might he be?"

"I would not depend upon it, Papa," said Elizabeth. "Charlotte has written to me of Mr. Beasley, and he appears, by her account, to be a man of uncommon good sense and one whose good offices are looked upon well by families of consequence in the country. It is possible that *he* might be captivated by Kitty; but we can hardly expect my sister to favor a man offering her merely intelligence, constancy, and the prospect of a substantial living in good time."

"You are severe, Lizzy," said Jane. "I have remarked to you before that Kitty and Mary are not beyond salvation. We may have accomplished little there; but if this Mr. Beasley is really a man of parts, then Kitty at least may surprise us all."

"Do you speak of Kitty?" said Mary, then entering the room with her mother. "How she does tarry at Hunsford. I cannot think what might be keeping her. There is nothing there but gloomy cottagers at their prayers and not a book to be found but the Bible."

"The Bible need not do you harm, Miss," replied her mother. "I was myself reading the Bible to my own Mama, when Mr. Bennet saw me first—was I not, my love? Wearing a dress of blue muslin with the sweetest flounce at the hem, I can remember now how he looked upon me. I have had a particular fondness for the Book of Lamentations ever since."

"Holy works may serve to attract some suitors," said Mary. "Had *I* such an intent, I should choose rather to be surprised over the works of Livy. But then I do not seek such attentions; they should distract me too much from my study of Tristan and Isolde."

Elizabeth, at this, cast up her eyes and Jane but smiled.

"Well," said Mr. Bennet, "now I think upon it, I shall not wait too eagerly upon the increased discernment of either of my remaining daughters. However, nor will I call for Kitty yet, if only to avail myself of the opportunity to fret my cousin Collins for a few days longer."

CHAPTER 41

WITHIN YOUR MORE fashionable marriages, ardor soon cools to affection. Attachment once secured, the vows exchanged, and the wedding sweetmeats consumed, impassioned gazes are at liberty to subside to kindly glances, the once agitated heart to still to an altogether more comfortable rate.

So lamentably out of mode, however, were Mr. and Mrs. Darcy, that his homecoming, eagerly anticipated as it had been by both, in its occurrence only surpassed their every expectation. Within *their* union, that which had begun in raillery, had only ripened to a frankness of exchange, a true accord of mind and inclination, bringing to Elizabeth such satisfaction as she had never imagined possible.

Nor was her husband's situation any the less to be envied.

"My Lizzy," sighed he quite soon. "Endless have been these last lonely weeks without you. And to think that but two years ago I knew you not. I suppose there was indeed such a time; but truth to tell I cannot remember it."

"And that is scarcely to be wondered at," replied his wife, "considering the measure of vexation my family has caused you since then. We are ever to you a source of disquietude and distress. I wonder that you do not look back lovingly upon the days when you knew the Bennet family not at all."

"Say not so," cried he. "To you I owe my every happiness; such assistance as I may have been able to afford your family is but a paltry thanks for you, my Lizzy. Nor, to tell truth, can I myself disclaim responsibility for many of the sad events of the last years. Had I exposed Wickham's character earlier, with less attention to my own private affairs and more to the public good, he should never have been able to continue so in his treachery. But with my poor sister's reputation to shield, how other might I have acted?"

"None other," assured his wife, "you did only that which was proper. Your sister deserved all protection at the time, so young as she was, and so wronged. But Mr. Darcy, it is the Georgiana not of then, but of today, who excites my more particular compassion. I had not before confided to you that I detected in her a preference for the scoundrel, Captain Heywood. And now I see her, listless, pale as never before. It is a bad business, indeed. Does she suffer very much?"

"I fear so," replied her husband gravely. "Oh, Lizzy, how sorely you were missed in London. However much my sister might sorrow, she would never confide it to me. Now she is at home, I can take comfort that she will turn for counsel towards you. *I* can but observe her pain, and wonder at my lack that I might not be entrusted with its expression."

"What high expectations you do entertain of fraternal candor. Can you not know that a young girl will confide in a pet rabbit before her own brother? And particularly in affairs such as these. But depend upon it, I shall speak to Georgiana, and do for her what I can. Her heart is surely not wounded beyond repair: at eighteen, the more certain one may be that she will never recover her spirits, the more secure it is that she *will*."

But when at last she was alone with her sister, Elizabeth discovered her discomposure not easily overcome.

"I cannot reserve from you, dear Elizabeth," began she almost immediately, "that I have fallen sadly into misjudgment, nay, into folly. Often before this have I boasted to you of my heart's proof against the more tender affections—only now to have bestowed them upon the least worthy of recipients. I need scarcely explain that I speak of Captain Heywood. A blackguard, indeed, who might—would—have caused the ruin of my dear Lizzy's aunt. And yet to me he seemed so particular, so tender. His actions, his attentions could not but suggest his partiality. How blind was I to be thus taken in by fair address and consequential situation. While he. . . ." And she gave way to tears.

"Oh, my poor sister. Too soon do you learn the bitterest lessons of life. But you must take some comfort at least, in the knowledge that the Captain duped not only you, but every one of us; even, for a time, your Aunt Catherine. If nothing more, you were among superior society."

"We were used ill," said Georgiana. "The Captain wooed us all; until he turned his gaze towards me, I believed him intended for my cousin Anne. And all the while he was plotting only harm. And the end of it was, that any fortune—no matter how odiously got—would suffice him. He deceived us wickedly."

"Let us not denounce the Captain for intending to marry to his pecuniary advantage. For such as he, expensive in his tastes, unused to self-denial, *that* was only prudent in him. Where he should—must—be decried, is in his duplicity. Whether it be to your cousin, to your self, or to my unfortunate Aunt, his whole behavior was founded upon lies and deceit. You have had a happy escape, Georgiana; with a Captain Heywood, consider how far could tranquility have been from your life."

"But dear Lizzy," then burst forth Georgiana. "How may one judge the measure of a man? Not only was Captain Heywood's manner beguiling, his family was unexceptionable, was connected indeed with my own. If he cannot be supposed to be righteous, then who can?"

"So proper a question," replied Elizabeth, "merits no less than an exact response; how unreasonable is it that there is none. But this much I do know. An unexceptionable lineage is no more a guarantee for virtue than it be for the shade of a man's hair, nor a courtly air, of benevolent intent. It is not in his family, or in his air, that a man's worth may be estimated, but in his deeds. Consider your brother, or my uncle Gardiner; or, for a more apt example, the young architect James Leigh-Cooper. *He* has neither a noble family, as the former, nor a beguiling address, as the latter, to further him; but, Georgiana, only think of his conduct. I understand that his part in uncovering the villainous scheme was little short of heroic. You see, sister, there is probity in mankind after all, although, I greatly fear, your present unhappiness might make you doubt it."

"I thank you for your compassion, Elizabeth," said Georgiana, "but, in truth, I do not merit it. I have thought long since I left London; nay, since before I left, guided in large part by the wisdom of your excellent Aunt Gardiner. It was she who exposed to me how little understanding of true gentility was mine. Too little have I considered others, too much myself. Sister, I have been vain, foolish, presuming; it has led me to permit attentions my judgment should have warned me against. Nor, as you too well know, was this my first such error.

"Yet," with a sigh, "I shall not so err again. Believe me, Elizabeth, from henceforth my feelings shall be governed by good sense, civility and restraint. My every endeavor shall be to be of assistance to my brother and to you."

Elizabeth rejoiced to hear this recital. Admiring the resolution of her sister's tone, and assured that self-sacrifice so eager must certainly expire ere it need cause anxiety, she took her hand and pressed it warmly.

"But tell me," continued Georgiana after a moment. "How does your Aunt Philips? And more particularly," blushing at the dreaded name but resolved to exert herself, "your unfortunate brother Wickham? Surely, to have him now in prison must be for the family a hardship as great as the former?"

"There, nothing is yet certain," replied Elizabeth, recollecting now her own woes. "Mr. Darcy had hoped that for my sister's sake he might yet again intercede and the Lieutenant be freed; but it appears that more is involved than we know of, that, in short, this matter requires such influence as even your brother does not wield. As for the Captain and his lady, none know yet where they are. It is thought that they have fled overseas."

She looked over with some concern to her younger sister, to see how she received the intelligence of him who had most lately done her ill. But Georgiana had scarcely heard her. Already she was preoccupied in devising the fashion in which she herself might step forward to champion the Bennet family in this, their present adversity.

CHAPTER 42

I T WAS GEORGIANA'S custom, on arriving at Pemberley
after an absence, to call as soon as she might, upon her
beloved godfather, Sir Geoffrey Portland. That good gentleman awaited her visits in high anticipation. Darcy, he had
loved as a child and now esteemed as a man; but *her* beauty
of face, her sweetness of temper—even those very high
spirits, so frowned upon by her Aunt Catherine—cheered him
as could little other.

But when the occasion for her call arrived, it was not solely
the company of his young friend that he welcomed, but news
that she might bring of Mrs. Fitzwilliam Darcy. Little as he
might incline to acknowledge it, he had come, over the last
weeks, to regard the new mistress of Pemberley with esteem,
if not admiration. Apprehensive he had been when, weeks
earlier, Darcy had left her on her own in Derbyshire, that she
might turn to him to solicit the support which in all decorum
he would be unable to offer her. On the contrary, he had
discovered her mien to be rather haughty than importunate.
Elizabeth Darcy, standing alone in her misery, had shown
herself to care for neither his, nor the neighborhood's censure. Her head she held high; she continued in every particular the very mistress of her own life.

Sir Geoffrey was an aristocrat born, and far be it from him
to hold in regard one not of his own rank; but, in all condescension, he must own that had Mrs. Darcy only shown the
good taste to be born to a more prominent family, he *must*
extol her. Her carriage, her fortitude, above all, her refusal to

gratify him, all would have shown themselves impeccable, had her ancestry but allowed. Moreover, Sir Geoffrey, who usually kept scrupulous distance, had caught sight of her once by accident at an evening at Mrs. Celia Montague's, and had observed her fine eyes to be only improved when flashing in defiance. Seemliness might—did—prevent such considerations from having influence upon his conduct, yet to his most private self he would acknowledge her a worthy adversary, if nothing more.

Certain it was, however, that no measure of command on the part of Mrs. Darcy could ever touch the heart of Lady Catherine—as a letter he had received from Her Ladyship that very morning, had apprised him.

Dear Sir,

Now what say you to the Bennets' presumptions? Since the entire country speaks of it, you can surely not have failed to learn of their new business. My misgivings upon the Bennet alliance are well known. Yet even my own wildest expectations could not have supposed them to include a common thief! Through their late addition, the vile ingrate Wickham, they have destroyed all, even, it grieves me to say, that most unfortunate young man of my late husband's family, whom you yourself entertained at Denby Park.

My unhappy cousin, whose undoing Wickham contrived, was led to straits which must excite the compassion of any by a pitiable series of gaming debts. So heartrending was his plight, indeed, that I myself was forced to send him from Rosings and the courtship of my daughter Anne. Yet the Captain was, if nothing else, a man of an acceptable family; what a disgrace it is that he should be led to his downfall by the son of Darcy's steward!

Alas, the Bennets' ill does not end there. A younger sister of this tiresome family, staying now at Hunsford Parsonage, has so far succeeded in beguiling my new curate—an able person, if something overzealous in the pursuit of religion—that I greatly fear for him. Such a match would mean a Bennet in my view daily; the girl can but be about it for spite. Although I have dispatched my parson to alert Mr. Beasley to his danger, the young man remains obdurate even in the face of my expressed displeasure.

Now you must see, Sir Geoffrey, that naught but misery can possibly come of intimacy with those in the lower positions of society.

For myself, I have done. I will not discuss the matter further, and I charge you most particularly, from henceforth, on no account whatsoever, to refer in my presence to such odious people as these, unless your communication be such as would confirm my sagacity.

Yours very sincerely,
C. de Bourgh

Sir Geoffrey perused this missive in some disappointment. He had hoped it might contain some explanation of how so seemingly gracious a young man as Captain Heywood had fallen thus into ruffianly deeds. The antics of Wickham—low of birth, and ruined moreover by his patron's indulgence—could surprise him little; but that a Captain Heywood should stoop was a source of puzzlement for the excellent gentleman—and one he had hoped Lady Catherine might illuminate. But all that *this* communicated was its author's rage against the Bennets and their familiars. It was true that Elizabeth Darcy's connections remained improper, but even they could surely not be held culpable for debts incurred on the other side of the Continent. He thought it unjust in Her Ladyship for all her consequence; had their positions been reversed, he was secure that Mrs. Darcy would not have used *her* so.

But it was only later, when the warmest greetings had been exchanged with Georgiana, together with expressions of his concern over his dearest girl's pallor, clearly a result of her recent sojourn in the City and immediately to be repaired by the servant's bringing hot tea and biscuits, that he could pursue his path of inquiry.

"I can scarce hope, dear Georgiana," began he, "that you remain altogether ignorant of the deplorable events within the Bennet family, events which have so far reached to drag down not only the abominable Wickham, but your own cousin, Captain Thomas Heywood. Let it stand as a lesson to you, my dear girl, that a young person of gentility cannot be too careful in the choice of his associates. It was a caution your own aunt gave to your brother before his marriage, but one which he unfortunately elected to ignore."

Sir Geoffrey had chosen his words with care, knowing how fierce was Georgiana's loyalty to her sister, and confident that the coda to his speech would elicit an outburst in Elizabeth's defense that must contain intelligence of her situation. But to his disappointment, his young friend addressed instead the import of his earlier remarks.

"Dear Sir Geoffrey, you would extol breeding above all, but my recent stay in London has taught me other. You have, I believe, heard something of my sister Elizabeth's Uncle and Aunt Gardiner of Cheapside. A man and woman of great civility and elegance, yet he, at least, commanded no early fortune. While others there are, born to every propitious circumstance, who.... You see, Uncle," catching herself, "that I have been thinking long of late and I have come to know that good breeding is nothing; is indeed," a most fitting image striking her upon the sudden, "no more a guarantee of virtue than it be of the shade of a man's hair."

Sir Geoffrey was given pause by this curious proposition.

"My dear Georgiana, you are untried," said he after a few moments. "But allow me, as your elder and the more experienced, to assure you that it is very vexing not to depend upon the solidity of rank."

Georgiana, understanding by this that she and her old friend had come to think very differently, nevertheless evaded contention. Her purpose was other. The situation of the Bennets, while changed, was by no means resolved, since it appeared that Wickham's offences were so desperate that even her brother was unable to help him now. But Sir Geoffrey she knew to enjoy influence that the younger man did not: could she but prevail upon him to exert some of that interest on the Lieutenant's behalf, what joy would it bring to Elizabeth! To that end, she would apply each resource of beguilement that was in her power—even to the extravagant extent of feigning acquiescence where in truth she felt none.

"Untried, I doubtless am," said she softly, "and can only wonder at your wisdom. But dear Uncle, let us not, I pray you, look too harshly upon those who have not been nurtured with the advantages enjoyed by ourselves. There is one, for instance, and one indeed, raised among us here in

Derbyshire, who lies now wretched in prison in London. True, it is Lieutenant Wickham's own misdeeds that have brought him to such a pass, but reprobate though he be, I cannot bear to think him thus. His father was dear to my own. But one word from you, dear Sir Geoffrey, could alter all. I implore you, if not for his sake, for my own, to exert your power in his interest."

Sir Geoffrey heard these words in some surprise, since he had not for two years heard Georgiana so much as speak of the steward's son, much less concern herself with his welfare. It showed once more her tenderness of heart that she would apply so to his compassion, and on behalf of an outright villain. But the more he considered her petition, the more he inclined to fulfill it. Georgiana's confidence was far from misplaced: his influence could indeed have the young ruffian out of his bondage and on board ship to Antigua before the fortnight's end. Sir Geoffrey could refuse his goddaughter little, and less when her fancy proved so arduous of answer that he must appear the more to advantage in dispatching it. Moreover, it occurred to him that those to whom such an execution would cause wonderment included not only his goddaughter, but the indomitable Mrs. Darcy.

"Wickham is a wretch," he said somberly. "But miserable as he be, is as much your own father's doing as his own. He was born with little character, it is true, but my good friend's indulgence of him did not foster its development. Since he is no longer with us, it must fall to myself then to address this sorry situation. Dear child, the matter is now in my hands."

Georgiana could not speak, such was her pleasure. Taking her old friend's hand, she embraced him in gratitude.

CHAPTER 43

I N THE WEEKS that followed, Georgiana, much heartened by her success with Sir Geoffrey, found an ailing spirit to respond commendably to an admixture of youth and self-gratulation. Some dejection remained, it is true; but as the days passed, she began to think upon, not that which she had not, but the good fortune she had, and to resume her life in useful application of her proper pursuits. To her books, she had been inclined even since a small girl; now, she turned with equal ardor to copying out musical pieces, to perfecting her needlework, to undertaking a portrait of Elizabeth, in short, to making herself so very perfect a model of an accomplished young woman, that even her brother observed and was discomfited by it.

Elizabeth, however, took only pleasure in her sister's recovery. "I rejoice to see in you, Georgiana," said she one morning upon their ramble, "at least the appearance of good spirits. Your heart may not feel cheerful now; but depend upon it, if you but proceed as if it *were*, in time it will be. We are gullible creatures all, and you will be surprised to learn what folderols we may persuade ourselves to believe, if we do but apply ourselves."

"In time I hope I too may benefit from this particularity," sighed Georgiana, "although, for now, dear Elizabeth, only you can know how little I have yet done with oppression. Still, I would wish for no change, after all. Imprudent I was; but think not that I am not seasoned from my errrors. *Now*, I can confidently discern whom I should—and whom should not—hold in esteem, and for that, I must thank the brave Captain, although the lesson was most cruelly taught."

Her sister witnessed her determination with approval, only smiling to herself at the happy expectation that never again might Miss Georgiana Darcy be deceived by man or woman for so long as she should live.

"Enough, then, of my own woes," soon continued Georgiana. "My brother brings me the happiest of intelligence. Sir Geoffrey Portland himself has intervened in behalf of Lieutenant Wickham. I know not how he effected it—my godfather's influence you know to be substantial—but the wonder is, that at this very week's end the Lieutenant shall be released from prison and on his way to Antigua, to employment on Sir Geoffrey's own sugar plantation. Was that not excellently done of him?"

Elizabeth had indeed learned of this reversal early that morning, allowing her time enough to marvel at it and conjecture as to its provenance. That Sir Geoffrey should thus exert himself in the interest of those he did not esteem, was a circumstance she had little anticipated.

"A kindly intervention," agreed she, "and a most immediate solution for our family. Lydia and my mother travel to London today to bid the Lieutenant godspeed; my sister means to follow him abroad as soon as she may. I am most grateful to Sir Geoffrey for his efforts on our behalf, but do confess myself something perplexed. I cannot but wonder whether I see the hand of my newest sister in this gratifying turn of events?"

Georgiana, blushing, denied this suggestion with energy, and their talk turned to other affairs.

It was only later, when alone in her room, that she permitted herself the indulgence of reflecting upon this exchange, at some length, and with no less pleasure. Sore had been the temptations in the days since she had prevailed upon Sir Geoffrey, to exult to her sister in that gentleman's enlistment in their cause; but always she had resisted, fearful that too high an accession of Elizabeth's hope might only result in the greater misery, should his endeavors come to naught after all. Now that Wickham's liberty was all but achieved, she elected no mention at all of her part in it, preferring to enjoy, in the solitude of her own heart, the knowledge that she had done well for those she loved, and that knowledge made only the sweeter for needing to be shared with none.

From her earliest years, Georgiana's natural inclination, fortified by her reading, had excited within her yearnings to philanthropies. Unfortunate was it, that growing up as she had, lacking companions of her own age, and herself enveloped in every luxury, the opportunities for selflessness had proved but slight, and her benevolent impulses, perforce, been harnessed to the fancies of splendid deeds, rather than to their more commonplace execution. Now, for the first time in her life, she had contrived a real, and not insignificant, service to another—and that other, her sister, Elizabeth, one she held unreservedly dear. Small matter that the instrument of her assistance was the irreclaimable Wickham: that Elizabeth's lot was made lighter was the essential. The measure of gratification that this brought to Georgiana's truly warm heart can be only surmised.

So stunning a success might indeed have caused our young heroine to recover her mettle a little *too* assuredly, in short, to think again too well of herself. Happily, a most substantial reminder of her yet less than perfection was provided in these days by her still unimproved relations with James Leigh-Cooper. She had seen him but once upon her return to Pemberley. The meeting with the young architect had been brief, and his manner, despite her every placating effort, distant. And then he was gone. Where before he had too eagerly engaged her in converse, now he but bowed and went about his business, confining their exchanges to the barest permissible by courtesy. She had foreseen that it would be thus—and that the breach was of her own making, she too well knew—but the reality, the cold inclinations of the head, where before they had exchanged frank glances, the indifferent, "Good day, Miss Darcy," where she had been wont to expect lengthy discursions, all these caused her more pain than she could have imagined possible.

One morning as she walked alone in the park, meditating upon this division, and the singular degree of perturbation it was causing her, she observed the stalwart figure of Mr. Leigh-Cooper himself concluding some business with the bailiff, Merkin. She watched him for some moments from afar; he spoke with vigor, but as soon as the other left him, she could not but mark how his head sank in dejection. Often had she seen him arrogant, then, of late, unconversable; but never before had he shown himself melancholy. On the sudden, she determined to approach him, and ran down the hill towards his retreating figure. "Mr. Leigh-Cooper," she began, directly she came up with him, "I cannot, no, I will not, countenance this uncordiality between us. We have, I think, always been friends. I did offend you in London, I know it, and can only beseech your pardon. I entreat you, do not let us quarrel forever about what is past. Come, can you not forgive me?"

Leigh-Cooper started at her approach, nor did his astonishment in any way lessen at her words. He hardly knew how to look. But as he gazed on her, his anger—which had indeed been great—could only melt, both at the openness of her address, and the very candid appeal which he read in her eyes as she turned them upon him. "My dear Miss Darcy," he began; but color soon overspread his cheeks and emotion prevented his continuing.

Georgiana saw this discomfort and wished only to relieve it. "Then it is settled," said she heartily. "We are to be friends once more. Now, let us talk as we were used. You, Mr. Leigh-Cooper, shall exposit upon what you will, whether it be the stream yonder, or Derbyshire marble, or the poetry of your friend Mr. Hugh Jones, and I give you my word, I shall listen enrapt. But how beautiful is Pemberley this morning. Is it this uncommonly lovely spring, or rather your own handiwork, that inspires my admiration?"

He answered her now with greater command, being able to employ for that purpose the amiable expedient of speaking that which he knew well. "A little, I fancy, of both, Miss Darcy," said he. "It is small credit to *my* skills, if your eyes are delighted by the flow of the river, by this fine lawn, or by the chestnuts on the hill yonder. My own part in your present pleasure has been to allow the poetry of the park to be freed. Too long have the natural virtues of these grounds been suppressed by man's imposition of order—well-intentioned though that was when conceived. Their liberation I have effected since you left about your travels, and I flatter myself not ill. But let me show you all." As once before, he offered his arm, which now she accepted gladly, rejoicing in the return of their accord. They walked together the great gardens, he chronicling his accomplishment, she at once engrossed in his words and captivated by his vision, able for the first time since her return to Pemberley to admire the changes he had wrought that, until this, she had been too oppressed even to see.

"A sweet view indeed," said she at last. "I confess to you I had hardly thought the vistas of my childhood capable of improvement, even by one so gifted as yourself. I was quite wrong, as you have shown me. Nature must indeed submit to man's order; can even flourish under it; yet how much lovelier it is when granted leave to thrive, unfettered by artificial arrangements! Alas, I have been mistaken in so many things. But Mr. Leigh-Cooper, I am not the same returning from London as she who left; I believe my understanding to have itself undergone improvement. I have seen that people of fashion are very well; but too much perfection of manner can only confuse. How grateful am I to be at home again in the country, where what attracts is nature's own elegance, altogether free of deception. I do believe that looking about your landscape this morning has made me truly happy for the first time for many weeks, and for that I thank you most kindly."

She looked upon the young man earnestly and for some moments he was again speechless, so many changes had his own temper known during the course of the morning. He had been heavy-hearted—she had sought him. He had been angry—she had softened him. He had displayed to her his work—she had admired. Her discrimination and candor set her peerless among her sex: let come of it what may, he must speak.

"Miss Darcy," said he, "It is in my power to be silent no longer. I know you to be a creature of all goodness, and trust your honor to be such as will overlook distinctions that can signify little in the end. True, our situations are not alike—but what of that? I am a frank man—some have said too much so—and now I must speak out. Miss Darcy, you will know that I have long admired you. I ask you in all plainness—will you accept my love?" Georgiana was quite confounded. That *he*, so intransigent a young man, so little courtly in his speech, so ready to tease or cavil with her, should stand now before her professing his tenderest love! How might she have suspected—

how have had an idea—of so improbable a circumstance? His behavior had given her no sign, his manner towards her no warning. And this, to conceal emotions so powerful that they must proclaim themselves even across differences of station! Truly, it was beyond expectation.

And how infinitely greater was her amazement when his declaration aroused in her, not indignation, but so exquisite a flutter of joy as she had never dreamed possible, and that hardly had he framed his plea before she had accepted him with all the ardor of a loving heart.

CHAPTER 44

WHAT SWEETER CONVERSE than between two beings discovering their love? Our happy pair walked the park hardly knowing the hour, and without a moment of disharmony or of silence, for there was much to tell. On *his* side, was the open expression, at last, of those emotions for so many months—he had feared forever—repressed within himself; on *hers*, the wonderment, that this best and most fascinating of men had stood before her so long and she had known him not. Such pleasure did both the explication and the comprehension of these sentiments afford the pair, that they must recount them again and again until their attachment was proven fast—for had they not been most devotedly in love, tedium would assuredly have claimed one or both ere the morning was out.

"I do believe I have loved you from the start," said he. "If my manner did not reveal it, nevertheless, it was so. Indeed, I fear that the more I felt for you, the greater was my need to conceal it. Still, I was intrigued even at the moment I saw you, at your brother's ball that first night at Pemberley so long ago. How should I not be? Loveliness itself you were, and so surrounded by admirers that—although your brother presented me—the very next morning you remembered me not at all."

"Gracious creature that I was," replied she, blushing at the recollection. "So aloof, so insolently forgetful—and of *you*—I wonder only that you did not entertain an immediate aversion for me."

"Insolent—no! Your distraction only beguiled me the more. You were quite captivating, all enthralled by your dreams of the evening's triumphs, not to speak—'with a smile that held yet a question in it,' of the good Lord Byron."

Georgiana was checked for a moment at this allusion to her earlier folly. But she persisted, for between them could be no subject unexamined.

"Alas," she sighed, "His Lordship led me sadly astray, and might too easily have carried me further still, with the help of an unprincipled other. Mr. Leigh-Cooper, though my desire is small to revive painful memories, I must speak to you of your offices on my behalf in London. Nay," for he would interrupt her, "I *will* finish. My brother has told me of the exertions of you and your friend Mr. Jones—for myself, and in a different fashion, for my sister Elizabeth. Then it was that I began to understand your worth as superior to most, perhaps to all men, although for tranquility's sake I would own it not. But think not my love for you springs from cold gratitude; I can see now it has been growing," with a smile, "even since our first altercation. Nevertheless, your actions upon *that* evening were such that I can *never* repay, nor shall cease to marvel at."

"My reward shall be your never speaking of it more. But," quickly noticing her expression, and with an urgent change of tone, "is it then my fate to be ever Mr. Leigh-Cooper to you, Miss Darcy? My Georgiana, cannot you pronounce me James?"

"I believe I can contrive it," said she laughing, and for the first time careless of the color in her cheeks, "since my own name sounds so sweet in your voice, dear James. Yes, you see, I can. Were ever two creatures happier than we?"

"I cannot think they were," said he after a moment. "But fair speeches are not among my arts, Georgiana. Only know that my love for you is fixed, nor shall anything temper my devotion. But, dearest girl, so precipitate have I been to claim you for my own, that, selfishly perhaps, I have left you little leisure to consider all that our match must entail. Your generosity prevents your remarking upon it, but the truth is that the disparity in our stations will not go ignored. If *you* regard it not, make no mistake but that others will. Are you sure—dear Georgiana, are you certain—that this is what you choose?"

And with so sober an inquiry did he look into her eyes that one would almost suppose that he remained yet in the least doubt of her answer.

Nor did she show herself now variable, having already responded thus to the same question several times that very morning. "What is rank to love," cried she. "No position in society, however exalted, can rival such perfect understanding as we two now feel. Dear James, together we shall be happier than any deserve to be—the rest of the world signifies naught."

"A charming picture," he laughed, "but only wait, Georgiana, until that insignificant 'rest of the world' begins to intrude—as it will, and in ways you cannot now imagine. *Then*, I fear you will discover it not so trifling after all."

"How little you yet know me, dear James. It is not our family's way to be guided by the neighborhood. Let others say what they will, you and I shall be happy and there's an end to it. My one fear is that my brother might set himself against us, for he is proud, as you know—and something too solicitous of me. But," her romantic fancy once again taking flight, "I would hold our love a paltry thing were I not ready to do battle for it. My brother's approbation, he may reserve, but depend upon it, I will vouchsafe his consent, at least, before the week is out."

With such fervor did Georgiana prepare to bear down whatever opposition her brother might place, in order to secure her love. Let him talk of impetuosity, let him rage over impropriety; let him say what he would of union to a man without alliance—*she* would prove only the more persuasive in pleading her lover's cause. James Leigh-Cooper might be without connection, but his constancy of heart and brilliance of mind were incontestable. Darcy *would* in the end know his consequence as did she.

Imagine therefore, our young lady's bafflement, upon confronting her brother, with case prepared and resolution fixed, to find him, once he had recovered from his astonishment, welcoming the match with the most unaffected of pleasure.

"How should I not rejoice," said he, "owing as I do my every happiness to one I myself had first dismissed as having inferior connections—I speak, of course, of my own dear Elizabeth—shall I then deny you the same prospect? Nor, in truth," with a sigh, "might any words of my own serve to dissuade you from that which you intended; too much in that do you resemble your esteemed Aunt Catherine.

"I will own surprise, however, sister," continued he in a graver tone. "James Leigh-Cooper is a proper man—his genius has never been in doubt, either to myself, or to the rest of England—but, *you*, Georgiana, have shown him to my knowledge no special favor, rather a kind of impatience. Do anything, dear sister, before marrying one you love not. Georgiana, do you love?"

With tears in her eyes, his sister declared most solemnly that she held James Leigh-Cooper dear above any other.

"Then I congratulate and give you blessing. Leigh-Cooper's fortune may not be quite equal to your own, but it is not inconsiderable either. You shall not want for money. More important than what your betrothed has, is what he *is*, in mind and heart. Georgiana, I can scarce express my satisfaction that, since you have fixed your affections, they are upon such as he. You will be a happy woman."

Elizabeth's response to the match was all exultation. Too long had she observed her architect friend undergo the agonies of uncertain love; now, she might commend her sister for extending to him the clemency of accepting a lifetime of felicity.

"I compliment myself upon your emergence, my dear," said she. "You have the assurance at least of a marriage that will never lapse into sulks, since I have not yet heard that young man silent for ten minutes together. I can well cry up a spouse of lively spirits. Mr. Darcy and I have long settled it that no couple is to be happier than we; but I charge you most solemnly upon our sisterly affection to strive as you may to be *almost* as happy."

With what success our young couple fulfilled this commission during their long life together must be left to the reader's determination. Suffice it to say, that they achieved a degree of bliss far from disgraceful to two who wanted not for money, and whose union, begun in real affection and the ardor of youth, only ripened in mutual confidence and esteem with every year that passed.

The neighborhood endured their good fortune with tolerable grace, and that made simpler over time by the growth of

Leigh-Cooper's reputation, and the social embarrassments attendant upon scorning one whose friends included the Prince Regent. Even Sir Geoffrey unbent, although slowly. He saw his beloved godchildren made happy by their marriages, and, at last, declared that for their sakes he would overlook the improprieties so far as to acquiesce to intercourse with all. If truth were told, it was less the well-being of either Darcy or Georgiana, than the company of Elizabeth, which enticed him; but since truth never was told, both he and his higher-born friends were allowed to go to their graves in the comfortable reliance upon *his* unusual condescension and *their* undiminished superiority.

The prosperity of Mr. and Mrs. Darcy was secured not long after the marriage, by the appearance at Pemberley of a cousin for little Elizabeth Bingley. Geoffrey Fitzwilliam Darcy was a good-natured and comely infant, but oddly solemn, which his mother proudly attributed to a sagacity uncommon in babyhood, and which she made it her particular business to laugh him out of, ere he had reached his fifth year.

Lydia Wickham had bade farewell to her husband with many tears and affecting promises to join him at earliest opportunity. As soon as she had secured the money, she would be at his side—then, as soon as she had recovered her health from the pain of their parting—then, as soon as she had completed the rug she had promised to her Mama before Michaelmas. It was not long before it became evident that so many "as soons" must needs add up to one "never" and indeed, Lydia, having discovered that the privileges of matrimony were quite as well to be enjoyed without the unnecessary extra of a husband, chose to remain forever steadfast at her mother's side, confining her wifely duties to the occasional glance at a portrait of her absent loved one, and the shedding of a tear when she remembered, or was observed.

Mrs. Bennet, delighted to have her favorite restored to her, soon settled to her good life again. Many a profitable evening was spent by the two, in the bracing company of Mrs. Philips, once she had recovered from her ordeal, in such essential pursuits as playing whist, and discussing the probability of another regiment's being billeted at Meryton.

Mary, thus deprived of being her mother's only solace, soon removed herself to Hunsford parish to be near her sister

Kitty. Kitty had indeed married Mr. Beasley, and being much improved in temper and understanding by the match, welcomed her sister warmly; which favor Mary dutifully repaid by supplying the poorer families with soup from Kitty's kitchen, and such uplifting homilies of her own, as to leave them in scarcely less cheerful a state than they had enjoyed before her arrival.

As for Captain and Mrs. Heywood, they were never to be seen in England again. Bingley heard often through his sister's letters of their travels about the Continent, of the sights they encountered there, and the much that was made of them in every capital. These communications he read eagerly, and marveled at; and too exemplary was his nature ever to wonder, if these welcomes were quite so zealous, why therefore the pair never rested in one place above a twelvemonth.

Lady Catherine, who had long predicted a sorry end for her niece, was, for the once, less than gratified to be proven correct; her compassionate heart must be affected by the pitiful sight of Georgiana, like her brother before her, marrying for reasons other than the conservation of rank. Even the reports that came to her during the years of the couple's modishness in London society assuaged her not. For Her Ladyship, a person of obscure birth must remain ungenteel, however much he be solicited at St. James's. A marriage between unequals—she frequently assured her daughter Anne, who sensibly refrained from all danger of following either cousin's example—was nothing short of an infamy. Never to be countenanced, nor even contemplated—for it could accomplish nothing more substantial in the end than trifling levity, and more contentment than was either seemly or becoming.

And thus it proved.